Free Loner

Jennarose Milette

Order this book online at www.trafford.com
or email orders@trafford.com

Most Trafford titles are also available at major online book retailers.

© Copyright 2015 Jennarose Milette.
All rights reserved. No part of this publication may be reproduced, stored in a
retrieval system, or transmitted, in any form or by any means, electronic, mechanical,
photocopying, recording, or otherwise, without the written prior permission of the author.

Print information available on the last page.

ISBN: 978-1-4907-5508-3 (sc)
ISBN: 978-1-4907-5507-6 (hc)
ISBN: 978-1-4907-5506-9 (e)

Library of Congress Control Number: 2015902550

Because of the dynamic nature of the Internet, any web addresses or links contained in
this book may have changed since publication and may no longer be valid. The views
expressed in this work are solely those of the author and do not necessarily reflect the
views of the publisher, and the publisher hereby disclaims any responsibility for them.

Any people depicted in stock imagery provided by Thinkstock are models,
and such images are being used for illustrative purposes only.
Certain stock imagery © Thinkstock.

Trafford rev. 03/04/2015

Trafford
PUBLISHING® www.trafford.com
North America & international
toll-free: 1 888 232 4444 (USA & Canada)
fax: 812 355 4082

Dedicated to:

My parents. Thank you for always being there for me and believing in me. I love you both dearly!

My friends. You know who you are! Thank you for your encouragement and just cheering me on throughout this process, I couldn't have done it without you!

Contents

Chapter 1: Trouble on the Bus 1
Chapter 2: In the Spur of the Moment 5
Chapter 3: Eighty-Six, Drake Street 18
Chapter 4: Keeping Cool 27
Chapter 5: Twenty Years Older 36
Chapter 6: Pinching Fire 41
Chapter 7: The Past Relived 52
Chapter 8: Best Christmas Ever 60
Chapter 9: Of Good-Byes and Railways 81
Chapter 10: Second Meeting 88
Chapter 11: Mall Adventures 100
Chapter 12: Of Things Higher 106
Chapter 13: Family Relations 116
Chapter 14: Whisperings of New Beginnings 122
Chapter 15: Settling in the Midst of Chaos 137
Chapter 16: Pain of a Different Kind 153
Chapter 17: Taking the Leap 173
Chapter 18: Of Seemingly False Starts and Bigger Pictures 184
Chapter 19: The Big Night 199
Chapter 20: Burning Summer's Heat 209
Chapter 21: Brothers in Arms 224
Chapter 22: Future Plans 231
Chapter 23: Camera Flashes and Salt Air—Older and Wiser 242
Chapter 24: I Do—Epilogue 251

Chapter 1

Trouble on the Bus

Day dawned, if you could call it a dawn; the sun remained blanketed in a thick gloom of gray clouds. It was the kind of weather that would make people feel miserable. Misty tendrils of fog hugged the damp ground and hid depressions in the rutty back road, making him stumble if he wasn't careful.

School was the last thing he wanted to do on a day like this. He hunched his shoulders and jammed his hands into his jean pockets, yawning even as he told himself to stay awake. A gust of wind blew along the road, showering him with wet leaves and whispering down the collar of his jacket as it sent chills racing up and down his spine. Shivering and feeling gloomy, he hitched his backpack higher on one broad shoulder and made for the bus stop at the end of a seemingly never-ending muddy old road.

No one else was there, and not in the mood for being sociable anyhow, he sat on the curb, propping his backpack between his legs, and let his mind wander in no direction in particular. That was a mistake, for he didn't like the route it took. Everything in him wanted to be free of his life, the things surrounding him, but he didn't know how to stop or know where to start to make things easier.

Here he was, eighteen years old with no life to speak of. He sighed dismally. He went from school to work and then back to the broken-down shack his dad called home. Dad. What a name. If that was what all dads were like, Sheldon fervently wished no one had one. To him, the word "dad" meant beer and whiskey, cigarettes and drunken rages. It meant days spent in fear of coming home, nights out in the shed. It meant a different girlfriend every week, each one worse than the last, all of them seeming more interested in Sheldon than in his father. Sheldon hit the road when they were around. It wasn't as if he had anywhere else to go. Nobody at school seemed to want to hang out with him; his dad's reputation was too much to contend with.

The bus lurched to a stop and spewed exhaust all over his face, the doors opening to admit a new prisoner. They seemed to swallow him whole as he dragged himself to his feet and trudged up the rusty steps. Sputtering, the old vehicle crawled forward as it picked up speed. Sheldon raked his blond hair out of his eyes and faced a long busload of earbuds and hazy morning stares.

"Classic," he mumbled as he stumbled to the back and sat down in an empty row.

School was the same; it never did seem to change. Classes were pretty much identical to yesterday's, chaos in the halls and finally homework, and lots of it. "The one thing I can rely on," he undertoned as he crammed it all into his backpack.

He was tired when he climbed the steps up into the return bus. The driver flashed him a cheerful grin.

"Long day, huh, kid?"

"Sure, not over yet." He slumped into a seat and leaned his head back. The girl behind him playfully pulled his long hair and stared back at him from black-rimmed eyes. He didn't recognize her and edged closer to the window, propping his chin in his hands. She'd soon figure out not to even try to mess with him. Most girls did. A few just didn't know when to stop. With those types, ignoring them only provoked them to further foolishness. He learned soon enough what sort she was when she slid into the seat beside him and slipped her hand just inside his loosely buttoned shirt. He drew a quick breath and grabbed both her hands, practically throwing them on her lap. She looked him in the eyes, a slight smile playing across her lips as she moved closer to him.

"Hey, hey, hey, cut it out!" he cried, shrinking away in disgust.

"Why? You know you could have a lot of fun," she said, glancing at him sideways.

"Heck no! Leave off." He lowered his brows. "Go back to your seat and quit being stupid." She flipped her hair over one shoulder like a snooty model but surprisingly enough listened to him. Sheldon let out a low whistle of relief and rolled his eyes. *What a freak!* he thought, disgusted with the loose way she'd conducted herself. The really frightening thing was she'd obviously thought he'd find her attractive enough to spend a night with her. He suppressed a shudder.

Sheldon got off in the middle of town with a bunch of other kids and hurried to get to work on time. Loading groceries into bags, he wondered if it was really worth eight dollars an hour. *It's better than nothing,* he thought with a shrug, dropping a loaf of bread next to some jam and plunking the bag into the cart. He worked four hours after school and eight on the weekends. Sundays were off.

He was thinking of Sunday as he trudged the four miles to home a few hours later. The day he could sleep in until noon, occasionally take himself out to the one decent breakfast he got a week, and do whatever he wanted to. *Long ways to go.* He let himself in the door quietly, ears tuned for sounds that signaled a hasty retreat. Cold and wet as he was, Sheldon was glad that all he heard were snores. Bounding up the stairs, he deposited his backpack on his bed and put his paycheck in the safe he'd cut out of his wall behind a picture of his mother. He studied it in silence for a moment, wishing his mother was back, wishing she'd lived. She'd died in a car crash when he was ten, and it had seemed like all the lights went out of his young life. That was why his dad went from the perfect picture of fatherhood to the lazy drunk he was today. That was why they lived in such a dump.

He traced her features with one finger; that firm jawline so familiar in his own face, the straight nose, high cheekbones, he

3

had them all. But his eyes were a piercing blue while hers were gray, and they were deeper set and larger. She was a brunette, he a blond. But their resemblance was absolutely striking. Sheldon dropped his hand and turned away, lonely and the hurt cutting deep. Not at all hungry now, he undressed to get out of his wet clothes and stretched out on his bed in his boxers. He lay there for a while thinking until he was finally overcome by sleep.

Chapter 2

In the Spur of the Moment

The next few weeks followed in a similar manner. Sheldon would have a few tangles in the hall with the girl from the bus, and he'd come home to either a drunk father or a sleeping one. The man hadn't been sober in weeks. Walking home from work became harder as December hit, and the snow began to fall, becoming deeper with each passing week. Sheldon quit his job at the grocery store as he'd done the previous winter and took to shoveling snow out of people's walkways and digging their cars out. He got better pay for this and made close to sixty dollars per property, depending on the person he was working for. But that was only when there was snow to shovel. He set up posters all over town advertising his name and cell number, hoping to get more customers. Apparently, the few people on his customer list approved of his work, for he got so many calls he had to take his posters down. Eventually, he had to put the highest payers first on his list and let the others go if they weren't willing to wait until the following day.

One Saturday, he got home from work feeling totally exhausted, all his muscles aching and his back screaming out for a hot shower. He was so tired that he didn't even care if his dad had any of his girlfriends over. Luckily, upon closing the door behind him, he found he had the house to himself. Dad was most likely out at some bar. Sheldon flipped on the kitchen light and glanced around with disdain at the empty beer cans and the general sense of disorder and chaos. He was too tired to do anything about it and crunched over a few cans on his way to the bathroom. He threw all his clothes in a heap and let the water run for a moment, brushing his teeth during the wait. He spit, rinsed, and ducked into the shower. The water running down his back and over his sore shoulders felt so soothing that he groaned. He worked his fingers into the knotted muscles of his neck, letting the water give him total relief, and then sank down and sat with his head between his knees as he fully surrendered to the luxury. Before too long, the water began to feel a little cold, and Sheldon stepped out, dried his body off, and quickly draped a towel about his slim waist as he opened the bathroom door. A wave of cool air hit his damp skin and made his teeth chatter momentarily, and his hair steamed as he raced up the rickety stairs to his bedroom. Locking himself in, Sheldon took off the towel and rubbed his hair until it stood up in spikes all along his scalp. Then he pulled on a pair of boxers and jumped into bed, yanking the blankets up to his chin.

"Gee, what am I gonna do for Christmas?" he mused out loud to nobody. He didn't relish the idea of "spending" it with his dad, like he had done the previous year. It was just the same as every other day of the year. But there just wasn't anyone who he could impose upon! Suddenly, he thought of his grandma, whom he hadn't seen since he was thirteen yet who still wrote him letters. They seemed to come out of the blue. He loved getting letters from her; they filled up a hole in his heart for a few days, just helped him keep going. And they were always there for him to read again and again and again, until the pages became worn and frayed.

He turned on his cell phone and pulled up his contact list. He only had a few people in it, and they were either his customers or his boss in the summer, namely the store manager. He knew his grandma's number was in it somewhere. He scrolled through it a few times and, upon finding it, dialed before he had time to think twice and reason himself out of his hasty decision. The phone rang once, twice . . . three times. On the fifth ring, he told himself to hang up as he was probably interrupting or she wasn't there. He began to pull the phone away from his ear when he heard a voice on the other line.

"Hello?"

"Hi . . . This is Sheldon." There was silence.

"Sheldon?" The voice had a glad ring to it that thrilled him, and suddenly, he knew everything was going to be all right. "Oh, honey, I haven't heard from you in ages! It's so good to hear your voice!"

"Yeah, I know, good to hear yours too, Grandma."

"All right, let's have it. You'd never call me unless there was something on your mind or a good reason." He grinned.

"Are you doing anything for Christmas?" There was no use beating around the bush with her.

"Oh, nothing but the usual."

"The usual?" His throat tightened as a sudden crushing disappointment hit him.

"You know, me, myself, and I, make a Christmas dinner and watch a movie, wishing I had someone special to share it with."

He was quiet and then said, "Do I count as special?" He could almost feel the love in her voice vibrating through the phone in his hand as she replied.

"Oh, Shel, you are the only special person in the world for me. I love you so much. I'd love more than anything in the world to share Christmas with my grandson." She choked. "You know my home is always open to you, as is my heart."

"I'll be there. Wait for me." Sheldon hung up the phone, knowing that she'd understand.

Two hours away from where he was, an elderly lonely woman stared at the silent phone in her hand. Putting it down, she cried her heart out for her grandson, tears of joy as well as sorrow for his pain.

The eve of Christmas Eve dawned with a cold brilliance, and Sheldon grabbed some clothes from his dresser, clumping down the stairs to the bathroom. The house looked the same as before; Dad must have pulled an overnighter. Locking the door out of habit, Sheldon pulled on a pair of comfortably faded jeans, his usual T-shirt, and a black-and-red sweatshirt. He carefully combed his blond hair, smoothing his slanted bangs just so over one blue eye. He shoved his PJ pants into a corner and headed back to his room, toothbrush clamped between his teeth. Working it around in his mouth, he pulled a duffel bag from beneath his bed, raising a mini dust storm in doing so. He felt a sneeze coming and saved his toothbrush from a crash landing on a dusty floor in the nick of time. Returning it to its rightful place in his mouth, he opened his dresser drawers and began shoving things into the bag: jeans and T-shirts, underwear, socks, and all manner of masculine paraphernalia. He nearly sliced his finger badly on an open razor as he zipped it into a pocket. He spat a mouthful of toothpaste foam into a wadded tissue and popped the finger into his mouth. He gave himself a quick spray of Axe and tucked the bottle inside the bag as he stood, swinging the loaded pack to his shoulder. He collected his wallet and, after raiding the kitchen for a bowl of cereal, headed for the train station, hoping to catch a lift on the way. But he didn't seem to be in luck, and an hour later, he sat out in the cold at the station, waiting for the next train.

Dad crossed his mind, and he pushed the thought away resolutely. After all these years, he could take care of himself, if you could call it care in the remotest sense of the word. Sheldon amused himself by evaluating the people at the station. There weren't many, about six or so, but it was something to do. One was an older man who looked like he should be back in bed with the hot water bottles of his day and age tied to each foot. The only parts of his face that were visible were his eyes and his eyebrows, which waggled up and down, making his opinion of the newspaper he was reading easy to assimilate. There were two women, obviously friends or even sisters, each with a steaming mug of Starbuck's coffee; Sheldon suddenly felt cold and very covetous. There were two younger men, very different; one was your average professional young business man, all spiffed up in a suit and tie, the effect of which was rather marred by the heavy winter coat he was bundled into. The other couldn't seem to decide which he liked to fiddle with more, his straggly hair or his earrings. Sheldon's attention span ran short, and he yawned and dropped his head, staring at the ground. That was when he realized he wasn't the only person on his bench. He looked up from a pair of high-heeled leather boots into the face of a very pretty girl. She met his eyes and then dropped hers, confusedly bashful.

"Hi, I didn't know you were there," he said, glancing down the tracks. A train whistle sounded in the distance. He turned his head back to the girl, grinning. "Train's almost here! Sure is chilly out here, huh?" She nodded, shivering almost imperceptibly. "You cold?" She didn't look like she was dressed for the weather.

"I didn't have time to get a proper coat," she said with a rueful smile.

"Do you mind?" He unzipped his own coat. She looked at him quizzically and not comprehending what he was saying. He shrugged out of it, his hair fanning across his eyes, hiding a light in her own.

"Oh no!" she cried as he made to pass it around her shoulders. "I couldn't possibly take your coat! You'll be needing it any minute, not as if you don't now."

"Just until the train. I'll be fine." His teeth flashed as he smiled. "No fun spending Christmas sick in bed!" She returned his smile as he pulled the coat close around her. "Already warm too."

"Um, very." She cuddled down inside it.

"Glad to help." He slumped in the bench and pushed his hands into his hip pockets, his chin on his chest. She watched him, beginning to warm up to the world and to him.

She hesitated, and then asked, "Are you from around here?"

"Oh, sure, go to school here. Not like there's a school other than this here regional one for miles around. Unless you count the private school." Those white teeth gleamed again in a devilishly disarming grin. She laughed suddenly, making him think it was because of his comment. It was the only thing she could do in light of the realization that he was the most irresistibly handsome young man she'd ever met. That grin only intensified everything. And she found that she'd forgotten everything they had just said. "You?" his tone was questioning. Her mind raced frantically, trying to remember some thread of the conversation. Suddenly, the whistle shrieked again, much closer, like it was just around the bend. She pounced on the diversion shamelessly.

Turning back to Sheldon, she said apologetically, "I'm sorry. I didn't quite catch what you were saying."

"That's fine. Are you from around here?"

"Oh yes, about ten minutes away." Was it just her imagination or did his eyes gleam suddenly in the darkened shelter? He rose to his feet and slung his duffel bag hastily to his shoulder as the train steamed to a halt in front of the platform, making their eyes smart. He felt a small hand on his arm and looked down at the girl beside him. "You'll be needing this." She unzipped the coat.

"No, no, you can keep it for now, just have to ride in the same car. You don't look like you're warm enough yet." Heat rushed to her face, and she quickly dropped her eyes, pretending to fiddle with the zipper, her heart pounding so loud and fast that she feared he would hear it. She steadied her voice.

"Of course! Long train rides are no fun unless there's someone to talk to." He took her arm as they boarded the train, eager to continue the conversation, completely unaware of the emotional conflict she was experiencing.

He sat down across from her on a shiny leather seat and handed a few dollar bills to the conductor, who punched his ticket and slipped it into a slot on the top of the seat and passed on. Sheldon jounced his feet up and down, suddenly feeling a little awkward.

"Say, do you mind if I put my feet up?"

"No," she said, wishing he'd sat beside her. He propped his feet up, lazily crossing his ankles, and stared out the window as the train began to pick up speed. "You have small feet for a guy," she observed, for lack of anything better to say.

"Some of the guys in senior high wear size thirteen. I'll take my nines any day. Gotta wonder what it feels like to have flippers for feet, you know?" She laughed.

"So you're a senior?"

"Yeah, thank god, I couldn't take another year. I'm moving out as soon as school's through." She was quiet for a moment, studying his sneakers.

"Life doesn't really agree with you, huh?" When he didn't answer right away, she looked up and found him regarding her with a strange expression in his eyes, nearly hostile, calculating, as if he was speculating just how much she could be trusted and how much he could tell.

"Not really." He twirled his hoodie tie around one long finger. She didn't know if she should draw him out or if she even could, so she decided to let the comment go. His piercing eyes flickered up for an instant, and she saw that they had gone dark, nearly a midnight blue. "I never talk about it. No one has ever asked. Don't know you pretty much at all, so forget you even asked." Although his answer hurt her, there was a certain quality to the anger in his voice that suddenly made her heart ache. Behind the pain, she thought she saw a chance he was willing to give her, a chance at knowing him enough to get inside. Maybe she just wanted that so much she only saw what she wanted to see; perhaps she was reading into his comment too much. She wondered at herself, at her attraction to this boy she'd only just met, and whose name was a mystery to her still.

"There's still nearly six months of school left to get to know one another. It's going to be interesting going to a new school. Maybe you can help me to get to know some people." She saw her mistake as he looked up, a bitter twist to his lips.

"Yeah, like me, myself, and I." She saw his hurt and thought quickly of a way to keep him light. She smiled, sensing that she was treading on thin ice, the uncharted waters familiar to none but him.

"That's cool. I hate meeting a million kids at one time, 'cause then I feel like I have to get to know them all. It never works. I'm more of a one-on-one person, so I work better with fewer people, and I'm glad I met you first!" He looked into her eyes steadily, sizing her up, seeking for something contrary to her words. For all his caution, he only found genuine frankness, and he was at a loss of what to do.

"You really mean that." It was more of a statement than a question.

"Of course, I do." She saw the black fade from his eyes, leaving them a beautiful clear blue. A slow, doubtful smile played around the corners of his mouth, and he leaned toward her, dropping his feet to the floor.

"That's the best Christmas present I've gotten in years." He tilted his head to one side. "Thanks."

She smoothed her hair around one ear and opened her mouth to speak. "No, please don't say anything." He touched her knee. "It's a big deal to me. Maybe not to you, but it really is for me." He removed his forgotten hand and raking the fingers through his blond hair, returned to the shallower waters of conversation that were easier to navigate without touching too close to the core of things. "So did you just move here? You said the new school and all."

"Yes, we did, two weeks ago, just in time for Christmas break, so I'm really not from around here. Sorry I lied!" His eyebrows quirked, and a crooked smile played around his mouth for a moment.

"Far from where you lived before?"

"Yeah, just a little far removed! North Carolina is sort of different. This is a big change and it's so cold!" That explained the soft twang of an accent in her voice.

"Oh, OK, yeah, I can see how New Hampshire would be different. We're pretty far up here, not many people around. There're only ninety or so kids in senior high this year."

"Wow, that's crazy small!" He grinned.

"Everybody knows who hates who and who likes who . . . Easier to stay out of company or in."

"And I guess it would be easy to remember a lot of people's names."

"Yeah, especially the ones who hate you."

"You don't seem like the kind of guy who gets beaten up."

"No, I've got the height, but being ignored is just as bad. You want in, don't hang with me." Her eyes narrowed, a hard determination shining in their green depths.

"Maybe I don't want 'in.' Maybe I don't care what anybody else thinks of me. Maybe I like you better than I would them anyhow. I hate bullies. They don't deserve any respect, and furthermore, they don't need another follower." She stopped, surprised by how far she'd gone on in such a bold manner and even more so by the stunned but skeptical look on his face. She figured she might as well go all the way and clasped her hands tightly in her lap, saying slowly, "But it's always best to know who you're hanging with, and anyways, I only remember the names of people that I have reason to remember. Since we're going to be friends, partners on the outside, so to speak, my name's Richelle." She hesitated and then held out her hand. A smile lit up his eyes and flashed out in a bigger grin than she'd thought could fit in a human face as he took her small hand in his.

"And I'm Sheldon. Gosh, this is already the best Christmas I've had in years!"

"All I have to say is, boy, am I glad I took the 9:15 train! School isn't really the best setting in which to get to know someone." Sheldon let go of her hand and leaned back, his head inquisitively to one side.

"So where are you heading?"

"One of my friends wanted me to spend Christmas break with her, or at least part of it. So here I am. All my stuff is already there. I go there so much when I'm on vacation that her parents literally bought me my own bed and all kinds of clothes for me so I don't have to pack! It's crazy, but they like having two daughters once in a while, and I love being spoiled." Richelle smiled.

"Yeah, that's what grandmas are for, happens to be where I'm heading."

"Oh, that's sweet! My grandma lives way out in California, and I've only seen her a couple of times, but we write back and forth. She's the sweetest thing."

"Yeah, mine too. She's pretty much all . . . Oh, never, hey, we're slowing down, there's a station coming up. Can you see anything out your window?" He twisted in his seat and pressed his face to the glass.

"Yes, next station I'm off." She made her own conclusion to his choppy sentence. Sheldon looked at her.

"Maybe I'll drop in and say 'hi' on my way home if that's all right." He stopped and rolled his eyes, exasperated at himself. "Forget it. That would be like really awkward. Guess it's not the coolest idea in the world, sorry." He trailed off, embarrassed. Laughing, she pulled a pocket notebook out of her purse and quickly scribbled on it.

"That's the address, and we'd love to have you for as long as we can." She pushed the page into his hand.

"You're sure?" His hand closed around it, and he tucked it away into the back pocket of his wallet.

"As sure as you are!" Richelle laughed as he shook his head with a silly grin.

The train stopped, and people made the on-and-off transition. He resumed the conversation as the train picked up speed once more.

"Do you have any siblings?"

"A younger brother, fifteen. He's a little like you."

"Really? In what sense?"

"You both are confident. You seem like you know what you want out of life. Matt is a pretty intense person."

"You think I'm an intense person?"

"Definitely. Maybe it's just an impression, but you probably accomplish whatever you set your mind to."

"I've always felt like I was stuck, like there are too many things holding me back. You know what I mean?"

"Everybody has felt like that at some point or another in their lives. I certainly have." He acknowledged this with a slight nod.

"Do you live with your parents?"

"Yes, Matt and I are lucky."

"Sure are." He rubbed his chin as she looked at him with concern.

"Are yours divorced?" she asked softly, wondering if she should have asked.

"No." He stopped. "Mom was killed in a car crash." His voice was quiet. Richelle didn't know how to respond to his pain; saying "it's OK" would be stupid and pointless. Impulsively, she reached out and clasped his hand tightly in hers.

"I shouldn't have asked." His ghost of a smile didn't reach his eyes.

"How could you have known?"

She squeezed his hand and whispered, "I'm sorry."

"I know." He ducked his head. They sat in silence: one in deep empathy and the other struggling to put long unearthed emotions and pain back behind his mask of nonchalance, his hands locked together, the knuckles whitened with the force. He raised his head, one eye concealed behind a screen of blond hair. "You'll find you really can't talk to me, can't ask me questions about myself without dragging something up. I'm not used to bringing things out. It's hard."

"I didn't mean to. Please, don't be angry at me."

"No, I am not angry at you. It's just painful for me, but I feel like maybe I could trust you with knowing me. If you'd be OK with it, if you're cool with it, you know." His cheeks reddened, and he looked out of the window.

"It would certainly be a privilege to know you that well. Whenever you feel like it, I'm here. I've always been good at listening." She pressed his hands as he let go.

"I might take you up on that, someday." His mouth made an attempt at a smile that came out queer. Richelle tactfully changed the subject.

"My station's coming up quick." He passed a fist over his nose and sniffed.

"OK, next question in the interview, are you the kind of girl who's got a million hobbies?"

"Maybe not quite a million, but I do have a few." She giggled slightly. "I am definitely an outdoors girl. I love drawing what I find, going on hikes into unknown places with a notebook and pencils, and that kind of thing. Makes me feel one with nature, so to speak. I like to sing—music is how I communicate a lot. It's because music speaks to me, I guess. So I'll write my own songs if I'm in the mood and all kinds of miscellaneous little things, you know. So what do you like to do?"

"Oh, I like to tinker with stuff, like motors and that kind of thing. I definitely prefer the outdoors to in, especially when it comes to work. Never really had the time to develop any hobbies, but I love reading. Whenever I get the time, that is. I love the kind of weather at the end of summer, when it's cool and windy in the evenings. And spring mornings, when it's warm and wet with dew. You know what I'd love to do?"

She propped her chin in one hand. "What?"

"I'd love to go gliding. You know, jump off a cliff and have a crash landing in the ocean?"

"Oh, me too! It is so fun. My uncle takes us gliding in summer. You *have* to come sometime!"

"That would be cool. I don't suppose he lives around here though." He laughed.

"Yes, he's kind of far away." She looked regretful. "But maybe you could come down sometime." There was a reduction in the speed of the train. "Oh. I'd never thought I'd live to see the time when I wished the train would never stop." She looked at him. "Well, this is good-bye."

"For now. I guess I'll drop in for a stay a few days after Christmas. They don't happen to have a cheap motel up there, do they?"

"No, not a single one." He looked uncomfortable. "Silly, I am not going to invite you only to turn you out for nights! You'll stay with us." She shifted in her seat as she removed his jacket and handed it to him. "Thanks, it kept me nice and toasty. It's been wonderful getting to know you."

"And you too. Sorry there isn't more time. Until next time then." He held out his hand. They shook, and Richelle stood up as people began moving out. Sheldon followed suit. "Well, good-bye," he said, not knowing what else to say as they stood there awkwardly looking at each other. Suddenly, she wrapped her arms around his waist and rested her head on his chest. Surprised, he returned her embrace lightly. She met his eyes for an instant as she drew back.

"Good-bye, Sheldon." She picked up her purse and ducked into the flow of people heading for the door. He caught a glimpse of her on the platform, looking back at the train, her red hair blowing around her face in the chill winter breeze. Their eyes met through the window glass and held, but people walking to and fro obscured one from the other. As the train moved out, he saw her, still standing there, gazing after the retreating train. Then she was gone.

Sheldon sank back into his seat, feeling alone with only his thoughts to accompany him for the remainder of the trip. He suddenly realized that she was the first girl he'd ever really hugged, and he thought that it was only right. She was now his best and only friend. Again, he felt her in his arms, close to his body, the perfect fit. He thought of how hungry her arms had felt, as if she needed to be held. Then he remembered the look in her eyes and realized that it was not to be held that she had hugged him, it was to hold. It was pain for his pain he'd seen in her eyes, and she'd tried to let him know she cared in some way because she didn't know what to say with only words. She couldn't convey enough. His heart went out to her, and he wanted to reach out and pull her to him. So far he felt like she fulfilled everything he'd dreamed of in a friend, and he'd only just begun to know her.

He reached for his jacket and pulled it around him, trying to get comfortable as the train sped closer to its destination.

Chapter 3

Eighty-Six, Drake Street

An hour later, he stood among other passengers at the station, waiting for his grandmother to come pick him up. At last he saw a snowy head coming toward him, and the next thing he knew, a warm pair of arms wrapped around him and held him close. Grandma looked up at him.

"My, how you have grown! You must be six feet!" She hugged him again as if to make sure he was really there. "Grammy's so happy to see you again, Sheldon. You're still her little boy even if you are half a foot taller than her!" Sheldon laughed.

"Are you ready for Christmas, Grammy? 'Cause I am! This is gonna be the best Christmas ever!" He passed an arm about her plump waist and headed toward the parking lot.

"Of course, I am! You can't imagine what a flurry I've been in to get ready since you called! Your room's all set for you."

"The same one Momma had? Where are you parked, Grammy?"

"The very same, honey. It's been yours for years now. I'm over there, same old Subaru." Sheldon led her to it and handed her in on the passenger side, explaining that he'd drive. He settled down into the seat and hitched his seat belt. He put the car in reverse and carefully backed out of the lot.

"OK, right or left? Haven't been here in years. Wait, it's a left, right? No pun intended . . ."

"Yes, it's a left. It'll all come back soon." Sheldon zipped along at thirty-five mph, free and happy. He loved driving but never really got time to practice.

"I've got to buy my own car one of these days. It's no fun having to drive around in the truck back home. I swear one of these days I'm going to find myself sitting on the ground while the rest of the contraption drives off by itself." She chuckled.

"There are some for sale around here. I saw one going for nine hundred the other day."

"Oh, I'm sure, but I want one that will last, not one that needs a zillion things fixed."

"I know what you mean. You're taking the next left up ahead, Shel."

"How far are you from the station?"

"Oh, about fifteen minutes. Now a right, onto Main Street. How long are you planning on staying?"

"Well, I packed for a few days. I've got nearly two weeks off school, but I met this girl on the train and . . ." He told her about Richelle and their plans.

"She sounds like a wonderful girl, Shel. But be careful who you let inside and what you tell." She looked at him with motherly concern.

"But she's different, Grammy, not like those girls at school. I can't put my finger on what it is, but I know she cares, no really!" he said, seeing the look of doubt in her wrinkled face. "There were tears in her eyes when she asked me about my parents and I mentioned Mom. She didn't fake it. You don't think I could tell?" Sheldon passed a hand over his face. "I've never let anyone in since I was ten, Grammy, because there was no one who could look past things and treat me for who I was, for myself. But Dad's reputation precedes anything I've ever tried to strike up with anybody. There's just been no one I felt comfortable enough with to tell in the first place, you know that."

"Yes, I do. I just can't help feeling concerned for you, after all that you've been through. You haven't told her very much?"

"No. Trains are not really the best place for that kind of conversation, just a tad too intense, you know?" He concentrated on driving, content to let her make conversation if she so choose.

"It's a right onto Drake Street, Shel. My number is eighty-six." They pulled in a moment later.

"Hey, it's painted since I was here last. Looks good!" He surveyed her quaint cottage-style house, liking the way it looked with all the lights, like something out of a painting. He popped the trunk and grabbed his luggage, his grandmother leading the way up the shoveled walk.

"Surprise!" she cried, throwing the front door wide. The interior of the house was arrayed with Christmas lights and holly, and mistletoe ran along the tops of doors and the mantelpiece. The crowning glory was a huge tree in the center of the living room. There were candles lit everywhere, and it smelled like holiday cookies and pine. "Merry Christmas, Sheldon."

"You didn't, not all for me?" He hugged her, joy filling him.

"All for you. I had no idea when you were coming, but knowing you it was going to be at a moment's notice. I wanted to make it a beautiful Christmas for us to share."

"Oh, this is awesome! And I literally just called you yesterday! You did all this?" He couldn't believe it.

"If I fall asleep, you'll know why. It was worth it all just to see the expression on your face as you walked through the door." Her brown eyes glowed warmly. "Now let's get you settled, and then we'll have cookies and milk, just like old times." She headed up the stairs. Gripping the banister in places where there wasn't so much mistletoe, Sheldon followed on her heels.

His room was very masculine, model airplanes hung from the ceiling, deer and wolves gazing out of rustic-styled frames on the mossy-green walls, and the feather bed was covered with an earth-toned plaid comforter. The dresser in the corner had family pictures scattered tastefully over the surface: his grandparents, his mother when she was a girl, and one of him in her arms as a little fat baby. *That has changed,* he thought as he patted his stomach pensively.

"You just put your clothes away in the dresser and join me in the kitchen."

"OK, be there soon." His door closed behind her, and her footsteps receded down the hall. Sheldon tucked his clothes away none too neatly and looked at the pictures on the top of the bureau. He saw one of Grammy and his grandfather when he was alive that he'd never seen before. Sheldon picked it up and realized it was one of their wedding photos. They looked so happy, but he wondered vaguely if they were any happier than he himself was at that moment. Somehow he doubted it, if two very different types of happiness could be compared. Putting the picture back in its place, he unzipped his hoodie and threw it on the bed, flinging the door open and thumping down the stairs.

"There you are, Sheldon. All unpacked?" Grammy placed two mugs of warm milk beside a large platter of cookies on the kitchen table.

"Yeah, I'm good. Wow! These look amazing!"

"Boys! All you do is eat!" She laughingly pushed him into a chair and sat down beside him, wrapping her hands around her mug. She took a sip, watching Sheldon devour a huge bite from a gingerbread cookie.

"You were always the best when it comes to cookies." He shot her an appreciative glance and washed the mouthful down with a swig of milk. He dropped the remainder of his cookie into his mug and regarded it contentedly, waiting for it to become totally soused and soggy. It got a little too saturated, for when he carefully drew it out of the milk, the whole thing fell apart and slipped down out of sight below the surface. "Aw, come on! This always happens to me! My poor soggy cookie!"

"Here's a spoon."

"Thanks, you know me too well." He fished the sodden mass out of the mug and popped it onto his mouth, slurping as it nearly slipped off the spoon again. "Hmm, perfect!"

"Would you be interested in coming to a Christmas Eve candlelight service with me tomorrow night?"

"Sure. I haven't been to one in years though. Oh, I don't really have anything to wear, as far as dress clothes go. Don't have any actually. I do have a button-down shirt, but it's pretty casual, plaid and all. Is that OK?"

"What matters is that you go. As long as you are neat, and you don't play with fire or candles!" She held up her finger as a look of puppy dog innocence came over his face.

"What? I never play with candles, right?" He grinned hopefully, still attempting the puppy face. "All right, all right, I won't. I'll be good." Ignoring this, she went on with her own train of thought.

"But you are always neat. We'll be fine, Sheldon." She patted his arm. "My, you are so tall! I remember when I could hold all of you in only one of my arms. And you had the chubbiest little hands! Look at them now!" She spread her hand over his palm. He laughed.

"I got you there!" He squeezed her hand tightly. "But yours are full of memories, and prettier than mine!"

"Now, now, don't you sweet talk me!"

"They are! Look it." He held her hand up. "They are the most perfect pair of grandma hands in the world." She got up and pressed a kiss on his blond hair.

"I love you, my dear, dear boy."

"I know. I love you too."

Sheldon lay on his bed, his stomach contentedly full of cookies and milk. He'd been an obedient grandson and gone upstairs to rest after his "long tiresome trip." So here he was, trying to keep his mind from flying in a million different directions and go to sleep. But there were so many things to think about, like no school for a few blissful weeks, seeing Grammy again, his new best friend, no Dad for a good long while, and the list ran on. He pulled his iPod out of his pocket and played a few mindless games to give himself a break, but his personality was too restless, and it didn't last long.

He decided to listen to music instead and lay quietly, but his rebel mind broke free of the melodies and soared off on its own. Soon, he was daydreaming of gliding in the summer with Richelle, taking her places, protecting her from senior-high's bullies like the sister he'd never had. He wondered what it would be like knowing a girl, letting her in on everything that went on in his mind. He tried to imagine what a real friend would be like: one who could see behind his mask and not care about all the junk people had thrown on his life, someone who wouldn't be afraid to call him "friend." Brother. The word rose unbidden before his mind's eye. Sister, answered a whisper of a voice somewhere deep inside him. Unwelcome noise invaded his reflections, and he automatically pressed a button, changing the song for one more suitable to his mood. Maybe he could get her a job if she needed one; he knew all the best places and employers. It would be fun working with Richelle.

He rolled over and pulled out his earbuds, resolutely determined to catch a nap. He flopped a pillow over his head and shut his eyes.

He had an awful and very disoriented dream that involved candlelight services where the candles were beer bottles and therefore explosive to some extent, trains running through the church, and girls with strange makeup chasing him down the street where he apparently ended up at Richelle's house, which could fly by means of gliders festooning its roof.

His grandma got a graphic version of this fantastic nightmare when she came up to his room to tell him that it was two-thirty and he could eat a late lunch if he was so inclined, cookies not being much in the way of nutrition.

"You have the strangest dreams. I think the cookies did it. My mother used to tell me not to sleep on a stomach full of sweets. From your experience, I would deduce that they do things to the subconscious mind."

"Hmm, probably what did it. It was pretty cool, explosive candles! Wouldn't that be awesome? Imagine the reaction in church, with all those people. It would be a sensation! I've got to . . ." His voice trailed off into incoherent mumblings under her reproving eye. "I was just kidding about the church. Got to try it in school, it would be hilarious!"

"Right. Wonderful idea. Getting put in detention isn't a part of that plan, I suppose?" she inquired mildly.

"OK, outside then. Gosh, maybe it would wake Dad out of one of his everlasting naps if I lit one under his chair and bolted." His tone was light, but his eyes were hard. She touched his shoulder.

"I made you a grilled chicken club sandwich, and there is no way I'll ever fit it. You'd better come down and tuck it away." He glanced up and stretched, the mood gone, swinging his legs over the side of the bed.

"Another thing you're the best at: Grammy's famous chicken club sandwich. Where's it hiding?"

Bottles rattled in the fridge, and her head popped up for a second.

"What would you like to drink, hon? I've got a mango–orange juice mix, a pineapple–grape one, I think, and orange juice."

"The mango-orange sounds good. Hey, look, it's snowing!"

"White Christmas after all. That would be nice. Sheldon, I've got to do some grocery shopping for Christmas dinner. Would you like to come along? You don't if you would rather not."

"I'd love to. Rather not stay here all by myself, you know." He took a bite out of his sandwich. "This is really good!" He tried saying around it, his voice coming out muffled. Swallowing, he said, "I'm definitely ready for some good cooking. School lunches are just totally disgusting. I bet the cook wouldn't think the leftovers fit for her dog to eat."

He polished off his lunch with the juice and took his dishes up to the sink, rinsing them for his grandmother. "Do you want to go now?" he asked, wiping his hands off on his shirtfront and waving them around in the air.

"That would be good. Just to warn you, the store is probably really crowded."

"It's an obstacle of course! That's fine. Just let me grab my sweatshirt." He pushed his chair in and bounded up the stairs to his room. He unraveled the hoodie from the blankets and pushed his arms into the sleeves, zippering it up over his chest.

Sheldon turned the windshield wipers on, the snowflakes making it difficult to see.

"You be careful now."

"I know, Grammy. There's no accumulation on the roads, I just need the wipers on."

"Shel, I actually have some errands to run later on tonight after dinner. Will you be OK with staying home?"

"I don't mind. Oh, wait, don't they have a gym around here?"

"There is a YMCA down the road a bit, not quite a half mile. Did I tell you they put in a swimming pool since you last were here?"

"That's cool. I think you might have mentioned that some time in one of your letters. Anyways, I brought my swim stuff. Yeah, I'd like to go for a swim while you're out. Float around and relax. Maybe lift a bit so I can say I've got some muscles." He grinned at her with one eye on the road.

"All that snow shoveling keeps you fit," she protested.

"True." He turned the heat down a notch. "OK, where is this store? I know it's here somewhere."

"It's on this street. Give it a moment. Coming up fast." She paused. "On your right."

Sheldon parked and helped her out, taking a quick survey of the parking lot as he did so.

"You were right," he stated. "It's packed."

"We don't have too many things to pick up. I've got everything I need for baking at the house. I just need a turkey and the traditional trimmings."

Soon they were walking down the aisles, Sheldon pushing the cart while Grandma followed, telling him where to go to get what, her nose glued to the list in her hand.

"Man, I'm gonna kill somebody. Can't see a thing round these corners." He pulled out into the main aisle and nearly collided with a girl in red striped stockings. "Gosh, I am sorry! Can't see anybody around these corners!"

"That's OK. I'm still in one piece." She gave him a bright smile and walked on by.

"Victim number one. Where did you say the turkeys were?"

"That's fifty-seven dollars and eighty-three cents, ma'am." Grandma handed the cashier a check.

"Exact amount, please."

"Here's your receipt. Have a nice night. Merry Christmas!"

"And to you, thank you." Sheldon pushed the grocery cart out of the building and rode it, balancing precariously, across the snowy pavement to the Subaru. Together, they loaded the groceries into the trunk.

"Thank you, Shel. That didn't take too long. Thanks to you."

"That's what I'm for, right?" He laughed.

"Sometimes. OK, you drive me home."

"Hey, no carrying those! I'll get 'em. You go inside and keep warm, OK?" Sheldon lined grocery bags up along his arms and walked quickly up the snowy walkway into the kitchen. "I think I made some mud puddles. Sorry about that," he said as he put them down and brushed the hair out of his eyes. She was already mopping up the mess.

"Oh no, problem, that's what you're for, right?" She winked at him, brown eyes twinkling merrily. "Help me put these away, and I'll bring you down to the gym." He looked at the kitchen clock, which registered quarter to four.

"All right, incoming turkey. What are the apples for?"

"Apple pie." He moaned, rolling his eyes up to the ceiling.

"I'm gonna get fat. Suppose I'll have to visit that gym regularly when I'm here, no kidding." She poked him in the stomach.

"Long ways to go to get fat. You've got a six-pack I'll bet. Hard as a rock."

"Ow, that hurt!" He dodged her finger.

"Give me that ice cream before you drop it all over the floor, you goose." He handed it over and collected the grocery bags, waded them all together, and crammed them into a cupboard. "Well, that's that. Go grab a change of clothes and your swim trunks. I'm in the car."

Chapter 4
Keeping Cool

The Subaru pulled up in front of the YMCA, tires spraying wet slush over the sidewalk. Grandma handed Sheldon some money to get in and drove off to do her errands. He walked in and gave the lady at the desk his cash. After politely refusing a membership, he went to the men's locker room and crammed all his stuff into an empty compartment.

Sheldon sauntered into the weight room, glancing around casually. There was an older man working out a pair of rather pathetic biceps and a few women on treadmills, burning off excess holiday fat. His mouth quirked at the thought as he took a quick sip from the bubbler and headed over to the weight system. The layers came off one by one, and he eventually got down to his undershirt, completely soaked through with sweat. He hadn't done bench curls in a while. He worked on his shoulders and then his biceps until his muscles burned, and his stomach quivered every time he pulled at the bar. Then he got on the treadmill and took a quick fifteen-minute run to even out the burns and aches to all over his body. It was a little awkward being the only guy, and he was glad when it was over and left as soon as he took a drink from the bubbler.

Back in the locker room, he stripped off in the shower and rinsed the sweat away, pulling on his swimming trunks as the water ran down over his body. Dripping water onto the floor, he pulled open the pool door and walked out to the diving board. Taking a quick breath, he raised his arms over his head and plunged in.

The water closed in around him and held him in a rippling embrace as he sped through it, relenting its hold as he broke the surface, sputtering. Sheldon treaded water for a moment and then struck out across the pool for a few laps. After ten, he turned over on his back and floated around, gazing up at the ceiling far above him. There was a network of pipes that he found fascinating, and he traced their courses with his eyes.

Suddenly, there were voices and a few splashes as people jumped into the water, and he looked over in their direction, mildly interested, as he had been the only person in the pool. A couple of college students, obviously experienced swimmers, cheerfully raced each other down the pool's length, their voices echoing loudly in the huge room. Sheldon figured it was time to leave and climbed out, leaving watery footprints as he padded back to the locker room.

Soapsuds slipped off his skin, his body tingling from the scrubbing he'd just given it. He lathered his hair, suds flying about the stall, and watched them wash away down the drain. He shut the faucet off and reached for his towel, rubbing himself dry.

His dark jeans were stiff and rough after the soothing water, and he sprayed on some deodorant and pulled a shirt over his head. On went his sneakers and jacket, and grabbing his stuff out of the locker, Sheldon headed out through the lobby and struck out for home. He felt his damp hair freeze slightly and hoped he wouldn't be deathly ill for Christmas as he thought about what to get his grandmother as he trudged along the messy sidewalk. Walking fast, he reached the house before too long, grateful for the streetlamps that lit his way through the freezing slush.

The smell of good food and the sound of his grandma's cheerful welcoming voice quickened his steps into the kitchen.

"How was your swim, Sheldon? You just drop your things in the laundry room, I'll take care of them and wash up for supper! I made one of your favorites." Sniffing hungrily, he chucked his clothes into a laundry hamper and returned to the kitchen to wash his hands. Curiously, he peered over her shoulder as she stirred something on the stove.

"Oh my gosh! You're the absolute best! Where's the cranberry sauce?" he demanded.

"In the fridge. Can you get it for me?" She placed two large biscuits on his plate and lathered them generously with gravy thick with chunks of chicken. She added some peas on the side and set the plate on the table. Sheldon pulled out his chair and sat down, slicing off a piece of cranberry sauce for himself and another for his grandmother, who'd sat beside him with a distinctively smaller serving. He looked from her plate to his and grinned. She smiled and held her hand out, grasping his as she prayed for the meal, thanking God for provision and a holiday spent with her grandson.

"Grandma." She glanced up from her book and peered at him questioningly over her reading glasses. "Could I borrow the car for an hour or so?"

"As long as you don't go places you wouldn't take me, that's fine. Watch out for telephone poles, and pedestrians are really airheaded this time of year."

"Thanks! And you know I don't go to places like that, come on. So I'll watch out for more girls with striped socks, right?" She laughed.

"Don't be long, I'll get lonely. Pick us out a movie for Christmas if you get a chance."

"I will. See you later." He went upstairs, coming back before she could find her place in her book, and closed the front door quietly after himself, his jacket flung over one shoulder.

Sheldon revved up the motor and backed out of the garage. Cruising slowly through the busy downtown streets, he found what he was looking for and parked on the side of the road. He joined the pedestrians on the crosswalk a moment later and was soon inside a little gift shop. Walking thoughtfully up and down aisles, he discovered that he was none too good at picking out gifts for women. There were way too many choices, too many things to pick from. Finally, he saw something that caught his eyes, a chain necklace with the word "grandmother" for a pendant. He found one with his birthstone in it and added a fuzzy purple and silver scarf. He poked around the store for a bit and then moved to front to pay for them. As he put his purchases on the counter, he spotted boxes of gold-foiled chocolates on the shelf behind the cashier.

"Could I add one of those chocolates to this, please?" The woman smiled and reached over her head to take one down. She rang up his total with an air that spoke of years of practice.

"That's twenty-eight ninety-nine." He pulled out his wallet and gave her three ten-dollar bills. "One dollar and one cent for your change, happy holidays!" He pocketed the money and turned toward the door, bag clutched in one hand. He turned back.

"Hey, you're gonna hate me, but I just realized I could use some wrapping paper and tape. Don't suppose you have any?"

"That's fine. You're not used to shopping, are you?" She laughed. Sheldon pulled a face that was clearly an affirmative.

"Not really."

"Right over there." She pointed. "The tape is on the shelf above it, if I remember correctly." Sheldon picked out one with a nice pattern of poinsettias and got a roll of tape.

"Eight ninety-nine."

"Hey, sorry about that. Here's another ten."

"No problem! I'm getting paid, you know."

"Yeah, I know. I work at a grocery store, and it's really annoying when people have a sudden brainstorm and go tearing off to get all this junk and leave you hanging, you know what I mean?"

"Yes, I do. Is there anything else you forgot?" Her eyes laughed merrily at him.

"Na, I'm good. Merry Christmas!"

He ran back across the street and unlocked the car door, hopping in and starting up the engine.

"Now to get them inside without her knowing. This ought to be good." He rolled into the garage and killed the motor. He unzipped his jacket and crammed the bags inside, holding the bulky bundle tight against himself as he walked up the steps into the kitchen.

"Back so soon?" Grandma called from the living room. Sheldon froze, feeling like a guilty little boy caught red-handed with a stolen apple, glad he was out of sight.

"Yeah, I'll be right back." He skirted the table, trying to conceal the wrapping paper poking out of the bottom of his jacket and went upstairs, simultaneously praying that nothing would fall out and cursing the architect who designed the house with the stairs in the living room. His bedroom door slammed shut, and there were mysterious rustlings and cracklings; she could hear the bass in his voice as he talked to himself about something.

"What on earth is that boy up to?" she wondered aloud to herself, shaking her head, settling her glasses more firmly on the bridge of her nose.

Packages wrapped and safely under his bed, he came down to the living room some time later. A smacking sound pulled grandma out of her book, and she looked up inquiringly. Sheldon stood there, his face in his palm.

"I forgot the movie," he mumbled, feeling like a perfect idiot. "What a night! I need a coffee or something. Half my brains left my head, I don't know what's wrong with me. I'm sorry."

"We'll get one tomorrow, don't worry about it. And nothing is wrong with your brain, you're just tired. Would you like a hot chocolate?"

"Sounds good! We didn't eat all those cookies when I got here, did we?"

"No, I made a lot. *You* ate most of them, and don't you forget it!"

He drank his cocoa quickly, the pleasant warmth coursing through him, and put his mug in the sink. He went to his grandma's chair and put his chin on her curly white head.

"I think I'm gonna call it a night. It's been a long day, really tired and all that jazz. Love you, Grammy." He leaned over and kissed her cheek. She returned the gesture lovingly.

"Good night, dear, I'll see you in the morning. What would you like for breakfast, pancakes or French toast?"

"Don't overdo yourself! But French toast would be awesomely amazing. OK, good night!"

Lying on his bed, he pulled out the extra cash and his wallet and flipped it open. His license, credit card, and a wad of greenbacks poked out from various pockets. He added the rest of the cash and shut it, bored and sleepy. A small piece of white paper fell out and floated onto his chest. Wondering what it was, he picked it up and realized it was the address Richelle had given him and her phone number, apparently.

"She didn't tell me about that, cool." He grabbed his cell phone and added her in his contacts, along with her friend's address just in case something happened to the paper she'd given him. He looked at her number, contemplating. Then his finger was on the call button, the phone to his ear. It rang, and he realized he had no reason for calling her.

"Hello?"

"Hi." His voice was uncertain. "This is Sheldon. Just found your number, and I thought I'd ring you up and see if I got it right."

"Oh, hi, Sheldon." She sounded shy, girlish. "Did you get to your grandma's all right?"

"Yeah, it was fine, I'm in bed now. Just got home from the gym, and I'm totally wiped out."

"That's cool. Is it a nice gym?"

"Yeah. They just put in an indoor pool last year or so. Thought I'd try it out. It seems funny taking a swim two days before Christmas!"

"That's awesome!" She laughed. "We don't have a pool at the YMCA in Natalie's town. That's my friend, by the way."

"I figured! She has a pretty name, not really common. So anyways, by the time I see you next, I'll probably have gained like fifteen pounds. My grandma is taking full advantage of having me here and literally stuffing me! I haven't even been here for twelve hours yet. She's an awesome cook and I'd forgotten how to truly appreciate good food. School lunches are going to kill me after this."

"Hey, it's Christmas break. Quit talking about school, you!" He could hear the smile in her voice.

"Yeah, I know, it's like the only thing I have to talk about that's in common with you." He pushed a hand through his hair.

"People don't have to be exactly alike in every aspect to get along and be friends. It's the differences that make it special, not the similarities. It's seeing past the differences, making the most of them, even appreciating them. But hey, we're just getting to know each other, I'm sure we'll find a lot of things we both have in common."

"Huh, I wouldn't know, but that was pretty good, what you said. Yeah, you're right."

"Give yourself a chance!" she said with a laugh. "It sounds like you're being properly spoiled, good for you! You need some spoiling and someone to make a good healthy fuss over you. I've got a few ideas of what to do when you come over. Oh, by the way, I asked Natalie's parents about having you, and they would be delighted to meet you and borrow you for a few days. Question, do you have your license?"

"Yeah, I do, don't you?"

"Not quite. I'll have it in a few months."

"OK, I probably had more reason to be motivated than you did."

"Probably. Have you had it for long?"

"Kinda, I got it somewhere around eight months or so ago. I'm thinking of buying my own car soon. The evil contraption I use around the house is ready to sign into the junkyard. I don't drive it too often. It's really too dangerous to be on the road."

"Really? My dad's thinking about selling his old Honda. He was talking about it the other day." Sheldon's interest was piqued.

"How much was he thinking of selling it for?"

"I think he said eighteen hundred, not bad for a car, especially a Honda."

"No kidding! Is the motor good? The body in good condition?"

"Yes, no rust on it that I remember. It has an imitation leather interior, AC. It's not convertible, but it does have a sunroof. It's got automatic windows, no radio on the wheel or anything fancy like that, but it's in really good shape."

"I'm interested. A lot. Don't you dare let him sell it! I'll kill myself, I swear. It's too good to be true."

"I'll tell him he's got a potential buyer. Would you like his cell number?"

"Definitely, could you text it to me? I seem to have misplaced my iPod, and there's no paper anywhere."

"I will. I don't know when he was going to put it out, but he didn't want it out in the weather. I guess the winter isn't the best time to sell a car, but you can talk to him about and he'll give you the particulars."

"Sweet, that's great! I hope you've got the price somewhat close to being right, 'cause I'm not exactly rich. Money doesn't grow on trees for me."

"It doesn't for most people."

"All righty, Richelle, I got to go. I'll call you or send you a text when I figure out when I'm coming, OK? Just so you know, I'll have to go back home to shovel out some people if there's a storm. Haven't checked the weather yet."

"OK, it's looking good so far . . . Wait, it looks like there'll be a few inches on Friday in the early morning."

"If it's over around four inches, I try to call people who have someone as a back up. There's only so much one guy can do. I only do a few if it's over that, for the money, but there's no way I have the strength to do ten plus customers with over four inches. I'm totally wasted when I do three inches. It takes me over an hour per customer, depending on how long their walkways are, but I have no idea why I'm telling you this."

"That's OK. I like hearing you talk so much. It's good for you." She tried to rescue herself from the hole she'd got into. She didn't want him suspecting anything. "It looks like there'll be three to five inches, so far. Keep an eye on it, Sheldon."

"Oh, I will. Do you have a massage therapist down where your friend lives?" She giggled as a pathetic note crept into his voice.

"My dad says I'm good for sore shoulders, but I couldn't say."

"I'll let you know what I think if there's a storm while I'm over." He yawned, teeth clicking together. "OK, Chelle, I'll see you in a few days. Have fun. Merry Christmas."

"You too, Shel. Hey, that's funny!"

"What is?"

"You called me Chelle, and I sort of zoned out and called you Shel. It's the same name, just different spelling. Do you mind me calling you that or are you uncomfortable with it?"

"That is funny! No, I don't mind. I actually like it. Just don't call me 'honey' . . ."

Richelle snickered. "All right, honey, you git yurself a good night sleep, and we'll see y'all in the mornin'." She drawled in a southern accent. "Or maybe 'sugar' would be more southern."

"Hey, I meant it! That's just weird!" He laughed. "OK, really got to go. Bye, Richelle, have a good night."

"You too, bye now." She listened as he rolled over and pulled the phone away from his ear. She heard him yawn again as he hung up. She sighed, a little lonely now that his voice was gone. Somehow it made her feel like he was near. She blinked, shaking her head at herself as Natalie walked into the room.

"Oh, you done talking to your boyfriend?" Her eyes were teasing, playful.

"He's my friend," Richelle said shortly, her voice sharp. She missed him a lot, she had to admit, and was in no mood to be teased about him.

"Boyfriend. He's all you've talked about since you've got here. I bet I could draw a portrait of him based on your description!" Richelle blushed.

"Wait 'til you meet him," she shot back weakly.

"You know I'm only kidding." Natalie laughed, putting her hand on her friend's shoulder.

Chapter 5
Twenty Years Older

Sunlight danced across his bedspread, making strange patterns as it shone through the gnarled branches outside his windowpane. Sheldon stretched luxuriously, pulling his blankets over his head. He was too cozy to get out of bed, but the smell of sausages and French toast frying down in the kitchen was incentive enough. Grumbling, he reached out and unplugged his phone from its charger and sent a text to Richelle.

"Good morning! Hey, I've finally got someone to text! Happy Christmas Eve!" He pressed the "send" button and, with a yawn, he rolled out of his blankets and stumbled sleepily into the bathroom, calling good morning to his grandma down the hall. Her cheerful reply floated up to him through the kitchen vent.

Sheldon brushed his teeth and dressed in yesterday's clean clothes. He'd only worn them for about three hours anyway, and they smelled fine, maybe a little funny in the armpits, but that was what the masking scent of Axe was for. He applied a generous amount and flung open the bathroom door, choking helplessly.

"Are you going to survive up there?" Grandma shouted.

"Yeah, I'm fine. Just inhaled some Axe. I'm OK, coming down in a sec." He threw the can of Axe onto his bed and hurried downstairs.

"Are these sausages homemade?"

"You bet they are. I buy them from a country farm a little ways from here."

"Never had anything like them or this toast. You should seriously open up a restaurant 'cause I bet everyone else would go out of business." He popped a sausage into his mouth and chewed blissfully. "So I talked to Richelle last night, found her number she wrote on that address. She said there'll be some snow coming in on Friday."

"I didn't think you could talk to yourself for that long. It sounded like you two had a nice conversation."

"Yeah, we did. She's like no one I've ever met. I feel comfortable talking with her and it's kinda like I've known her forever. So anyways," he said, spearing a piece of French toast, "if it snows like it looks like it's going to, I'll have to catch a train back and do some shoveling. I hope there'll be a train back late at night 'cause I don't want to be stuck there. Did I tell you I'm thinking of getting an apartment this year?"

"It will certainly be good for you to get out. You're old enough, and I'm sure you could take care of yourself better without your dad around. I figured you might have to shovel, but hopefully, you won't have too much to do."

"The forecast isn't saying there'll be a lot. But yeah, I think it'll be great to have my own place." He finished his breakfast and leaned back in his chair with his coffee. "I'm not sure if I could afford an apartment. I might just rent a room and eat my meals out. I don't know, I guess I'll figure it out when I get there." He smiled at her over his mug. "I'm not so sure about that now." His face clouded over. "Before, I was set on clearing out as soon as school is out in June, but now I have something holding me back. And it's a friendship." He paused, his eyes flickering up to hers for a moment, then stared at the coffee cup in his hands. "It's just that I've always felt like something was chaining me down, preventing me from moving on. But Richelle is the best thing that has happened to me in years. She's my only friend, and no one should ever leave a friend behind. But I don't want to be near the old man. I don't want to feel responsible for him, I want to be my own person. And I don't want to hate her because of that. I just want to love somebody, Grammy. I don't want to hate anymore." He raised his head, meeting her eyes squarely. "I've poisoned myself all these years, and walled off my feelings so I wouldn't feel. I don't know how to get out. But when I'm with her, I feel like it's different somehow, like I could change." His voice came haltingly. "What do I do? I'm scared to death that I'll mess everything up."

"Do you like her?" His confusion was clear in his eyes.

"Like her? What do you mean?"

"I mean, do you want more than a friendship?"

"No!" His answer was decisive. "Not in that way, no. I want to know Richelle. I like her as a friend. Her as a girlfriend never even crossed my mind, I mean, I just barely met her!. But if I thought she was in it for that, I'd be done. I am just not ready for that, I've got too much pain to work through. I don't need a wishy-washy girlfriend hanging over my head, all temperamental kisses. No way! But what am I gonna do, Grammy?"

"I can't answer that, Sheldon. But we can pray about it. God always takes care of us."

"You think so? I'm not so sure," he said broodingly, dropping his chin onto his fist.

"Oh, but I am. Who do you think has protected you all these years? You?" She shook her head. "I can see God's hand all over your life, honey. He's kept you safe. No one else could've with what you've been exposed to: drugs, alcohol, sex, who knows what else. But you hate the very idea of doing what your father does. God's kept you pure in more ways than just physically. Can you see it?" He looked thoughtful, his coffee cold and forgotten on the table.

"Yes, I can."

"You know, the fact that you are even open to the thought of loving anybody is a miracle. You're not embittered as much as one would think, or as angry. I know there's so much pain, but you still can feel. And you can listen to me talk to you about God and not walk away. No, He has kept you from so much, from the world that preys on the innocent, and even from yourself, with the damaging anger."

"I need to talk to you more often 'cause you help me see myself in a different light. You're right, things aren't as bad as they could be." He got up to put his empty dishes in the sink and dumped the coffee down the drain.

"You could always move into town. Your father is four miles away or something like that. He's pretty far removed, and he doesn't go very far anyways."

"True. Richelle lives in town. I could always go to the next town over, but it depends on what's available. Thanks for listening to me, Grammy, it's good to get stuff off my chest."

"Come here, you!" She held out her arms and hugged him to her, rocking him back and forth. "I'm always here, always." He laid his head on her shoulder, his height making it a little awkward. She patted his back. "Would you like to go sledding? I've got a big old toboggan in the garage." He pulled away.

"That would be fun, sure, why not!"

Laughing and shouting, they sped down the steep hill, alone in the wild white beauty of the countryside.

"Are you sure we aren't gonna crash?" Sheldon shouted back to her, tears blinding his eyes. "I can't see a blessed thing."

"No, we'll be fine!"

They sat, gasping, as the toboggan slid to a stop at the bottom. Sheldon looked back.

"Wow, I think we went a mile that time! That was awesome! You up for another try?"

"Oh, I feel twenty years younger! I haven't had this much fun in a long time. Come on, I'll race you to the top!"

"Yeah, right! My legs are like twice the length of yours!"

"But I'm not pulling that sled!" She smiled, her face crinkling up with fun.

They went up and down the hill for hours until Grandma got so tired that Sheldon had to pull her back on the last run.

"OK, I'm done." He flopped into a snow bank. "Oh, my poor legs, my back!" She laughed as she got off the sled and walked to the car, pulling it behind her across the snow.

"Come on, Shel! Unless you'd like to walk home, which is fine with me," she said teasingly.

"Hey, wait for me!" He levered himself to his feet and hobbled after her. "I think you loaned me those twenty years, thanks." She laughed so hard that she had to sit down.

"Oh, you poor thing, just you wait until you're as old as I am. I'll drive." She hopped into the driver's seat. Groaning, he fell into the passenger side, laboriously shutting himself in. "I think a nice hot bath sounds like it's right up your alley, don't you?"

"Mmm, and hot chocolate. You have no idea how hard it was to pull you up that hill, didn't know you were that heavy." She slapped his hand.

"Don't you talk to me about my weight!"

"What? Not like you're two hundred pounds or something."

"Close enough."

"Yeah, right! That sled isn't exactly a lightweight. Man, I am famished!" His eyes popped. "Three o'clock? We've been out for hours!"

"You ready for a workout?" she teased.

"I think that counts! There's absolutely no way I'll be able to do anything more. What's for lunch?"

"I'm calling it an early supper. We'll have a midnight snack after service tonight."

"Oh, I forgot about that." He looked out the window. "Are there a lot of people?"

"We've got a good-sized congregation for so far up north, and as it is Christmas, there'll be more than the usuals. Probably two hundred or so."

"Oh yeah! Lots of fire!" He grinned. She clicked her tongue.

"You'd better be good."

"Just kidding. Oh, good to be home." He held open the kitchen door for her as she came up from the garage, bulky and wet in her snowsuit.

"Let's get this stuff off, and I'll heat up last-night's chicken gravy."

"Goody, give me your coat and I'll hang it up."

Chapter 6

Pinching Fire

Sheldon stood in front of his mirror, fastening the buttons on his shirt. He was looking as good as he was going to get without real dress-clothes, with his dark jeans free of holes and his blond hair tapering over one eye.

"I probably should shave," he mumbled to himself, digging through his top drawer for a razor. He shuffled down the short hallway to the bathroom and leaned over the sink, methodically lathering his face with shaving cream. Carefully, he ran the razor just above his jawline, over his cheeks systematically, and gave his throat a few strokes. He splashed water over his face and dried it off, peering over the folds of the towel at his reflection in the mirror to see the result. He traced over the thin line of hair he'd left on his jaw, quickly touching it up. Hurriedly, he slapped some aftershave on his cheeks and cleaned up his mess, swirling water around in the sink to wash all the stubble down the drain.

Back in his room, he fished his Converse from under his bed, taking care not to tear any of the concealed packages. He laced them up and joined his grandmother downstairs. "Not too bad? You look very festive." He surveyed her red-and-green sweater.

"You're just saved from being very unseasonable yourself with that red plaid. I like it, the narrow design is interesting."

"I thought it was pretty cool. I don't like the traditional plaid all that much, but this one was more me."

A little while later, they pulled into the church.

"Wow, I hope we find a space, this is packed! We should have come earlier." Sheldon glanced around at the tight rows of cars in the dim light cast by the streetlamps.

"I see one! Nope, then again . . ." They drove slowly around the parking lot and finally found a lonely space in the far back. Grandma shut the car off, and they hurried into the church. Organ music, lots of people, little children everywhere; Sheldon looked around with a rather bewildered air, feeling a little unsure of himself.

"Front row, Sheldon," his grandma whispered, and he followed her up the aisle, feeling like there were a million pairs of eyes boring into his back. He sat on the edge of his seat, tense and uncertain. "Relax, Shel, no one's going to eat you." He gave her a forlorn look and reshaped his bangs. "You missed a piece." She brushed his hair back with her hand before he could protest. The organ stopped. The guy at the pulpit gripped the edges and leaned on it, grinning infectiously out over the congregation.

"Good evening to all you, folks, merry Christmas! A special welcome to all our visitors, it's good to see your faces here tonight." Grandma poked Sheldon with her elbow, getting a smirk in response. "Please rise for our New Testament reading." The congregation rose to their feet, an older woman turning to the passage in her Bible and reading the words clearly into the microphone.

". . . She will bear a son, and you shall call his name Jesus, for He will save His people from their sins."

The next thing Sheldon knew, the organist was playing the opening bars of "Joy to the World," and many voices burst into song, like a huge choir. Then people began greeting one another, shaking hands and wishing merry Christmas all around.

"Hi, I'm David." A tall, slender, dark-haired boy held out his hand.

"Sheldon. Merry Christmas."

"You too." The woman standing beside David was apparently his mother, and she echoed her son in wishing Sheldon a merry Christmas as well. The preacher mounted the steps to his pulpit, calling his congregation to order.

"Please join me in prayer," he said, launching into a lengthy prayer full of joy and gratitude for God sending His Son to earth as a baby to become a sin-offering for His people.

The sermon was on gratitude, and Sheldon found it strangely applicable. He'd realized through his conversation with his grandmother that he truly had a lot to be grateful for, and he was. So when the pastor concluded his message with a prayer, Sheldon offered up his own, brief and awkward as it was. The lights dimmed after the closing hymn was sung, and the first candle was lit, the tiny flames popping up and spreading like wildfire all over the sanctuary. Grandma turned toward him, shielding the little light in behind her hand. He held his wick to hers and passed it on to David behind him. He grinned at him as the candle caught, the small flame flickering. Candles all over the room danced as the piano struck up "Silent Night," and Sheldon restrained himself from putting his finger into the wax dripping down into the candle holder. Soon enough, the lights switched on, and people began talking all at once, their voices rising to a dull roar.

Sheldon couldn't help himself any longer and turned innocently in the opposite direction from his grandmother, furtively pinching out his flame.

"Yow, how did you *do* that?" He looked up in surprise. The dark-haired boy was blowing frantically on his burnt fingers then gave it up as a lost cause and stuck them in his mouth. Sheldon put his own finger to his lips and jerked a thumb back at his grandmother.

"Shhhh!" he hissed under his breath, glancing guiltily in her direction. For all his caution, she wasn't taking any notice of him and was conversationally jabbering away with the woman who had read the New Testament passage. Slightly relieved, he turned back to the boy and leaned casually against the pew. "David, right?" He nodded the affirmative, eyes friendly and his manner open. "Takes a few times to get it right. Gotta do it quick and measured. Don't wanna be too scared, 'cause nothing will happen."

"Thanks! Might take some practice. Mom's always lighting candles all over the place." He smiled, glancing from Sheldon to his grandmother. "You visiting?"

"Yep. That's my grandma." And then David asked the question, and wasn't experienced enough to catch the guarded look that flashed into Sheldon's eyes, the friendliness snuffed out like a light. He noticed a definite change, but he couldn't figure out what it was.

"Are your parents here?"

"Just me." Sheldon's tone was tense in spite of his effort to keep it light, the result sounding a little funny. The other boy looked at him strangely.

"You OK?" Sheldon cleared his throat derivatively.

"Yeah, just something in the boom box, sorry," David snorted.

"That was a good one!" Sheldon was immensely relieved and relaxed slightly, glad the younger boy was easily distracted.

"Yeah, I come out with some weird stuff sometimes."

"I can believe it. You a senior?"

"Yep, almost done. Lucky, huh?"

"Sure are."

"Just born sooner, that's all. What grade are you in?"

"I'm a sophomore. Gotta few years to go. It's not that bad. I mean I like my school and the teachers are nice."

"The teachers really determine if the school is good, although of course, where you live is important. My school isn't that big. I'm figuring that yours isn't either, just 'cause this area isn't so populated. And of course, the kids you're stuck with are just huge."

"Yeah, true. Do you like your school?"

"No." David figured it was time to change the subject.

"So whatcha want for Christmas?"

"A car, and it looks like I'll be able to get one soon, probably a little late for Christmas, but I don't care. Just a little present from me to me. My friend's dad is selling it. I haven't even seen it yet, but it sounds cool."

"That's awesome! I can't wait 'til I can drive. What kind of car is it?"

"She said it's a Honda, an older one, but hey, not like it's a bug or something stupid."

"Hey, it's got a roof and tires, right?"

"Yeah, that's pretty much what it comes down to, only it's gotta have a functioning motor."

"Yeah, well, that's sort of a given."

"Just had to point out the obvious!" Sheldon laughed.

"Hey, it's been cool getting to know you, Sheldon." David glanced at his family. "They're gonna leave me behind if I don't get going. Merry Christmas, man." He gave Sheldon a fist bump and backed out of the pew. "Will you be here Sunday?"

"Nah, I don't think so. See ya." David hurriedly raised his hand in farewell, and Sheldon watched the dark head vanish around the doorjamb. Balancing on the back of a pew, Sheldon watched his grandmother talking for a while and then took out his phone. There was a text from Richelle.

"Merry Xmas Eve, Sheldon! Oh good! And you at least can spell! :P" Smiling at his phone, he swiped a reply.

"Hey! Yeah, I can spell. Sad, isn't it? I'm so behind times :P" He put the phone back into his pocket and looked around the church. A few people stood around in groups, deep in conversation, but the majority had left. Grandma showed no signs of letting up. He sighed dismally, bored. All of a sudden, his phone vibrated, and he was momentarily disoriented and nearly dropped it.

":P: P Silly! You sound like you think that's a bad thing!"

"Oh, whatever, at least you can read me."

"Oh hi!:) And yes, I can read you, just like a book!"

"Lol."

"Hey! It's text language!"

":D not totally outdated yet."

"Did you go to church?"

"Yeah, I'm sitting in a pew."

"I hope I don't have to call you a big bad boy, :P"

"No, I wouldn't text in church. Talk about disrespectful."

"Very. Are you a Christian?"

"Idk, to be honest with you." Richelle wondered what to say, thumbs posed over the screen, her mind racing.

"Hey, I'll pray for you, OK?"

"Take it that you are? Thnxs."

"Yes, it's like nothing you can think of, Shel."

"Huh."

"Hmm."

"Hmm."

"Lol. Whatcha doin'?"

"Texting you . . . duh . . ."

"O_o. Well, I know *that*, but besides!"

"Watching grandma talking to some woman. I'd be bored out of my mind if you weren't online."

"Watching her talk? What? Is she totally French?"

"What?"

"French. Does she use her hands to emphasize?"

"Oh, totally. It's hilarious, cuz I can't hear a thing she's saying."

"I love watching people like that! It's so amusing."

"Very."

"So how was your sermon?"

"I liked it. He's a good pastor, not that I go to church, but I liked his style."

"I'm glad you liked it. What was the topic?"

"Gratitude."

":)"

"Hey, she's done. I gtg, Chelle. Ttys."

"Bye, and merry Xmas!"

"You too! Ttys." Sheldon killed the screen and tucked the phone into his pocket.

"Sorry I took so long, Sheldon. I get to talking and well, stay talking," Grandma said with a smile.

"That's OK. I was texting Chelle."

"Who's that? Your double?"

"Richelle. It's c-h-e-l-l-e. She thought it was funny we have the same nickname. So yeah, I wasn't too bored." She raised her eyebrows.

"I see. I was rather surprised you didn't walk up and start poking me. Are you feeling hungry?"

"Yup! All that singing, I'm in need of some sustenance."

"You want to help me prep some food for tomorrow? I've got to get that turkey into the oven by six in the morning, so I need the stuffing. I actually made the pie dough the other day, so it's been chilling for a while."

He got behind the wheel and started up the car, rolling down to the road and looking both ways before he pulled out onto it.

"OK, what do I do?" he asked, one hand on the wheel.

"You can make the stuffing or peel apples for the pie."

"Can I do the apples? I can't really mess up on those."

"You've got to learn how to cook somehow!"

"Oh, that's what you women are for!"

"I guess you're going to marry young or starve or just go bankrupt!"

He threw his head back and laughed.

"I'll make a note of that—won't do to forget it!"

"The directions for the stuffing are on the box. Tell you what, let's do it together."

"That's more like it. Gotta have some Christmas music blasting good and loud, well, in the background. It'll be nice."

"You sound just like your mother. She refused to do anything around the holidays without Christmas music." Her voice was tender.

"Mom knew how to do it right."

"That's because she was my daughter. And you're your mother's son, all right. In more ways than the one written on your face. Your mother was a beautiful woman, and you really take after her looks."

"Now I'm beautiful, sheesh, what next?"

She laughed at his rueful tone.

"No, just too handsome for your own shoes."

"What do my shoes have to do with my face?" His eyes sparkled playfully as she fell for it, explaining that it was just a saying. "I'm just kidding with you, Gram. I never thought I was bad looking, but . . . you know what, this is just a weird topic."

"No, you're very handsome. If I was forty-five years younger, I'd fall in love with those blue eyes myself."

"All right, cut it out! That is creepy! Talk about sketchy . . ."

"I was going to stop, we're home anyway. Let's go forage," he snorted.

"Forage indeed! There's enough food in that fridge to feed us for a month."

She dug around in the fridge. "Let's see. There's spaghetti and meatballs, some wonton soup I made the other day with shrimp, a little chicken Alfredo—that probably needs some doctoring by now, because it gets dried out fast—and cookies for dessert."

"That wonton soup sounds good. Are the shrimp inside the noodle thingies?"

"Yes, it's rather complicated and time consuming, but there isn't a lot of me." Her mouth quirked humorously as she poured the soup into a small pot and turned the burner on. "I'll eat the spaghetti. The Alfredo will take too long to fix up. Oh, and grab that pie dough, it has to warm up a little. Cold dough is hard to work with." He transferred it to the counter, jabbing at it with a tentative finger.

"This stuff is bizarre. It feels like it's alive or something."

"There's probably something growing in it, like bacteria," she chuckled.

"Ew, that's gross! Technically you're right because of the yeast and all, but I'd rather not think of my pie as teaming with all kinds of nasty stuff, I'm good."

"Don't worry, they're all baked in by the time you eat it. Here, come take your soup. Careful, it's hot!" He gingerly took the bowl and perched on the counter, spoon posed over it. Selecting a wonton, he fished it out and nibbled a piece.

"Wow, that's hot!" He fanned at his mouth, huffing fretfully.

"Don't say I didn't warn you," she said dismissively, spiraling spaghetti around her fork. He bit his tongue apprehensively.

"I'm gonna wait until this chills out." He set the steaming bowl cautiously in the freezer. Singling out a likely paring knife from a drawer, he commenced to peeling apples. "With my luck, it'll be cold," he remarked concerning his supper, hacking away at the fruit.

"You polish this off for me. I've eaten enough." She handed him her half-finished plate and got the stuffing mix and an onion out of the pantry, pouring the mix into a large silver bowl.

"I love meatballs." He sucked up a noodle dangling out of his mouth.

"You like anything edible." He grinned and cleaned off the dish.

"Oh psh. Not necessarily." He pulled open the freezer and dipped a finger testily into the soup. "Not bad. I think I'll get this wife of mine a Chinese cookbook and sign her up for a class." He chewed up a wonton. Grandma regarded him, clearly mystified.

"Wife?"

"Well, you did advise me to marry young. I'm taking this seriously!" He heard a snicker, but she was innocently dicing onions. He slowly ladled his way through the soup. The little old lady sliced up a few stalks of celery, stirring them in with a little warm water and melted butter.

"I don't hear any music, Shel! What happened to it?" she observed. Sheldon wiped his mouth with the back of a hand and pulled out his phone.

"This will work if you don't want anything louder."

"It is background music." She winked at him. "You want to finish those apples while I roll out the dough?"

"Sure, I've got like four left." He turned on some Christmas carols, carefully setting the phone on the coffee machine. "I think it's easier to peel them if you quarter them first. And a whole lot faster," he said as he picked up an apple, quartered it, and cut out the core. Grandma looked up, rolling pin posed over the lump of dough.

"I suppose it could be, but I've always peeled the whole thing and then sliced it up, but then again, you can never teach an old dog new tricks." She set a pan by his elbow. "Just put those slices into this while you're waiting for the piecrust." The rolling pin pressed into the dough, flattening it out on one side. She turned it onto the other, rolling each side simultaneously as she tried to keep it somewhat circular in shape, until it reached the correct thinness. Holding the knife and the last apple, Sheldon observed the skill with which she flipped the dough into the pie fan, crimping it to the edge with her thumb all around the pan.

"Sheldon," she chided gently. He hurriedly resumed his task, peels dropping onto the floor. He sighed and bent over to retrieve them, taking care to work over the counter. Grandma began rolling out the next lump, and he asked if he had to peel apples for that pie as well.

"No, this one is going to be pumpkin. How are you coming along over there?"

"I'm doing, not very fast you know." He hummed along to "Jingle Bells" in a squeaky comical voice that made her laugh. "Aww, you messed it up!" he cracked up.

"What was there to mess up?" Sheldon pulled an offended face.

"Ouch!" He set the apple slices down next to her. Laughing, Grandma moved to the fridge and took out a bowl full of a brownish liquid. "What's that supposed to be?"

"This, my dear boy, is the pumpkin filling. It'll taste fine, trust me," she said in humorous self-defense.

"I'm sure it will when it's done, but it looks like somebody was sick!" Amused, she shook her head and poured the pumpkin filling into the waiting pie shell.

"Lovely! Now for that apple pie." She fluttered about the cupboards, sifting and sprinkling this and that into the apples, tossing them, and dumping them into the shell before crimping dough over top of them. She made a few cuts for ventilation in the top and placed both the pies inside the oven. "There! Now I might as well stuff that turkey. It'll be one less thing to do so early in the morning."

"OK, I think I'll go take a shower." Sheldon passed her the turkey. "Not touching this thing."

"Definitely marrying young." Snorting, he left her chuckling to herself and went up the stairs, closing himself in the bathroom.

CHAPTER 7
The Past Relived

A few moments later, he hurried to his room along with a cloud of steam which wafted away down the hall smelling of men's shower gel. Grumbling, he flung open his door and yelled down to the kitchen.

"Hey, Grammy?"

"Yes?"

"When you're done, could you bring up my phone? I'd get it myself, but I forgot to bring a pair of pajama pants." He heard muffled laughter. "Hey, just letting you know! You might come walking in on me and die of shock at seeing me in my boxers, I don't know!"

"Sheldon, you quit making me laugh! I'll be up in a minute, get yourself in bed so I don't have an early death."

"Thanks!" Snickering, he hopped into bed and tucked himself in. *She'll be so surprised tomorrow*, he thought, yawning sleepily. He stretched, running long fingers through his damp hair. The minutes ticked by and he'd nearly forgotten that his grandmother was coming upstairs when a knock sounded at the door.

"Sheldon? Can I come in?"

"Sure." He turned his head toward her, returning her smile cheerily, if not a little wearily. She sat on the edge of his bed and looked down at him lovingly.

"Tomorrow is going to be Christmas, wonderful, isn't it?." She stroked his hair back from his forehead. "I'm going to miss having you around when you go." Her voice was wistful.

"Aw, come on, Grammy. I'm not going anywhere just yet. I just got here, see?"

"Oh, I know. I just get to thinking. Life is so different with you."

"And with you, but I can't stay forever," he said gently.

"No, of course not." She smiled.

"Love you, Grammy."

"I love you too dearest." She kissed his cheek and stood. "Oh I almost forgot. Here's your phone." It passed from one hand to the other. "Have fun talking to Richelle."

"Accusation!" he squawked in protest.

"Don't give me that! I'll see you in the morning. Sleep tight!" The door eased closed behind her.

"Night!" His lips twisting into a sheepish grin, he shamelessly dialed Richelle's number.

"Sheldon?" Her voice was hushed.

"Yeah, it's me. Is this a bad time?"

"No, it's just eleven o'clock!"

"Oh, well . . . How come you're whispering?"

"I'm in bed and trying not to wake Natalie up!"

"I'm sorry! Guess I could call tomorrow."

"No, no, no, it's fine."

"Seems like I'm always in bed when I talk to you, weird." She laughed softly, trying not to make any noise.

"So what do you want to talk about?"

"Oh, I don't know, don't really care. I just really like talking to you. A friend is a new idea. You seem like a dream unless I can see you," he confined companionably, innocently ignorant of her synchronous delight and blushing face. She was vastly relieved that he was on the phone with her and not in the room. "You ever felt like you've known a person for like years, but you'd just met them?"

"Yes, I feel like that with you, in a way."

"Thanks. I totally feel that way with you. There're not many people like that you know."

"I know, there really isn't," she agreed readily. They chatted for a while, catching up and making small talk.

"So now what shall we talk about?" Sheldon asked. She was quiet, considering whether she should ask him.

"Do you want to tell me about yourself? I mean, you said you wanted to, back on the train, but maybe you'd rather not right yet." She bit her lip.

"I want to tell you, but I don't know how," he said slowly and paused. "Nobody really knows me for me, you know? Like how I think, who I really am. I'll try to tell you, but I don't know how this is gonna come out. Some people like voicing all their problems, but I never did, not even to myself." He became thoughtful. "Like if I didn't say it, it wouldn't be true, wouldn't be real, you know?" She nodded and, with a start, remembered he couldn't see her.

"Yes, yes, I do. You can just talk to me. It's OK, you can let it out." Her voice was soft in his ear.

"OK . . ." He swallowed audibly. "I remember when Dad had a job," he said in a funny tone that made it sound like he was talking about someone other than himself, like he was telling an old story almost. "I had lots of friends. Mom . . . Mom was the one who held us together. She loved us to pieces, and when she died, we just fell apart."

"How did she die?" she asked softly, beginning to draw him out.

"Dad got a call one afternoon, police. She'd gone shopping and never came back. Damn crazy drunk killed her." His voice took on a sudden raw and angry note, and it hurt her to hear him speak. "Dad screamed into the phone. I can't remember what he said, but I think his mind snapped, I really do. He was just never the same since. I don't remember much, it's just a blur, maybe because every day was mostly the same in my mind. Dad walking around, just pacing, all through the night. He didn't sleep for days, he was like a zombie. Then one day I got home from an awful day at school, everyone was horrible, and I distinctly remember walking into that house and not hearing a thing. No footsteps, nothing. He was gone. I think it was because I was so young, because I lost both my parents in a way, but I haven't trusted anyone for years, especially adults. Grandma was the only one." He was quiet, and then he said almost inaudibly, "Dad hated the sight of me. I figured that out soon enough. I look too much like Mom did. I'll show you a picture some time." His tone strengthened. "He abandoned me. Three days I was in that house, alone. Then one night he came back, roaring drunk, and when he saw me, he fell on his knees and started sobbing, crying Mom's name. I was just a little kid and I didn't know what the hell was going on. I got really freaked out and started crying, and he realized I wasn't Mom." The line went silent.

"Did he . . . did he hurt you?"

"Yeah, he hurt me, hit me. I don't know for how long. When I woke up, he was gone. After that, I never went near him if I could help it, although that didn't keep me very safe from him. His legs were longer than mine." His harsh laugh sounded more like a cough.

"He beat you unconscious?" She was appalled. "Oh, Shel." Her eyes stung. He went on as if she'd never spoken.

"So he quit the job, took to drinking, nightclubs, the whole damn thing, anything to escape I guess. We got kicked out of our house, and he had to use his savings to buy our shack. That's what I live in, a shack. 'Cause of him. Sometimes I get so mad at Mom, for dying, for going out that day." He choked.

"No, no, no, don't say that," Richelle said desperately. He got a grip on himself and, speaking very deliberately, went on.

"I hated people, the kids at school, the teachers with their condescending pity, everyone. When you're fragile like that, people just tear you apart. Friends left me in the dust and never gave me a second glance in the halls. They made me sit by myself and always bullied me. That did change to being ignored when I got older. I tried opening up once, new kid, but I got totally burned, so I never tried it again. You know, if I'd met you in school, I would've missed out on so much, so much." Richelle began to cry, whispering his name, echoing his pain back to him. "Don't cry, Chelle, I have to get this over with. I have to do this." She took a deep breath.

"Oh, I'm not going anywhere without you when school starts again. I won't let them hurt you." He smiled suddenly.

"No, *I* won't let them hurt *you*. See, I'm used to it, and you're not. You let me help you, OK?"

"OK." She sniffed rather emotionally.

"Now, when I was fourteen or so, I guess Dad figured I was old enough so he started bringing in his girlfriends, and after the third one, they just got worse and worse. Don't want to know where the heck he picks them up, it's frightening. One time I got home from work and walked in. Dad was gone, but there was this woman waiting for him. Gosh, she scared me to death, I won't ever forget what she looked like I think. I was so traumatized." He laughed harshly. "Anyways, she was next to me before I knew what was happening, and I swear she had snakes for hands, it was disgusting. She tried to kiss me, and I got the hell out of there as fast as my legs would go. Let me tell you, I've never gone inside the house when he's got his girls over. I've spent more nights in the shed than I care to remember. It's really bad in the winter."

"I'll bet!" She was feeling a little uncomfortable. Sheldon was quiet for a moment, and Richelle wondered if he had completely forgotten she was there, lost in the painful memories of the past he'd kept buried for so long. Just when she was going to say something, she heard him take a deep breath and let it out slowly, a little shakily.

"Dad tried to get me to drink, and I was sorely tempted a few times, but every time I picked up a bottle, I could hear him in my head, going off into one of his rages, and I couldn't bring myself to do it, 'cause I knew I wouldn't be able to stop once I'd let the devil out of the bottle," he said each word purposely, dragging forth his memories, getting it all out deliberately and slowly, yet the time seemed to stand still as his voice went on. Suddenly, it took on a fierce independent note. "I don't want to become like him. I hate the smell of the stuff, and I've got to live with it. Place reeks of alcohol, makes me want to throw up when I go inside. Surprised he hasn't started chewing on the walls. I'm sure the sheetrock is fermented enough." He ended sarcastically, disgust and bitterness permeating his tone. "So I've built up walls. I've felt free in my own cage. Hate is a prison, you know. Being bitter drags you down." Hope ventured its way into his words, lifting his tone. "You might think I'm totally weird, but when I'm with you, I don't feel so imprisoned. I feel like you can set me free. Richelle, I can't help myself. I wanted to run away and do something crazy. I never wanted to kill myself, but I've thought of it for sure. I was just so entangled in my own hate, so in love with it that I felt desperate enough to do anything to rid myself of him. I felt powerful, like I could take that hate and one day turn it against him and get revenge for everything he's done to me. When people shut me out, I determined to like being a loner and made myself believe it was my own choice. There was freedom in that, thinking it was my choice to be who I was." Richelle closed her eyes, tears running unheeded down her cheeks. "I don't know what to do when I feel love." His voice was so quiet; it was nearly a whisper. The pleading and pain in it was so strong, so lost that she wanted to reach out and pull him close to give him something to hold onto. She opened her eyes, listening to the sound of his voice, the sound of him breathing on the other line.

"Love makes me feel vulnerable. I used to hate that, 'cause I felt like I'd lost control of my life. Talking to Grammy, when I asked her if I could come over for Christmas, that all changed. Something inside me broke, and suddenly, I wanted to love. I wanted to *be* loved more than anything. It was kind of like a healing pain if you know what I mean. It was as if the hate had just cracked. And the next day, I met you, and it was like you didn't even belong here. You're so different."

"How?" she asked, wonderingly.

"There isn't any hate or spite in you, you're real. It took me a while to fully convince myself of your sincerity, but once I did, it was so foreign to me that it was like you weren't even human. Everyone else my age has only given me pain. You treat me like a person, a friend. I think you changed my life, Chelle. I know you did." Her control reached its limit, and she began to cry softly; he heard her, and suddenly, he couldn't speak for the lump in his throat. He dropped the phone, embarrassed that she would hear him crying.

"Shel?" She sounded distant. Struggling with his emotions, he held the phone to his ear.

"I'm here." His tremulous voice betrayed him.

"Shel." She was suddenly shy.

"What is it?" Then it all came out in a rush.

"Oh, Shel, don't you ever forget that I love you! Do you hear me?" She gasped, trying to speak though her voice kept catching in her tight throat.

"You really truly can still say that after all that?" He was incredulous.

"More than ever. Oh, I'm so, so glad that I met you, so glad!"

"I'm more glad than you'll ever know." Despite the intensity of the conversation, he yawned. Surprised at himself, he glanced at the clock. "Good gosh, Chelle, it's one-thirty in the morning! Hey, it's Christmas! Merry Christmas, you!" She giggled, smiling through her tears.

"You too!"

"We probably should talk later. I think we both could use a little sleep!"

"Yeah, now that you mention it, I suppose I could!"

"All right, then, good night, sis. Thanks for everything."

"Good night, Sheldon. I'm so thankful you told me everything, it makes us more friends than ever. You feel better?"

"Rather." She could hear his smile.

"Love you, Shel. Merry Christmas. Good night."

"You too, 'night."

Sheldon turned over on his side, his mind reeling from the memories he'd forced it to dig up; he was weary and utterly exhausted. He drifted into sleep, thankful for a chance at a better life and freedom from his hate.

Richelle lay down, her face still damp with tears. He'd experienced more pain than she could wrap her mind around. She had been so blessed with parents who loved each other and their children! She prayed for Sheldon like she'd never prayed for anyone before. How he needed someone to love him; he was desperately in need of guidance, a family even, for no one should go through life alone. She prayed that God would flood him with His love and send His Spirit, the Comforter. Slipping into unconsciousness, her eyes closed, heavy with sleep.

Chapter 8

Best Christmas Ever

Snow on the windowsill, a penciling of white on every branch. It was a Christmas out of a storybook, out of a dream.

Grandma bustled about the kitchen, baking cinnamon rolls. Water bubbled lustily on the stove top for hot chocolate. The turkey was roasting slowly under its aluminum foil, stuffed to bursting point. She lit a few candles, the scent of evergreen and apple pie floating up into the air to mingle with that of the rolls. All that was needed to complete the tranquil scene was, of course, the reason for all the festivity, Sheldon.

She wandered over to the head of the stairs, match box in hand, and looked up, dubious as to whether he was an early riser. She called his name inquiringly. There was a sleepy groan, sounding like he was stretching. "You awake? I made breakfast."

"Smells good!" he yelled and mumbled something inarticulate. "I'm up. I'm up."

"Come on down. We'll eat breakfast in our pj's." Sheldon shuffled sleepy-eyed out into the hall, pulling a shirt over his tousled head.

"Morning," he announced sleepily, grinning at her. "Beautiful Christmas, isn't it?"

"It is," she agreed. "Looks like you're having a little trouble there." He pushed his arm through and forced the shirt down over his trim torso. "How much sleep did you get? I fell asleep around midnight and you were still talking." Seeing a fleeting expression of anxiety cut across his features, she hastily went on to say that she was unable to overhear what he was saying. His eyes became amused.

"Oh, I looked at the clock at one-thirty and nearly had a heart attack and probably went to sleep pretty soon afterward. Here, I'll serve. You've been doing too much." He sat her down at the table and pushed her chair in. "Wow, you made cinnamon rolls?" He brought the heaping basket to the table. "Oh, these are heavenly," he gloated jubilantly, pouring boiling water over hot chocolate mix into two mugs. She watched him adoringly as he seated himself, passing her the cocoa. He consumed a roll in blissful silence, savoring it on his tongue. Sipping his cocoa, he inhaled suddenly, his eyes filling. "That soup last night," he choked, "really singed my tongue. Totally scalded it! I'm going to use a spoon, go ahead and call me a baby."

"You are." He looked at her peevishly. "You're my baby."

"Spoiled beyond hope or repair." He grinned carelessly and picked up another pastry, dunking it into his chocolate.

"The last time you did that, you lost a cookie in milk. Good thing you've got a spoon."

"This is a different texture. It's not so crumbly." He sloshed it up and down in his mug and popped it into his mouth appreciatively.

"Well, it being Christmas, I've got you a little something when you're done." His face registered obvious surprise. "You didn't think I'd get you a present? That's the fun of having you for Christmas, I must spoil you all the way." Her eyes twinkled with fun.

"Whatever you say," he laughed.

After they'd finished breakfast, Grandma grabbed Sheldon's hand and towed him into the living room like she was a little girl again. There around the base of the tree were various boxes of assorted shapes and sizes. Sheldon looked at her, utterly astounded.

"Wow, Gram, really, this is too much!"

"Nonsense! You are my only grandchild, after all." He shook his head.

"Hold on a sec, this needs something more." He turned and disappeared up the stairs. A few more packages from underneath his bed were added to those under the tree.

"I think we surprised each other equally today," Grandma remarked as she warmed herself before the fireplace. She held her hands out over the dancing flames.

"The best kind of surprises are the ones you weren't expecting." Grinning with anticipation, Sheldon sat down beside his grandmother, pressing a small box into her hand. "You first!"

"Oh, Sheldon, it's beautiful!" She lifted out the necklace. "Would you clasp it on for me?" She held it out to him, the silver chain sparkling in the firelight. He moved behind her, fumbling with the clasp as he managed to hitch it together. "Is this your birthstone?" she asked, touching the tiny red gem as she straightened the pendant.

"It is," he said.

"This is lovely, sweetheart. Thank you. Now I know that this isn't the most practical thing I could've gotten you, but I fell in love with it the moment I saw it." She plunked a large rectangular box in his lap. He tore off the wrapping paper and lifted the lid. Tissue paper. He dug through it and pulled out a shimmery black formal suit.

"You got me a tux?" He laughed.

"Don't you love the material? It's so unusual that I just had to get it. You have to have something to wear to prom." She looked away from his suspicious eyes innocently.

"It is really nice. The prom . . . Grammy?" He looked at her suspiciously, eyes narrowed.

"What?" She lifted her hands. "I must see you put it on! It should fit. I got your sizes from your laundry." He looked embarrassed. "And here are the shoes to go with it." The shiny black leather dress-shoes were a perfect match for the suit, according to Grammy. She took another package from him and unwrapped it.

"How did you know I love purple? And it's deliciously fuzzy!" She put her scarf around her neck.

"I thought you'd like it," he said, pleased with his choice. She smiled and unwrapped her last gift. "Chocolates, my favorite."

"I bought that for *you*, no sharing!" He took the proffered chocolate in his fingertips and popped it into her mouth.

"Oh, perfectly delicious! This is good quality, so nice and creamy. You really must try one!"

"No, I'll have enough sweets today. That pie is calling my name." He laughed at her.

"I've got one more thing for you," she said around the mouthful of chocolate, reaching for the last package. It was a leather study Bible, with his name embossed on the cover. Sheldon Eric Trindell. "It's an ESV, a very good translation, and you'll find the commentary helpful."

"Thank you, Grammy. This is awesome." He hugged her affectionately.

"Merry Christmas, dear. Now go try on that suit! I want to see if it fits you."

"All right, all right, if you insist." His face screwed up into a grimace.

"And I'll be wanting a picture, so go all the way!" Sheldon gathered up his things and padded up the stairs to his room.

He pulled on the pants, the material silky and elastic on his skin. He liked the streamlined fit; loose clothes made him feel large, awkward, and sloppy. Buttoning up the white shirt, he knotted his tie and slipped into the jacket, admiring the tailored lines in the mirror. It fit him just right, setting off his slim waist and broad shoulders to perfection. He combed out his tangled hair and nearly forgot the shoes on the way out the door.

"All right." He tapped her on the shoulder. "What do you think?" She looked him over scrutinizingly, one hand holding her glasses to her nose.

"Do you like it, Sheldon? I think you look rather stunning. Those lines are ingenious, it's clearly from a good designer."

"I really like it! The tighter look is just my style. I don't like the baggy stuff. I didn't know they had suits like this. And I'm shiny!" He smiled that crooked grin that Richelle loved.

"You know, I was serious about the Senior prom. It is coming up." His eyes narrowed.

"I hope that's not why you bought me this!"

"It's a timelessly classic piece that every man should have," she explained derivatively, with a dismissive wave of her hand. "Now I want that picture. How about you stand over there, by the fireplace?" Grumbling, he walked over to it and obediently struck a casual pose, one arm draped across the mantel and his knee bent with a careless, lithe grace that made him look like a model in the studio. She snapped the picture and studied it. "That's a good one. The quality is excellent. I'm going to get this framed." She looked at him expectantly. He crossed his arms over his chest and leaned back against the wall, gazing into the leaping flames with a serious, thoughtful expression. "Perfect." The camera clicked. Laughing suddenly, she remarked, "If you're ever in a tight place, you should seriously consider modeling, because you are a natural." He looked up with a quizzically doubtful smile, a snide retort on his tongue. "Hold it!" she exclaimed, camera posed. "I've got some good ones. Come and see." He moved to her shoulder and peered at the little screen as she paged through the pictures.

"Wow, I look pretty hot!" he snickered.

"Very sexy."

"Grammy. Don't start. I can't marry you, I'm sorry!" he said in mockingly apologetic tones. She burst out laughing and pulled him off his knees. "Hey, could you e-mail those to me?"

"I certainly will." She kept back a comment concerning Richelle and smiled to herself. "I will e-mail them over later. I want you to run down to Red box and get a Christmas movie for us to watch. I've got a few things to prepare for dinner. We'll see it after, with pie and ice cream."

"I hope there's going to be an interval between dinner and dessert," he groaned. "I'll pop if there isn't!"

Sheldon shuffled his feet on the doormat, leaving a thin layer of snow as he slammed the door against the cold.

"I think it might snow tonight, Grammy," he said, dropping the DVD on the table. "I got *It's a Wonderful Life*." He gestured with one hand, unzipping his jacket with the other.

"Oh, *the* Christmas classic." She smiled, fluffing potatoes while attempting to keep them in the bowl and from going all over the wall, the hand-beater purring loudly as it whirred through them. "I thought the storm was coming in tomorrow. When does it say?" Sheldon turned on his phone.

"Hold on a sec." His voice trailed off as his thumb pressed in a Google search. "OK, it says it'll be coming in early in the morning, around five. I'll have to skip down." He sounded annoyed.

"Oh, that's too bad. We'll make sure we don't stay up too late. So you can get some sleep." She poked him in the ribs, grinning mischievously up into his eyes. "And no texting you-know-who, you hear me? I'll meet a zombie at the station if you do!" His laugh ended in a concealing cough, or at least he tried to make it sound as such.

"I'll have to get out of here by six. I'll still be a little late." He looked up the train times. "We've got one going out at six-o-five. I'll have to take that. It gets there about eight-thirty."

"You'll be back late?"

"Yeah, I've got a few places to shovel. Gosh, I wish I had a snowblower," he added as if on an afterthought and sighed dismally. "I'll call you when I'm done. It'll be pretty late, two and a half hours to get back with all the stops the train has to make."

"I don't care," she said vivaciously. "You're not going to spend a night in that house on your vacation." His mouth twisted into a half-hearted smile, yet he was appreciative of her determination. "I set the table in the dining room. Would you mind carrying in the turkey?" He took it carefully in his hands, getting a sense of balance. "I'm following with the mashed potatoes, right behind you. Look out, the carpet!" She seemed to hold her breath with anxiety. Sheldon looked around the room, the table overflowing with food and candles and evergreen scattered tastefully around in strategic places.

"We're going to eat all this?" He laughed dubiously as he set the turkey in the center of it all.

"Leftovers, my dear boy, leftovers."

"Yeah, sure thing. For a good long while."

"That's why you're here, hon." She reached for his hand as they sat beside each other. "Let's pray." She blessed the food, thanking God for the gift of his son. And so followed turkey and stuffing, mashed potatoes and gravy, corn, candied sweet potatoes, a raspberry jello salad with marshmallows that Sheldon couldn't get over it was so good, shrimp platters with hot sauce, a green bean casserole, and baby creamed onions. Afterward, Sheldon retired to the living room and spent a while sprawled out on the couch, contemplating the pros and cons of eating too much food and those of holidays as well.

"I think I know exactly how that turkey felt," he moaned to his grandmother, who chuckled sympathetically and popped *It's a Wonderful Life* into the DVD player. The screen came to life, and James Stewart's face collided with Sheldon's line of vision. Halfway through the movie, Grandma paused it and got a tub of coffee ice cream and the apple pie, cutting a very generous wedge for Sheldon. He whistled admiringly as he took it, watching the creamy mounds melt down over the warm pie.

"The food of the gods." He licked ice cream off his lip.

"We all good?" She sat down, hitting the "play" button.

"Hmm." He stuck the spoon in his mouth and sucked on it, amused by the weird noises it made.

"Hey, I can't hear the movie, you!" She poked him, nearly upsetting his pie all over his lap.

"Wow, that was close!" he yelped, rescuing his plate and running a finger around the rim.

The sky grew darker as the day drew near to a close, clouds gathering on the horizon, bringers of the snowstorm. Oblivious to the weather, Sheldon and his grandmother watched the movie to its conclusion, mesmerized by their full stomachs and the continual noise into a tranquil state of apathy. Grandma yawned as the credits scrolled by, turning down the volume and looking at her sleepy grandson.

"It's only five o'clock, but don't you feel like a nap? I know I do!"

"I could totally sack out right now." He raised his arms over his head and stretched down to his toes. "I want those pictures though, pwease?"

"OK, I'll send your pictures on over. Silly." He closed his eyes lazily. She picked up the dessert dishes and disappeared into the kitchen. Impulsively, Sheldon curled up on the couch and dozed off. The clattering of dishes in the sink receded into the distance, and he fell into a deep sleep. His grandmother walked in wiping her hands on her apron, her mouth open to ask him to help her with the dishes. She closed it and regarded his sleeping form with a funny mixture of exasperation and affection. She decided to do them herself and let him sleep, for she knew he'd been up late and had a long day of work ahead of him.

"If I know that boy, he'll want to talk to Richelle despite all the snow in the world, so he might as well catch a wink while he can," she said to herself as she splashed suds over a dirty plate.

Sheldon woke with a start. The house was dark, and he didn't hear anything. He sat up slowly, waiting for the blood to circulate down to his cramped legs. He walked out into the kitchen and noticed with a feeling of guilt that she'd let him sleep while she'd cleaned up everything herself. The clock over the stove read 9:00; he had slept the whole afternoon into oblivion!

"I feel like a lazy butt!" he muttered and stalked up to his room. "Gosh, I've got to shovel tomorrow!" He clapped a hand to his head suddenly. "And there's like no possible way I'm going to sleep right now." He flopped on his bed in a state of indifference and stared listlessly up at the ceiling. His phone rang, and Sheldon dove for it, nearly jumping out of his skin at the suddenness of the blaring noise.

"Hullo?" he mumbled sleepily.

"Hello," came an uncertain male voice on the other line. "Is this Sheldon speaking?"

"Yes, it is. Who am I speaking with?"

"My daughter said you were interested in looking at my Honda." Sheldon realized who was on the other line with a jolt and he came more awake.

"Well, sir, 'looking' isn't the word I would use."

"Oh?"

"From what Richelle told me, I think I would buy it outright in a second, but I suppose it would be wise to look at it first, unless you've found someone else who's interested in buying?" The man laughed good-humoredly.

"Actually, she made me call and tell you I wouldn't even think of putting the car out until you'd seen it. She said that you really need a car?"

"Yes, I do, and I'm really hoping this will work out."

"Me too! I don't need an extra car sitting in my garage."

"I can't say how grateful I am. Thanks for being willing to give me a chance."

"Oh, not at all. Looking forward to meeting you, Sheldon."

"Thank you, Mr . . ."

"Callahan. Mr. Callahan."

"OK, thanks, never did get your name from Chelle—Richelle, I mean."

"You seem to be great friends. Richelle is so excited to have made a friend before school starts. Well, it was great talking to you. Merry Christmas, young man."

"You too, sir, good-bye." Sheldon ended the call and laughed. "Sweet!" He sent a text to Richelle.

"Your dad just called. Thnxs for everything. Hope you had a wonderful Xmas."

Noticing he had an e-mail, he found that his grandmother had sent him the pictures of him in his tux. Grinning over the one of himself looking into the fireplace, he sent it to Richelle.

"Hey!"

"Hey, Chelle! What's up?"

"Got your text. Glad Dad got in touch with you."

"Yeah, me too. Thnxs. Lol."

"What?"

"I was not expecting him to call. I had just woken up when he called and sounded like it. Haha."

"Ooops . . ."

"The convo went fine. You've got a nice dad."

"Yes, I do. *Wow*! That pic you sent! I *love* your suit!"

"Lol yep, my Xmas present from Grammy."

"You look like a magazine model."

"Rofl, Grammy says I could be a model if I ever got into a tight place. I guess I'm a natural."

"I have to say I agree with her."

"LOL. Glad you like it. I really like it myself. I'm shiny!"

"Haha, I noticed."

"What did you get?"

"I got a five-piece emerald jewelry set. It's absolutely beautiful."

"Five-piece?"

"Yeah. Necklace, earrings, ring, and bracelet. I fell in love with it the moment I saw it."

"Sounds pretty."

"Oh, it is! Natalie got a kitten, among other things. I luve kittens!"

"That's cool. Cats seem to like me for some reason."

"Do you reciprocate the feeling?"

"Lol, yes!"

"Yay, a fellow cat lover."

"Haha. So you had a nice Xmas?"

"Very! You?"

"I did too. I don't want to see another mouthful of food for as long as I live."

"Meaning until tomorrow morning, when you will have pie for breakfast."

"Probably exactly what will happen too. Lol."

"Probably! :P"

"I got a bible today."

"Awesome! What translation?"

"ESV. It's a study bible."

"That is wonderful. Now you can read it!"

"Yep. Grammy said the footnotes will really help me understand a lot of things I might find confusing."

"True."

"I gotta hit the road tomorrow. Go shoveling."

"Ick, that's too bad."

"Sure is, but hey, I gotta buy that car somehow!"

"If I was home, I'd help! Long day, I'm sure."

"Yes, it'll be a very long day. Grammy refuses to let me stay overnight."

"Oh."

"No, I don't want to, just wish I didn't have to travel two and a half hours to get to bed when I'm done. Rather wet and fall over tired."

"Hope you don't miss your station!"

"I'm going to set an alarm."

"Good idea. Hey, you get some sleep, boy!"

"Lol. I took a 4hr nap or something like that."

"O_O a nap on Xmas?"

"Yeah! We stayed up pretty late last night. You must be getting tired."

"I'm not going to lie."

"Sorry . . ."

"No, don't be! But you still shouldn't stay up past 11:00."

"Yeah, I think I'll be able to sleep by then."

"I can't wait to see you again."

"Can't wait to see you either! I think I'll let you get some sleep, Chelle."

"Thnxs, I'm having a hard time staying awake. Glad you had a good Xmas. I wanna see that suit on you!"

"Oh come on . . ."

"Haha. OK, good night you."

"Night, Chelle."

"*Hug*"

"What was that for?"
"Oh, everybody in general, you in particular."
"Lol, OK . . . I returned it, jsyk. OK, go to sleep!"
"Yes, master, cya soon!"
"Yup, bye!"

The phone's alarm went off at 5:30 in the morning. Sheldon rolled over with a groan and picked it up in fingers weak with sleep. The screen was so bright that he felt like his eyes were being seared out of his skull. Killing the incessant buzzing, he heaved his body into a sitting position and pulled the blankets up to his chin, staring bleary-eyed at the lump his feet made at the end of the bed. The thought of disentangling himself from the warm blankets and having to pull on cold clothes was not appealing. Grumbling to himself, he threw off the bedclothes and hopped out onto the carpeted floor. The jeans were cold and felt rough as he thrust his legs into them. Shivering, he pulled on the remainder of his clothing and grabbed his snow gear.

He wrote his grandmother a note while he waited for the water to boil for hot chocolate. He didn't want to wake her up to drop him at the station. So he decided to let her know he had the car. *Hopefully she doesn't need it or anything,* he thought to himself as he laid the sheet of paper on the table where she'd see it. After a short search in the cupboard, he found a large mug and filled it with water, stirring the cocoa mix in. Balancing a cinnamon roll on top of the mug in one hand, he yanked on his boots and quietly closed the door behind him.

It was cold outside, and Sheldon was grateful for the warmth of the chocolate as it coursed through his body. The Subaru crept out onto the road, quickly gaining speed with the pressure applied to the accelerator. There wasn't much time until the train came in, and he didn't want to have to wait for the next one. He stifled a yawn and licked the last of the sticky glaze from his fingertips, turning on the radio. Blaring country music helped him wake up, and he felt more alive as he finished his cocoa and parked the car. He was careful to get his gloves and hat before he stepped out, zipping up his jacket. Experience had taught him that shoveling with no gloves was one of the most miserable things a human being could ever endure. There was no need to repeat it.

The train was on time, kept rigidly on schedule. It was pleasantly warm inside the car after the bitter cold of the outdoors, and the cracked leather seat felt very comfortable as he settled down for the long ride. He rolled up his ski-pants beside him and put in his earbuds to block out some of the noise, deciding to go back to sleep, which he did, and very promptly at that.

A few hours later, he trudged quietly up to his house, and upon observing the deserted atmosphere, he moved on to the shed to get his snow shovel. It was dark and musty inside the little makeshift building, but Sheldon knew his way around it and found the shovel hanging on its hook from memory.

The snow was light, but Sheldon knew that the more the day wore on, the heavier it would become as the sun melted it, so he tried to hurry as fast as he could without burning himself out.

The hours crept by, and his muscles burned and ached; his legs and arms felt so heavy, and he was wet through. Sheldon shoveled out another car, the banks of snow piled high along the walkway. He sighed and leaned against it, hot and tired. He made a face at his watch, 11:45.

"Gosh, no wonder I'm so hungry! I've been doing this for like four hours!" Finding new energy at the thought of food, he finished up and briskly knocked on the door of the house.

"Hi, Sheldon, how are things with you?" Mrs. Aldridge leaned against the doorjamb, scribbling out a check.

"Oh, I'm doing great, Mrs. Aldridge. How are you? Did you have a nice Christmas?"

"I'm doing very well myself, and yes, we had a wonderful Christmas. Thank you for your hard work, young man!" She tore out the check and handed it to him.

"You're welcome. Have a good one!" He tucked his paycheck into his pocket and walked down the steps, surveying his work with a criticizing eye.

The restaurant was warm and bright, almost too warm because of the amount of time Sheldon had been getting used to the chill of the outdoors. He slid into a seat, taking off his jacket, and scanned the menu. Variety was rather slim, but they had his usual. It wasn't long before he was contentedly full and sucking on the end of his straw. He cautiously propped his feet up and glanced around, his keen blue eyes taking in everything. The waitress was texting behind the doorjamb, guiltily peeping over the top of her phone to make certain she was getting away with it. With a smirk, he realized he could either get her fired or at least a serious warning, depending on her boss's toleration.

"How's your friend?" he asked insouciantly. The poor girl jumped a mile and nearly dropped her phone. She cracked a nervous smile.

"He's fine." Her voice was uncertain, her eyes pleading.

"Nah, I won't tell on you, but I would like my total." His mouth quirked as she dropped her phone in her pocket and hurriedly pulled out her order pad.

"Here it is." She handed him a sheet of paper, her hands twisted in her apron. Sheldon winked at her encouragingly and pulled out his wallet.

"Here's a ten." She returned after a short delay.

"OK, a dollar fifty your change. Thanks a lot, by the way." She looked into his eyes for the first time, and Sheldon smiled up at her.

"Hey, no problem. A tip for the future, in case the next guy isn't as nice as me, don't do it, and there's no need to worry."

"Yeah, I know."

"See ya, kid!" He got up, tucking his change back into his pocket. "Got some places to shovel out." He raked his fingers through his hair, making it stand up on end, his hat dangling from one hand.

"Keep warm!" She had a sweet smile.

"Dry is more of my concern. I stay pretty warm. Bye now!" She raised her hand as he moved out into the street, the door swinging shut behind him, the bells jingling merrily. A moment later, they clattered as the door burst open and he ran back in. "Gee, I forgot to tip you, awfully sorry!" She laughed and tried to refuse the three dollars he held out to her, saying he didn't have to because he'd been so nice to her when her boss could be yelling at her right now. Anyways, she argued, she didn't deserve it. He insisted, and she pocketed the cash, watching him walk away. He was a very nice guy, not too bad looking either. She grinned and rolled her eyes at herself.

Toward evening, the temperature dropped drastically, and Sheldon found himself blowing on cold fingers. His gloves were wet, but they at least provided some protection against the cold. He slipped them back on and continued shoveling. He had three more clients and was making good time. Shuffling through the snow in one of his new customer's yards, he noticed a curtain shifting over one of the top-floor windows. He thought it mildly strange but soon forgot about it in the monotony of scooping up snow and chucking it off the asphalt.

Sheldon felt a little guilty ringing doorbells at night, but he didn't think his gloved knuckles would make much of a noise, so he jammed one long finger down on the button. He winced slightly as the chimes rang throughout the house, loud in the quiet of the evening. There was a ruckus like someone was running down a flight of stairs, and the door flew open. Involuntarily, Sheldon took a step back, and that girl from school regarded him with a sideways smirk he didn't like.

"It's so nice to finally get you alone. School isn't the greatest setting." Where had he heard that before? She was so different from Richelle.

"So that's what you look like under all that makeup," he said sarcastically, attempting to recover his customary cool. "I didn't recognize you at first, maybe because you don't look like you've been punched in the eye." Sheldon was not at all pleased to see this girl; he couldn't seem to get away from her. She glared at him. "Your parents home?" He peered over her shoulder, hoping for a rescue.

"No, just me." She leaned against the doorway, her hand on one hip. "You wanna come in for a while?"

"No, thanks. I just finished up, kinda need my paycheck."

"Oh, I know, but you'll have to come and get it." She tossed her head to one side, her white blond hair falling over half of her face.

"Look, just get me the check, OK?"

"You can have it. Just come inside for a bit." Her voice was soft, inviting. "You're making me let all the heat out." Caught off guard by this unexpectedly practical observation, Sheldon's polite instincts acted without reasoning, and he stepped inside. He couldn't believe what a fool he was when the door closed behind him. He knew exactly what she was thinking; this was all a game with one goal in mind, and she presently had the upper hand. She laid her hand lightly on his arm, trying to steer him into the living room.

"No, I'll wait right here. I got a few more hours ahead of me."

"But, of course." She walked out of the room, and Sheldon realized with a start how short her shorts really were. He blinked and looked away. "How much were they paying you? Seventy? I think my mom left you a check but she didn't fill in your name." she called.

"Yeah, it was seventy. I can fill in my name." She came back with the check in hand.

"Now I told you you'd have to come and get it." She giggled and dropped it down the front of her shirt. He growled angrily and lurched forward.

"Give me that check, you stupid girl!"

"Oh yes, please!" She pressed her body against his. He pushed her away and took her shoulders.

"Why are you acting like this?" Her eyes became slightly confused behind the bold playfulness.

"Why don't you pay attention to me? I don't understand! Come on, just a little bit of fun. You'll like it, I promise." She touched his cheek.

"Wait." He held up his hand, pushing hers away from his face. "You're doing this because I don't pay attention to you?"

"Yes," she sounded uncertain.

"The reason I don't pay attention is because you act like this. All you think about is sex. It's disgusting." He looked into her eyes, meeting her indignant gaze. "Look, no guy is going to ever love you if you're always pushing yourself on him. And the kind of guy you want isn't going to go anywhere near you if you act like this. You're just gonna get used. Don't you see? Please stop doing this to me, and I really need that check, so . . ." He put out his hand and waited with his face turned away. Suddenly, he realized she was crying, and he felt the piece of paper in the palm of his hand. "Thank you." He moved toward the door.

"I don't know why I'm crying," she wondered.

"Probably because I'm one of the first to care about you as a person and not be selfish about what you have to offer. There's a big difference." He walked out of the house.

She stared unseeing at the door in front of her, her mind bursting with the things he had said, spinning thoughts flying round and round. Did he like her? Had she finally made him see she could love him? Just that the results had been a little different than what she had expected. She shrugged. He would come round, eventually, and he'd see he was wrong; love was love. Love was not the fairy tale some people thought it was. It never worked that way. Love didn't turn out like it did in the movies. Love was cheap, easy, and fun. He had told her he cared . . . She grinned suddenly, more of a baring of teeth. Yes, he'd come round or she might just ruin a few things for him.

The train ride home seemed to take an eternity. Sheldon felt miserable; he was exhausted, wet, and sore. And he was upset about that girl; he still didn't know her name. Somehow, he didn't feel like he'd said and done the right thing. And he was continually berating himself for having walked through her door in the first place. Glumly, he pulled off his snow pants and rolled them up into a ball on the seat beside him. He felt a little better with the damp excess weight off his aching body.

Tired though he was, Sheldon found that sleep was eluding him, and he didn't feel like he was able to sleep anyways. His phone buzzed. He continued staring out the window. On the third time, the notifying vibrations wore through to his brain; he listlessly

Free Loner

picked up the phone and glanced at the number—Richelle. To his surprise, he found that he didn't really want to talk to her.

"Hey, Shel, thinking about you out there in the cold. Hope you're doing OK . . . Are you done with work yet?" Sheldon sighed and typed a brief response just to be polite.

"Yup."

"OK . . . Well, I take it that you are tired!" Richelle waited for his reply, which didn't come.

"Are you OK?"

"I'm fine." Sheldon didn't know if he wanted to talk about it or not, but he didn't feel like discussing it presently. Some things were really ominous until viewed on a full stomach.

"Rather not talk about it, huh? That's OK. You need some food and a hot shower." Relief washed over him.

"OK, thnxs for understanding."

"So do you wanna talk about whatever or you too tired?"

"I can't sleep. Don't worry about it."

"Awww, you so tired you can't sleep?:("

"Yeah, kinda."

"How much longer do you have 'til you get home?"

"Oh, I've been on the train for about a half an hour. Gotta ways to go."

"Ah. Late night, like you said."

"Rather! Not like I was flippin' burgers either."

"I'll say! How's your back feeling?"

"Miserable, to put it lightly."

"You need a good hot shower."

"Amen to that, sis." Richelle paused and bit back a sigh. She realized that she really had her hopes up, and her heart seemed to have lost a lot of the buoyant joy she had whenever she talked to Sheldon. Sister. She wanted so much more. A few minutes eclipsed.

"Hello?" Richelle shook her head, angry at her own feelings, and typed a quick response.

"I'm here."

"Yerp. Just making sure. Got nothing to do. Wouldn't mind talking to you." Suddenly exasperated, Richelle shot back a hasty reply before she thought.

"Don't mind talking to me. Well. Call your grandma, sheesh."

"O_o hey." He was surprised, at a loss as to what he had done wrong.

"Sorry *sigh*."

"Hey, what's eatin' you?"

"Nothing."

"Liar." He didn't like playing games.

"True . . ." She realized her hands were trembling, and her heart was thumping in her chest like she'd been out for a run. She couldn't let him know, not now, not like this!

"Well, you gonna tell me or what?"

"Oh, feeling a little blue. Don't mind me."

"You are full of it. Lol. If you don't wanna tell me, it's OK." He raised an eyebrow. This sounded sadly familiar. She'd only just said the same thing to him!

"What? I am!"

"OK, OK, I'll drop it. :P" Richelle felt relieved, yet somehow disappointed when he didn't insist.

"But you were fine a sec ago :/ Did I say something? O_o" Now she wished he hadn't insisted. Her thoughts whirled.

"No," she lied. "Something came up. Natalie's cousin is coming over. Did I tell you that?" Sheldon slouched in his seat. He knew she hadn't told him. What was up with her? He grimaced. If she started playing games on him, he was gone.

"Nope." He decided it was in his best interest to play along, and he might eventually find out what was up, hopefully.

"Guess that's not such a good thing, huh?" He fell for it? She couldn't believe it; guess guys weren't so smart if they could be so easily sidetracked.

"I don't like him at all. He's a jerk."

"Guy. IC." He blinked down at the screen as the words appeared in the "sent" box. He wrinkled his nose in annoyance.

What a brilliant thing to say. He had to almost laugh as she continued the conversation.

"Yeah, thinks he's a regular heartbreaker and is convinced he's in love with me. He's gross." She bit her lip and went with it. "Times like these when I wish I had a boyfriend or a big brother to give him a good-sized knuckle-sandwich."

"Dang. That bad?"

"Oh yeah."

"Well, you tell me if he tries anything on you, and if I ever see the guy, I'll give him an extra large special, for free. K?"

"He'd better hope he's gone when you get here, lol."

"XD, yerp. Hey, I might have a few things to talk to you about. When I see you, that is." Richelle glanced up from her phone, reached over, and pulled a blanket around her legs.

"Don't want to now? Everything OK over there, Shel?"

"No. Idk, Chelle, I might be overreacting, tired and hungry, but I don't think I'm OK. Don't feel right." Her brow furrowed, concern instantly flashed into her green eyes.

":(Sure you don't want to tell me?"

"I'd like to see you first."

"OK . . . Just tell me you're not hurt." Sheldon felt a smile coming on despite himself.

"What kind of question is that? Other than my aching muscles, doin' just fine. :) No, no one tried to kill me with my shovel or run me over with a plow truck . . . ;) ;)" Her cheeks smarted even though she knew he was just trying to make her feel better. He thought she was a little girl.

"*Rolls eyes* I gtg." She had to stop talking to him.

"OK, be at the station in a few. Ttys, Chelle. Have a good one." And he was gone. Richelle scrambled with the blanket and nearly tripped over it as she fled to her room, slamming the door a little too hard behind her. The bed creaked a protest as she threw herself across the mattress, the tears coming hot and fast. What on earth was the matter with her? She dug a clenched fist into the side of her cheek, grinding a tear into an angry salty streak. Unbidden pictures of the conversation, snapshots of his face across from her on that train when they'd first met, his baritone voice over the phone, they all flashed through her mind, and she found herself falling, giving up.

When Natalie came in a few hours later, Richelle was curled up in a fetal position, her pillow looked damp, and a few red strands of hair were plastered to her tear-streaked face. Natalie stood regarding her friend, puzzled and concerned. Her eyes narrowed suspiciously. If that guy, what's-his-name, had done anything to her . . . It seemed as if more than one guy was in for a preordered knuckle-sandwich . . . and neither of them knew it.

Everything was wrong. It often seems like that when at least one thing doesn't go right. Grandma had been very talkative and asked him all sorts of questions when he stomped in the door, banging snow off his feet against the jamb. He knew he'd been short with her, and the hurt look in her eyes made him feel awful. But he didn't want to talk. He ate his supper and took a shower, standing at the top of the stairs to wish her a good night. There was worry in her voice when she told him to get some rest. Lying on his bed with an arm behind his head, so many thoughts flew around in his mind that he wondered if he'd get any rest at all. He was angry at himself, at Richelle; he punched his leg, growling. He was an idiot; she was only playing with him and didn't trust him at all. Oh, he'd been such a fool! Grandma was right; Richelle was like every other girl he'd ever met. But how could he think that of her? He shook his head and sat up. All he knew was there was something she wasn't telling him, but maybe it was nothing other than the fact that he was exhausted and blowing things way out of proportion.

The room was swallowed in darkness with one flick of the light switch, and Sheldon dismissed the events of the day from his mind and resolutely flopped back onto his pillow, shutting his eyes.

Grandma knelt by her bedside, hands folded in earnest prayer. She didn't know what was troubling Sheldon, but she didn't have to know to understand that whatever it was, she needed to entrust him into the Lord's care.

Chapter 9

Of Good-Byes and Railways

Richelle determined not to call Sheldon—or text him. She laid down her brush with a sigh and looked into her own eyes reflected in the bathroom mirror. She'd already thought about this and didn't see a need to do it all over again. She twisted her auburn tresses into a long, thick braid and flipped it over her shoulder. Natalie looked up with a quick smile when she walked into the room, her arms full of pajamas and girly paraphernalia.

"Someone looks cheerful," she remarked as she dumped everything in a pile and knelt to sort it out. Natalie laughed.

"Nothing too out of the ordinary, I hope." She sat across from Richelle, her eyes soulfully concerned. "Are you . . . ?" She dropped her eyes. "Are you OK, Richelle?" Richelle dropped a shirt to the floor and met her friend's eyes for a moment in surprise. Then she blushed and looked away. "What is it? Tell me!" Natalie touched her knee.

"Oh, I don't know, Nat. I'm just being stupid, that's all." She smiled and laid her hand on top of Natalie's. Natalie chose not to push her anymore and grabbed her in a tight hug.

"Be careful, girly," she whispered and let her go with a pat to her back. "Come on, let's go grab some breakfast."

It was a long day. They all went to an old antique car show, much to Natalie's father's delight. The enthusiasm with which he raced from exhibit to exhibit made Richelle laugh, and her heart was so light that she was living completely in the moment, utterly forgetting the heartache of the previous night.

But on the way home, Natalie's mother turned around in her seat and said with a smile, "Tomorrow is when your friend gets here! We're going to have to go out for Chinese for supper! Just to celebrate." Richelle expressed the expected exclamation of agreement and then looked out the window at the scenery flying by the car. She wondered dejectedly what would happen when tomorrow got there. Natalie glanced over at her, noting the change in her demeanor. Involuntarily her jaw clenched; someone was in for some trouble.

That night, after supper, Richelle went to take a shower. She was tired and maybe just a little sore from all that walking. "It has been a long eventful day," she said to herself as she stepped beneath the stream of hot water spouting from the shower head. She ran her fingers through her hair, the water dripping off the ends. The shampoo smelled wonderfully refreshing, suds sliding off down her shoulders.

Clad in cotton PJ pants and one of her brother's oversized T-shirts, she slid between the sheets and pulled the blankets up to her chin.

"Hey, you got a text while you were in the shower," said Natalie, looking up from her book. She watched her friend as she reached over and grabbed her phone and pretended to be reading but noticed an instant tension in Richelle's face. She threw down her book. "All right, *will* you tell me what's going on?" she said, her voice managing to be concerned and exasperated at the same time. "This isn't like you not to tell me." The hurt tone melted Richelle's heart in an instant.

"Nat, I'm sorry! I'm not myself." She looked down at the phone in her hand.

"Well, I can see that! That guy, he'd better not have done anything."

"Oh no!" Richelle interrupted hastily. "It's just, last night. . . ." She paused. "Why am I trying to explain this to you when I don't understand it myself?" Natalie took off her reading glasses and tilted her head to one side contemplatively.

"You're falling for him?" It was out before she could stop herself. Richelle passed a slightly shaky hand over her eyes.

"Yes," she whispered softly. Natalie crossed her legs and rocked back and forth on her bed, looking across at Richelle with quizzical eyes.

"But, do you know him all that well?"

"He's told me a lot. He's sweet, a gentleman, but . . ."

"But what?"

"I'm just a sister to him. Little sister."

"Hey." Natalie sat next to her on her bed and passed a companionable arm over her shoulders. "You just met him! You should be thankful he wants to get to know you. You said he's a gentleman, right?" She waited for the assenting nod. "He would be a poor excuse for one if he decided he wanted to make you his girlfriend this fast. I mean, give him a chance! You don't wanna dive into something that serious on such a short notice, do you? And hey," she hugged her, "if he doesn't fall head over heels in love with you after he's known you for a while, something is totally wrong with him!" She smiled and got one in return.

"Thanks, Nat. I don't know what I'd do without you." Richelle put both arms around her friend.

"Daww, what's happening anyways? Did he decide not to come over after all?" Richelle showed her Sheldon's text.

"Hey, Chelle, I was wondering if the plan is still on for tomorrow. Haven't heard from you for a while, and I hope everything is OK."

"I didn't text him at all today," Richelle offered a vague explanation.

"Good, let him do the chasing."

"Whoever said anything about chasing?" Richelle said, indignantly. Natalie laughed and dodged the playful pinch. "OK, I have to send him a response." Richelle tapped out the words.

"Hey, Sheldon, yes, we're still on for tomorrow. Let me know what time you're getting here. Everything is fine. We all went to a car show today. I think you would've liked it :) Cya soon!" She hit "send message" and lay back on her bed, laying her phone back on the bedside table.

"OK, you, get some rest. I'm gonna go sleep now. Night!" Natalie crossed the room and hopped into her bed.

"Night, I'll get the light."

"Are you finished packing yet, Sheldon?" Grandma called up the stairs.

"Almost, I'll be down in a minute," came the muffled reply. Grandma continued dusting, picking up each picture on the mantelpiece and running the rag gently over the angles of the frames. Her hand moved slower, and suddenly, she put down the picture and the cloth and hurried from the room. Presently, she returned with a small frame and a glossy new photo; she'd had Sheldon's pictures printed out. Carefully, she pressed the picture to the glass and secured it within the frame, nestling it among the other family photographs jostling for a place on the crowded mantel. She straightened and surveyed the effect for a moment, a smile touching her lips as she compared Sheldon to his baby pictures.

"My . . . my, is he all grown up?" she whispered to herself, touching his photo. "I'll give him a copy, just so he has one." She bustled about the room, finishing her cleaning. Soon, she heard Sheldon's door open, and he came tramping down the stairs, his bag tucked under one arm.

"All set, Grammy." He smiled at her suddenly and, throwing down his pack, impulsively slipped his arms around her ample waist. He heaved a sigh, and she stroked his hair, his head on her shoulder.

"There there, deary. It's all right," she said comfortingly, holding him close.

"Sorry about last night, Grammy." He didn't say anymore, but she was very much relieved.

"That's all right."

"It was just me overreacting and tired. I should never have been rude to you though," he sighed again dismally and, squeezing her again, pulled away.

"I understand you weren't upset at me. But thank you for apologizing." She patted his arm. "So are you sure you got everything? You checked all the drawers and under the bed, nothing left behind? I don't want you leaving anything."

"Yup, it's all here." He gestured toward his duffel bag. "I made absolutely positively sure," he said, seeing her doubtful expression.

"All right, we'll see," she ejaculated, raising her palms. "What time did you say your train is leaving?"

"I'm taking the 2:00 train. A few hours yet, just wanted to make sure I get one more amazing lunch!" He winked at his grandmother, who couldn't hide the fact that she was vastly pleased. "You did promise me mac 'n cheese, ya know?" He followed her into the kitchen, peering over her shoulder anxiously as she surveyed the refrigerator's interior.

"Yes," she mused, "so I did." Cheese, butter, and milk lined up on the counter, and she set a pot of water to boil while she made the white sauce, humming as she whisked in a little flour. Sheldon leaned against the counter and watched it slowly rise to temperature and begin to simmer. "Now for the cheese . . ." Grandma stirred in the cheese, which melted into a thick, creamy golden mass of cheesy goodness, making Sheldon wish the pasta would hurry up and be cooked; he was hungry. "Give me the colander, Sheldon." He pulled open a cupboard and, upon handing it to her, voluntarily fished out a macaroni and chewed it up, declaring it to be in need of another minute or so.

Before too long, there was a heaping pile of mac 'n cheese on his plate, and he drizzled it liberally with ketchup.

"You really must visit more often, honey," Grandma said over the course of the meal. "I'll send you a check in the mail whenever you feel like it. It isn't fair for you to have to pay to humor an old lady." He laughed at this and was, on the whole, delighted with her proposal. "Then it's settled!" she said decidedly. "We'll keep in much more frequent contact, and you'll tell me when you have vacations!" Her rosy face glowed, and Sheldon couldn't possibly refuse her. He'd enjoyed his Christmas vacation immensely and knew it would've been awful had he stayed home. He nodded and savored another mouthful of cheesy macaroni.

"Did you get your gloves? Oh, let me run and see if I washed all your laundry." She was gone before he could tell her again that he was sure he'd packed everything. Her voice continued, and he heard something about socks disappearing to unknown places in the process of being cleaned and an unlikely theory of the dryer turning them into lint. He grinned and packed up his snow gear, jamming it all in with everything else. "See, I told you you hadn't got *everything*!" Triumphantly, she held up a lone sock, which he playfully snatched out of her hand and zipped up inside the pack.

"All set then," he said, simply for the sake of saying something.

"Yes, all set. Well, we'd best be going." Sheldon watched her lace up her boots and held the door as she resolutely marched through.

About halfway to the station, his grandmother broke the silence and began to say what a wonderful holiday she'd had and how she hoped to see him soon and how she hoped he enjoyed his gifts. She talked of school starting up again soon and seemed to have lots to say on that subject. The closer they got, the faster she talked, almost as if she were racing the clock. When they finally arrived, Sheldon ready to pull his hair out if she said one more thing about school, she let out a great sigh, like an engine blowing off steam. Sheldon turned his head toward her as he put the car in park. His mouth quirked in sympathy, for he understood how the little old woman felt. Sure, he'd miss her too, but it was different for her.

"Come on, Grammy," he said gently as he released both their seat belts and pulled himself out of the car. They unloaded his things and stood regarding one another.

"Oh, I'm going to miss you!" She held out her arms and wrapped him up in a tight hug.

"I'm going to miss you too, Grammy. But, hey!" He patted her back comfortingly, "Remember, I'll come up when I get breaks long enough to get away for a few days. We'll stay in touch. I promise." He released her and saw her furtively wipe at her eyes. Awkwardly, he glanced away.

"Yes, yes, I know, don't mind me. You just can't help it when you get as old as I am." He protested and picked up his bag, slinging it over his shoulder. The train was on schedule, and people were hurrying inside.

"I have to go now, Gram. Love you." He gave her a quick hug and walked to the train, looking back over his shoulder and waving once before he boarded. She waved a withered hand in response, straining to get a last glimpse and trying desperately to be brave.

Chapter 10
Second Meeting

The trip wasn't all that long, and before long, Sheldon found himself standing on the platform trying to get his bearings. He'd texted Richelle on the train to tell her he'd be arriving soon, but he didn't know if she'd gotten the message, for she had not yet responded. He moved over to a bench and sat, flipping through his phone's contacts to find the address Richelle had given to him. Ah, there it was. Sheldon stared at it apprehensively. Now to just track down some local townie who could tell him how to get there. He got to his feet and made off down the road in search of somebody. Half an hour's walking brought him to the right street, and he looked up at the house whose number corresponded with the one on his phone. He leaned against the tall wrought iron fence that surrounded what must be a beautiful front garden in the summer to catch his breath.

The door opened to reveal a tall middle-aged man, wiry and slender, with a shock of wispy light brown hair and friendly gray eyes behind a pair of glasses.

"Hi, I'm Sheldon Trindell. You must be Natalie's dad? I'm a friend of Richelle's."

"Oh yes, yes, of course! Rick Cohart, do come in." He gave Sheldon a firm handshake and pulled the door wide. "I'm terribly sorry, we didn't know when you were coming. Don't tell me you walked from the station." Sheldon told him that he had and also that he'd sent Richelle a text. Mr. Cohart expressed his regret that she hadn't gotten it, for he said, "They'd certainly would've gone down to pick him up." Sheldon told a little white lie and assured him it was OK while his shoulder, still sore from shoveling, protested against the weight of his duffel bag. "Run right upstairs, and the girls will tell you where to put your stuff. Just knock on the green door." Mr. Cohart wandered into the other room, clearly with other things on his mind. Poor Sheldon, left alone at the bottom of the stairs, stared nervously up the hall at the various doors along its length. He felt terribly awkward and very much out of place. *What a strange man,* Sheldon thought, trudging up the stairs. Did he always tell random guys he'd never met before to run on up to his daughter's bedroom? He certainly hoped not! Sheldon heard laughter and voices and wished he'd never gotten himself into this mess. There was no way he'd ever find the courage to knock on that green door. It was most awkward, and he wondered if he should just go sit on the stairs to wait until they came out.

"Oh, let me go get it. I'll be right back," came a girl's voice, close at hand, and the door was flung open, much to Sheldon's embarrassed confusion.

"Oh. Hi." The girl involuntarily took a step back into the room, brown eyes wide with surprise in her small white face. She looked up at him, utterly at a loss as to who on earth he was.

"Hi . . .," he said lamely. What was he supposed to say? "I'm . . . You must be . . . Your dad sent me up here." He jerked his thumb in the general direction of the stairs, feeling like an incoherent idiot. Imagine his relief when understanding flooded into her eyes!

"Ooooh, you're Sheldon! Richelle," she leaned her head back into the room, "he's here, you know." She turned back at Sheldon. "I'm Natalie, in case you were wondering." The sight of his red cheeks made her aware of his awkward situation, and she noticed his luggage. "Here, let me take that!" She reached out and secured his duffel bag, nodding at him to follow her as she started down the hall. "This is where you're staying." He glanced around the room. It was small and comfortable, painted in blue and gray, and Natalie dropped his bag on the bed.

"Sheldon?" He turned around feeling a bit overwhelmed and saw Richelle standing in the doorway, her eyes bright.

"Hi!" He tried to pull together the remnant of his shredded dignity.

"You're here!" her voice held a question, and once more he explained the text he'd sent. She looked embarrassed.

"It's all right," he said and passed a hand over his face. The girls looked at him in silence, and then both started talking at once. He was told to come see the house, take a nap, perhaps a shower, maybe hold the new kitten (Richelle remembered he liked cats), as well as have a snack. It was, after all, somewhat after five. Sheldon began to feel more at ease and plopped down onto the bed, kicking off his shoes as he grinned up into their eager faces.

"Well, what do you wanna do?" Richelle put her head to one side, her green eyes questioning. Sheldon leaned forward and hung his clasped hands between his knees, considering quickly.

"They all sound just fine." The girls looked at each other helplessly, just missing his mischievous smirk. Natalie laughed.

"He could just take a nap and dream about everything else."

"Come on, Shel," Richelle grabbed his hands in a vain attempt to pull him to his feet, "let's show you around." Sheldon suddenly felt a strong impulse to yank her down into a hug. He began to resist her and nearly gave into the feeling, but he pushed it away and stood up. Richelle found herself at a very close proximity to his shirtfront. A blush rushed to her cheeks, and she backed off quickly. Natalie felt an unholy delight in observing their awkwardness, which hadn't escaped her. She led them down the stairs, not bothering to hide her impishly gleeful expression.

"Feel like a sandwich? I can make you one quick." She held the fridge open, scanning its contents.

"Yeah, sure, if you don't mind."

"Oh, not at all. Just a little something to hold you off until supper. There're some chips over there in that cupboard." Richelle perched herself on the breakfast bar and watched him as he pulled open the cupboard. He was so tall, so athletic, just perfect! She'd forgotten just how handsome he was. How could she have possibly considered that eyes any other color could be attractive? Suddenly, he was looking at her, blue eyes inquisitive.

"Well, do you want any or not?" He shook the chip bag.

"Oh. Sure!" Natalie turned around to ask Sheldon if he liked mustard and mayonnaise and made a face at Richelle, communicating that she thought Richelle was being awfully obvious, not to mention silly.

"Yes, both please." Sheldon handed Richelle the bag and couldn't help snorting in laughter as he caught her carrying on the expressive facial exchange with Natalie. Richelle laughingly hid her face in her hands, imagining what her face had looked like. Sheldon put his palms on the counter and swung himself up beside her.

"Here you go, silly." He placed the chips between them and munched on one.

She caught her breath as his leg brushed against hers and then recovered enough to help herself to the proffered snack. Sheldon leaned back against the wall and closed his eyes, his face tilted up toward the ceiling. Richelle figured he was tired and found herself staring at him intensely. His eyes opened and he cracked a smile.

"Sorry, guess I'm tired. Hopefully, it's not going to be a late night, cuz I can tell you right here and now that I won't make it. Oh, thanks, Natalie." He took his sandwich and bit into it appreciatively.

"We're going out for supper in a few hours. Then we'll watch a movie. Nothing strenuous." Natalie took a seat on a high stool.

"Ah," He licking mayonnaise off his thumb. There was a ruckus somewhere in the house, and Natalie, with an exclamation of alarm, ran off to see what had happened. Alone with Richelle, Sheldon eyed her, thinking of the conversation they'd had. Was he naive to think she was genuine? Things were getting more awkward for Richelle the longer he stared at her, and she wondered if he was actually seeing her. She shifted uncomfortably beside him and dropped her eyes to the floor as the inevitable blush spread over her cheeks. Sheldon shook his head, dismissing something from his mind, and took another bite out of his sandwich.

"Is something wrong?" He chewed thoughtfully, regarding her with a sideways smirk. He didn't answer.

Then, he said, "I asked the same of you. Your answer was 'nothing,' so I guess I can say the same." He nonchalantly swallowed the remainder of the sandwich and turned a piercing, slightly accusational gaze on her flushed face. In a flash she knew exactly what he was talking about.

"I'm sorry I lied. I was having a bad day, was kinda emotional." That was the only part of the actual truth she could relay to him. She would only sacrifice their friendship if she was forced to tell him of her real feelings for him. His eyebrow was raised.

"I said something. What was it?" His fingers drummed on the counter.

"It wasn't you!" she cried. "I was touchy and chose to take your words the wrong way. I knew you didn't mean anything." Sheldon crossed his arms over his chest.

"Tell me." Something in his tone made her ashamed of her miserable conduct in how she'd deliberately treated him, yet afraid of him at the same time. He'd think her foolish and overreactionary.

"Well, you said you wouldn't mind talking to me because you hadn't been able to sleep and there was nothing else to do." Her eyes flickered up to his, their expression shamed and pleading. "I took offense and told you to go talk to your grandma. I was stupid. I'm sorry, you didn't deserve that." She lifted her hands and let them fall to her thighs.

"Gotcha. You're right. I didn't deserve that, but I could have phrased that differently. I would have been more sensitive had I known you were feeling a little blue.." He looked her in the eyes, sincere.

"Thanks," she said, smiling as he laid his hand on hers. She squeezed it, holding it a little longer than was strictly necessary. "Come on, let's go see what's keeping Nat." They slid off the bar and went in search of her.

The conversation at supper was general, light and fun, and they enjoyed the food as much as each other's company. Sheldon liked Natalie's mom. She was a slender woman with blonde highlights, and Natalie had her big brown eyes. She was blessed with a free and open nature which put people at ease around her, and Sheldon felt safe being with her. Her husband was very distracted and consequently rather vague.

"Business," whispered his wife to Sheldon confidentially, finding something to blame his preoccupied behavior on.

Driving home, there wasn't much conversation, full stomachs and the general sense of contentedness lent to the silence. Sheldon rested his head against the side of the car, suddenly feeling exhausted now that the stimulation of the lights and noises of the restaurant was gone. He would be grateful for a good night's sleep. But the girls weren't ready for that just yet, and when they arrived at the house, they dragged him into the living room to assist in selecting a movie. Sheldon, after declaring he didn't care what they watched, providing it was neither a romantic comedy nor a mushy chick-flick, dropped onto the couch and put his feet up. He was awake for maybe half an hour; then his consciousness wore off, and his head sank onto his chest. No one noticed him for a while, being completely engrossed in the show, but sleeping people are not usually entirely immobile and cannot remain in a fixed position indefinitely. Richelle leaned back into the couch, grinning at Natalie over an inside joke, when she felt something heavy against her shoulder. Mildly surprised, she glanced over and found Sheldon's blond head pillowed against her; he was clearly sleeping soundly.

"Nat," she whispered, directing her friend's gaze to the sleeping young man.

"Aww, he's so tired. Poor thing!" she exclaimed in hushed tones, careful not to wake him up.

"I know!" Richelle smiled; something about Sheldon's curled body made him appear vulnerable, even forlorn. The sight moved her strangely, and she ran light fingertips over the arm thrown across her leg. He seemed so helpless, yet she knew he was far from it, and the knowledge of the strength present in his slumbering form scared her because it was something, if ever aroused, she was powerless against. She was vaguely aware of the sound of crunching popcorn as Natalie finished it, but she had lost interest in the movie. She wondered, as she watched him sleep, just how much she really knew about him. What was he like when he was angry? How did he handle problems? Was he a passionate person? There, she might give an answer. She had sensed an intensity in Sheldon's character from nearly the moment she had met him. Passionate? Yes. Despite his horrible childhood, Sheldon was a person of feeling, very sensitive, no matter what he contrived to mask. He'd shown her he was capable of great emotion. He had a passion for life and a drive that would not be quenched. She could sense that, without knowing what his motivation was.

Sheldon shifted and moaned softly. Without thinking, Richelle ran a soothing hand over his hair. It was so soft, the silky fair strands rippling easily through her fingers. He inhaled deeply, moving his head a little as he let his breath out slowly. She realized she was still stroking his hair. She jumped as Natalie let out a loud affected yawn and stretched, the credits scrolling by. Sheldon opened his eyes and had no clue where he was. Richelle felt him stiffen against her side and looked down at him as she moved her hand off his head. He pushed himself away from her and sat up groggily, his hair falling over his eyes, making him appear unexpectedly boyish.

"You ready for bed, huh?" She felt a smile coming on.

"Yeah, gosh, I fell asleep." He was actually embarrassed.

"I don't mind," she assured him, letting him know she understood how tired he was. "Go hop in the shower, Shel." He yawned and stretched his long legs luxuriantly.

"OK, I'll do that." And he padded off, heading for the stairs. Natalie's elbow poked into her side.

"Dawww, he's so cute when he sleeps!" Richelle shot her a dirty look, knowing full well she was trying to make her agree with her. Natalie giggled and pushed her head into Richelle's shoulder.

"Hey!" Richelle burst out laughing and scooted away.

"I have to say, if looks matter so much, you aren't doing so bad." She bit the tip of her tongue, brown eyes dancing and playful. Richelle shook her head, exasperated, and let it go. She knew it was a pointless argument.

Clutching his dirty clothes to his chest, Sheldon stumbled out of the bathroom, eager to fall into bed and experience relief from his exhaustion. He met Richelle in the hall. She looked sleepy, her red hair tousled, shirt rumpled. She'd changed into pj's while he was showering, and my, was the T-shirt huge! He looked her up and down, eyebrows raised, and a most silly twisted turn to his lips. He forgot his fatigue momentarily and snickered.

"You should see yourself." She wrinkled her nose and pushed past him to the bathroom, brandishing her toothbrush at him.

"Whatever." The tube expelled a generous blob of toothpaste, and she scrubbed the brush over her teeth, up and down. "You going to bed?" she asked through a mouthful of foam.

"Yes, I am." He raked a hand through his hair; it stood up on end. The effect was irresistibly adorable. Richelle choked. "Well, don't die over there." His hand fell to his side. "You have a good night's sleep. See ya in the mornin'." He began to turn away.

"Hang on a sec." She rinsed quickly. "Tyson is coming over tomorrow sometime, Natalie's annoying cousin. Remember?"

"Oh yeah. Great. You'll be fine."

"I'm sick of putting up with him," she sighed and then looked at him as if she'd had a sudden idea.

"Yes? What's up?" he prompted.

"Can you make sure he can't sit next to me?" She bit her lip. "I'd really appreciate it. He creeps me out!"

"Sure. That's fine by me. Just stick around. OK, I'm gonna die. Good night!" He raised his hand.

"Thanks, Shel, good night."

She slid into bed, her exhaustion hitting her like a fist in the stomach as the blankets enfolded her tired body. She tossed her hair over the pillow and closed her eyes, welcoming sleep. Sweet dreams were with her.

As it turned out, Tyson wasn't able to make it; he said he'd drop by either Friday or Saturday. Mrs. Cohart had remarked that he most likely wouldn't make an appearance until the last moment. Sheldon, who was closely observing Richelle, saw some of the anxious tension relax in his friend's face. His brow creased in concern. Obviously she wasn't kidding when she'd told him Tyson creeped her out. Her lips twisted into a rueful smile as her green eyes looked up and met his observant gaze; then her attention returned to her breakfast.

Mrs. Cohart had been up early, busy making waffles, and had adamantly expressed her expectation of their ability to do justice to the large stack in the center of the table. Sheldon forked two more onto his plate, along with a sausage, and dumped syrup over the whole of it. He was none the worse from the late night before, judging from the appetite displayed this morning.

Everyone felt better after breakfast, and after hanging around the house playing games for a few hours, the younger group decided to go out for a walk down some old back roads in the woods just down the street. Sheldon's interest was stirred when Natalie had mentioned some abandoned granite quarries she and her dad had found exploring a few years back.

In the forest, where towering pines and huge sprawling oaks stretching their boughs to the cold grayish sky, the snow wasn't very deep, and in places along the rutted dirt road, it was bare, and curling brown leaves blew along underfoot. It was so quiet; their hushed voices and the distant scream of a jay were the only things to be heard besides the soft whisper of the chill breeze through the branches of the trees.

"It's beautiful, isn't it?" Natalie looked about her, up at one particularly enormous pine, her head tilted back. She was a small girl, and the awesome size of the tree dwarfed her into hilarious obscurity.

"It is." Sheldon touched his hand to the craggy gray bark, marveling at the sheer size of the gigantic conifer.

"Come on, you guys, I wanna see these quarries!" Richelle glanced over her shoulder impatiently. They looked at each other, shaking their heads, and quickened their pace to catch up with her.

The quarries were spectacular, huge and wide, like a deep, bottomless crater. A whistle escaped Sheldon's lips as the beauty of the scene sank into his senses.

"This has got to be utterly breathtaking in a summer's sunset." The girls turned and looked at him in surprise. "Gosh!" He shifted from one cold foot to the other. "I can appreciate beauty like this, ya know."

"Clearly!" said Natalie, warmly. Richelle hadn't said anything, but she was once again drinking in the landscape.

The sheer walls of the vast quarry plunged down a good fifty feet before they collided with a thick shield of ice that swallowed them up out of sight. Firs and pines crowded around the ragged lips of the chasm, some leaning drunkenly over where the edges had crumbled away, their tough weathered roots clinging to the earth and rock.

Richelle tilted her hooded head in Sheldon's direction. "I'd beg to differ. Think what this place would be like in the autumn." He nodded slowly in agreement, furtively blowing on his numbed reddened hands and stuffing them into his pockets.

"You guys ready to go home?" Natalie, who'd noticed Sheldon, had waited a few minutes before she asked the question. She glanced quizzically at the others, who affirmed that they were getting uncomfortable, and they all started off for home.

Kicking off wet shoes, they went laughing upstairs to get dry socks on their freezing feet. They all congregated in the living room, toes spread out to be thawed by the toasty woodstove.

"It was worth it though." Sheldon grinned and brushed a fair lock out of his eyes. "I bet you'd have a few photographers down there if people knew about the old place. I take it not many people do?"

"Not many, just some of the old townies, and they've forgotten. There's no need to remember things until they're needed."

"Gotcha." He gazed contemplatively into the leaping orange flames. A moment's silence fell over the room.

"So, Sheldon." His eyes looked into Natalie's suddenly laughing face. "I heard we're taking you to get an ear pierced."

"What?" he protested and shot a mildly incensed glare at a blushing Richelle. "I don't remember ever agreeing to this scheme or hearing anything about it!" He still kept his eyes trained on Richelle. Natalie tucked a dark chestnut tress behind a rounded ear.

"How about tomorrow?" Sheldon blinked and after opening and closing his mouth a few times, gave up trying to argue. "The mall is pretty close." She pushed her shoulder into his, laughing up into his blank face, brown eyes sparkling merrily. Richelle felt a smile coming and watched the two of them; Sheldon didn't know what to do with himself.

"Come on, Shel," she joined in the barrage, "you'd look great with an earring. We could get one together. I think I'd like a second piercing in my left ear." He still looked uncertain. "If you don't like it, you can let it heal up."

"True . . . OK, fine!" White teeth flashed. "Shouldn't be too bad."

"In my opinion," said Natalie in her honest, straightforward manner, "you have the face to pull it off. You won't look awful, that's for sure." *No, he won't,* thought Richelle. *Who am I kidding? He'll be irresistible, with that crooked grin of his . . .* She sighed softly. Sheldon sniffed and ran a hand across his nose.

"Sure," he laughed. For a while, they each were busy with their own thoughts and relaxed in the warmth radiating from the stove. Sheldon crooked his arms behind his head, lying back on the wool carpet, his feet up on the hearth.

"So, I think I'll be heading out for home Sunday." He craned his neck toward Richelle.

"But why? Classes don't start up until Wednesday!"

"Why not go home Tuesday, with Richelle?" Natalie propped her chin in her hands, waving her feet in the air carelessly. "You could get more time to hang out, and anyways, Richelle hates riding trains by herself, don't you?" She smiled mischievously at her friend.

"I don't love it, for sure," Richelle said honestly.

"Your parents won't mind?" He sat up a little and leaned back on his elbows.

"Oh no! In fact, they think you were planning on staying here until then and just leaving with Richelle." Sheldon shared a glance with Richelle.

"OK, that's fine by me. I just didn't want to outstay my invitation." Natalie dismissed this with a wave of her hand and flopped back down on the carpet, lazily closing her eyes. Sheldon shrugged and replaced his hands behind his head.

"Well, looks like we're in for another train ride, Chelle."

"I guess so!" Her smile was warm and sweet.

Chapter 11
Mall Adventures

The Coharts had agreed when Natalie begged them to let Sheldon drive them to the mall. Mrs. Cohart, in true motherly fashion, had anxiously exhorted them to be careful—Rick had waved and told his wife to let the kids have a good time. But she'd looked relieved when Sheldon assured her he wouldn't be taking any chances.

And so here they were, flying down the highway, the girls laughing and chattering, Sheldon grinning at all the noise. Richelle had turned on the radio, and the music added to the atmosphere of happy chaos. Occasionally, Natalie, being the more outgoing of the two, would burst into song, and Richelle would grin and sing along with her, Sheldon sneaking peeks in the rearview mirror and laughing at Natalie. It was a noisy party that arrived at the mall without mishap and piled out of the car.

"You ready for this, Shel?" Sheldon smiled down at Richelle.

"Ready as I'll ever be to have a hole punched in my ear." She grinned and lightly linked her arm through his. His blue eyes glinted with surprise, and he tentatively gave her more room, twisting his arm away from his body. Richelle loved the hard sensation of his firmly muscular arm under her hand, and she was pleasantly conscious of a measure of security with him beside her.

She was glad he was with them as they made their way deeper into the mall. Loud music blared in several shops; people crowded the main aisle, pushing and shoving, vacant stares, hurrying steps going no place in particular. It was a busy place.

Sheldon felt an increased pressure on his arm, and her fingers clutched anxiously at his forearm. He moved over further, pressing her protectively up to a wall as they pretended to be absorbed in admiring playful, furry puppies. There was a man watching them, particularly Richelle, with an expression in his cold eyes that unnerved Sheldon. He found himself staring the man down, and presently, he gave a disdainful shrug and strode arrogantly away.

"Hey, all clear, Chelle. He's gone now." He kept his voice down, his mouth close to her ear, keeping Natalie ignorant. Her eyes were frightened, and something in her white face awoke a fierce desire to protect her inside of him. He brought up a gentle hand and touched the curve of her cheek, wrapping a stray auburn curl around her ear. "I got you." The words were whispered. She squeezed his arm in acknowledgement as they continued walking.

Soon they were examining rows and stacks of displayed earrings, trying to pick out a pair they liked.

"What's the point of buying a pair when I'm only getting one ear pierced?" His complaining tone brought smiles to both girls' faces.

"Well, me too. It's not the end of the universe, you know." Richelle peered through a glass case.

"Did you find anything you like yet?" The girl on duty was a pleasant, plump thing who clearly supported her profession, judging from the rows of piercings marching up both ears. She had a stud in her nose as well as a small ring in her lip.

"Not just yet, thank you." Richelle smiled at her. "We'll let you know when we have."

"Hey, you guys." Natalie was looking into a glass display case. The two crowded about her elbows, following her indicating finger. It was a pair of small diamond rhinestone studs.

"Why not buy this set and each use one of them? There's no point wasting money here."

"Do you like them, Richelle? Cuz that sounds fine."

"Yes, I do. Trust Natalie's taste and good ideas!" She beamed at her friend. The assistant came over and took out the desired pair.

"So, what are we doing today?" She took out the piercing gun and pulled open a small drawer full of alcohol pads and a few sharpies. Richelle spoke up.

"He and I are each getting a piercing in one ear." She gestured toward Sheldon.

"And you're both using the same pair?" She was affirmed and then asked, "Well, who's first?"

Sheldon slid into the padded, imitation leather seat and felt like he was in a dentist's office. The cold alcohol pad swabbed off his earlobe, and the girl applied a small black dot with the sharpie.

"Ready?" Well, of course, he was ready. He was in this far, wasn't he? He couldn't exactly back out now . . . Ouch! Sharp stinging pain exploded for a second, and he distinctly felt the pointed end of the earring punch through the layers of his skin and pop audibly out the other side. He winced and then felt the pain subside to a dull throb. A glance in the mirror conveyed that all had gone well, and he decided he liked the effect the lone earring lent him and grinned back at the two eager faces in the mirror.

"Looking good, looking good, sweetie." The assistant popped her gum and gave him a slow perusal that clearly communicated she thought he was good-looking eye candy. His mouth tightened, and he rolled his eyes as he stood to allow Richelle to take his seat. The girl couldn't help a sharp intake of breath; then it was all over, and there was a little rhinestone where it smarted most. After instructions on care to prevent infection and the distribution of little baggies of supplies, Sheldon paid, and they began enjoying their day at the mall, or at least Natalie did. But after a bit, the pain from their piercings dissipated as they went from shop to shop. Eventually, the time sense built into their stomachs informed them in clear tones of empty hunger that it was time to grab a bite to eat.

"My dad gave me money for a movie," Natalie announced matter-of-factly and took a bite out of her burger. Sheldon looked up.

"Oh? Is there anything good showing soon?"

"I don't know, but we could check. When we're done, I mean," she added as an afterthought.

"Well, obviously." He realized she was nearly halfway through her lunch! Well, maybe that was an exaggeration, but she sure wasn't messing around. He took a swig from his root beer and returned an escapee pickle to his double-decker cheese burger.

Natalie, who was finished first, headed for the theater to see if anything worth watching was showing. Richelle reached up and absentmindedly gave her little stud a twist. She yawned and picked up a French fry, munching on it.

"Hey, you having fun?" He reached into the box of fries and helped himself to a liberal handful. She watched him squeeze ketchup out of the annoying little package and pop a dipped fry into his mouth. He'd forgotten to shave that morning. She smiled.

"Yes, I am." She leaned forward and propped her chin up. "Aren't you?"

"Of course!" He took another sip of his soda. "Despite my poor mutilated ear." Her merry laugh rang out, silvery.

"Oh, Sheldon, you're so dramatic!"

"Am I now!" His voice bordered on amused.

"It makes you fun to be with. One of the reasons." She smiled at him, leaning over and dunking a fry in his ketchup. Natalie returned and flopped into her vacant seat.

"The *Demolition of Smaug* is showing in about twenty minutes. I ordered tickets." She spread them on the table. "Everything else is just blah." Sheldon laughed at her expressive choice of words and tucked a ticket into his hip pocket.

"I don't know how long it is, but I don't want to be sitting here for the next twenty minutes. Come on, you two, let's walk around. My butt's gonna be killing me after all this sitting. Come on, come on!" He grabbed his tray and shoved everything into a trash can, depositing the tray on top of a growing stack. With the two girls in tow, he set off for a little more window shopping.

The theater seats weren't all that bad, and they dangled their feet over the backs of the empty chairs in front. Chattering died down as people took out their popcorn; bass shook their seats as the screen came to life, and they were all soon swallowed up into the unfolding epic tale.

"Well, that was cool. Did you like it, Shel?" Richelle's eyes were bright.

"Oh yeah!" he grinned. "I love *The Lord of the Rings*, so yep, I liked it." He discarded his 3D glasses and they walked out of the theater.

"How do we get out of here, Natalie?" Richelle paused and cast about her for some familiar point of reference. Natalie took the lead and led them down the long corridors, sidestepping groups of people, and thus, they eventually made it out into the parking lot. A breathy laugh escaped her as her eyes roved through the rows of cars, hoping for any sight of the right one.

"I do hope you remember where you parked, Sheldon."

"Umm, I've got the general area." That was vague and not at all inspiring. Richelle finally spotted the car after a few moment's hunting out in the raw cold of the exposed parking lot. He unlocked the doors, and they got in. Sheldon winced in pain as his earring caught on the seat as he strained around to grab the seat belt. "I bet sleeping will be rather uncomfortable with this blasted thing catching on everything and poking into you," he remarked with an edge to his voice.

"What, the earring?" Richelle adjusted the strap over her shoulder. "It'll heal quickly. Don't forget to keep twisting it." He grumbled and threw the car into reverse, backing out of the space, and soon hit the road. Richelle watched his sure hands gripping the wheel. Absentmindedly, she went over the day, stashing away memories to look back on in the years ahead. The headrest pillowed her head, and she let her eyelids drift shut. The thought of pajamas had an alluring prospect; she was as ready as the rest of them to relax. She became aware of Sheldon and Natalie talking nonsense, and she speculated on how wonderful it was that her two best friends got along so well.

The sky was a little bluer than the previous day, and a few pearly colored clouds chased each other over the great expanse.

Sheldon glanced over in a lapse in the conversation and saw Richelle gazing out her window. Pink was beginning to touch the horizon with a pale, rosy finger. He returned his attention to the road. The tires ate up the miles, and Richelle still hadn't said anything more when they pulled into the wide driveway. She was stretching when he hauled himself out and came around to her side of the car to assist her. Surprised, she took his outstretched hand and let him pull her to her feet.

"You OK?" He was attentive and even a little concerned.

"Yeah, I'm fine, just ready for pj's." She smiled and carefully avoided her tender ear as she brushed her hair back. He laughed lightly.

"Oh yeah. Me too, only I forgot to pack mine."

"You forgot to pack pajamas?" She laughed at him. "You can borrow a pair of mine. We already share earrings," she teased, her face visibly brightening as she winked at him.

"I might take you up on that offer if you have a pair of pj pants as big as that T-shirt you were wearing," he shot back playfully as she turned on him and prodded his arm with one finger.

"Hey! No dissing the T-shirt!" They shared a laugh and pushed their shoes away from the door to shut out the cold.

Chapter 12
Of Things Higher

Natalie was filling up the tea kettle to heat water for cocoa. Her dad called out a cheerful greeting from his study.

"Mom's visiting a friend, so who knows when she'll be back. But she says we can ransack the fridge for whatever." The kettle sputtered as Natalie settled it on the hot burner. She wiped her hands on her jeans and glanced at the clock. "I'm gonna go get changed." Both girls tramped upstairs, and Sheldon wandered into the living room. Sacked out on the couch, he didn't notice a small furry shadow stalking a little nearer, a little closer; he felt a tiny weight padding up his back. Whatever it was, it walked up over his shoulder, and he found himself being examined by a scrap of a kitten. It was very curious and amiable, nuzzling its cheek against his jaw.

"Hi, little guy!" He gently picked it up and turned on his side, stroking the downy gray fur. The kitten meowed, and a tiny pink tongue flicked out and licked his finger. Presently, it curled up against him and drifted to sleep, outrageously loud purrs rumbling out of its Lilliputian vocal cords, causing the small body to vibrate. Sheldon grinned and dozed comfortably with his head pillowed against the couch. He was just beginning to seriously wonder what had happened to Richelle and Natalie when he looked up and noticed them standing in the doorway. He looked down at the kitten cuddled against his chest.

"I've been adopted, evidently," he said.

"She's so friendly." Natalie smiled, affectionately regarding her fluffy gray pet.

"Yeah, she is." The kitten awoke at the sound of voices and yawned, rows of teeny tiny razor sharp teeth gleaming in the wide pink mouth. With a stretch, she plunked down on the floor, trotting away with her tail high in the air.

"Here, my dad lent you these." Natalie tossed him a pair of dark plaid pj pants.

"Sweet, I'll be down in a sec." He got up and disappeared into the other room, thanking Mr. Cohart as he ran upstairs. The door to the little blue room clicked shut, and he chucked his discarded clothes into the corner, yanking a clean shirt over his tousled head. The pants were a soft, worn flannel, and they felt good against his skin. Slightly revived, he joined his friends in the kitchen.

There were three mugs of cocoa steaming on the counter, and they were frying eggs for bagel sandwiches. He'd taken a lot longer than he'd thought. Richelle's teasing inquiry as to if he'd taken a nap received a sheepish ghost of a smile, and he leaned against the breakfast bar and watched Richelle flip the eggs.

"You do like your yolks runny, don't you?" She turned around, spatula raised.

"Yeah, sure." The toaster popped. Natalie retrieved the golden bagels and buttered them. Quickly, they assembled the sandwiches and set the food out, perching on stools. He pushed himself away from the counter and took a seat between them. Natalie took Richelle's hand and held out the other for his expectantly. Unsure of himself, he glanced over at Richelle and saw her hand outstretched as well. Then he realized what was going on and took each small hand in one of his. Natalie, being so tiny, had delicate, petite bones, but Richelle's hands were long fingered and fine without feeling like he could crush them. They closed their eyes respectfully as Natalie murmured grace.

"Anyone wanna do anything in particular tonight?" Her brown eyes flashed from Richelle to Sheldon over her mug of cocoa. They looked at each other.

"Guess not." He wiped up yoke with a bit of bagel.

"Wanna play Clue again?" Sheldon pulled a long face and hid behind his mug.

"OK, fine. We'll just talk. What's so bad about Clue anyhow?" Richelle coughed and nearly swallowed a whole bite without chewing. She recovered herself and laughed.

"What's so bad? We played all morning! Anything else for options?"

"Eh, not really. We don't play many games. Wait, we do have Uno."

"That's fine, faster than Clue at any rate." Sheldon winked before she could look flustered. They finished the meal with small talk and laughter and then cleaned up the kitchen and proceeded into the living room.

"I call couch." Sheldon felt too lazy to make a dash for it.

"First come first serve, me deary!" Natalie jumped on one end, Richelle on the other. Natalie put her legs up. Sheldon glared at her in imitative vexation and flopped down next to Richelle.

"Oh, I gotta go get the game, duh!" Natalie jumped up.

"How's the ear?" Sheldon tipped his head to one side and looked at it.

"It's fine. Doesn't hurt much. Do you like it?" she asked hesitantly, almost shyly.

"Course, I do. It's kinda cute." He gave his funny crooked grin. "What a day, huh?" She was quiet for a moment. Surprised at her silence, he looked at her quizzically.

"Yeah." She paused. "I'm glad you were there."

"Me too. It was a lot of fun," he said, carefree.

"No, I meant, well, about that guy."

"Oh. That." He passed his arm around her shoulders awkwardly, pulling her into a side-hug. "There's a lot of weirdos out there, Chelle. I'm sorry. Yeah, I'm glad you two weren't alone. He gave me the creeps." He looked into her upturned face.

"Tyson is coming over tomorrow." She let her words speak for themselves.

"Natalie and I will back you up. Don't worry about it. It won't do any good, you know," he said gently. She met his eyes, her own wide.

"Have you been reading your Bible?" Seeing his clouded face, she explained, "Jesus tells us not to worry. It's in the book of Matthew, I believe. 'And which of you by worrying can add a single hour to his day?' And he goes on to say do not worry about tomorrow, for tomorrow will take care of itself and we aren't guaranteed it anyways." She was thoughtful and leaned against his shoulder companionably. "You're such an encouragement to me. Thank you for being here for me, Shel," she sighed heavily. Sheldon didn't know what to say. He cupped her shoulder in his hand and pressed her closer for a second. She sat up straight as he let her go; they could both hear Natalie's quick returning footsteps.

"Is she always so energetic?" he inquired in a low voice as she entered the room. A smile broke over Richelle's serious face.

"Yes! She's crazy!"

"Talking about me, I hear. Yeah, we're all crazy, just some more so than others." She stuck her tongue out at them as she pushed a coffee table over to the couch. Squatting beside it, she took out the cards and dealt them.

"Here we go. Sheldon goes first." The top card was a green nine. He looked apologetically at Richelle and laid a skip.

"Hey!"

"Sorry! I'd be nicer, but my cards have determined otherwise! Fate has spoken!" Cards were slapped down promptly, and after a short interval, Sheldon held up one card.

"Uno!" he said a little dramatically.

It was a fast game; he was victorious for two successive rounds. Natalie beat them both soundly the third time around; then the game petered out, and they took to conversing for a while. An hour more went by, and the old grandfather clock bonged out the eleventh hour. By common assent, they shut off lights and tiptoed quietly up the stairway, conscientious of not waking Natalie's parents.

The house silent, Richelle clasped her blankets to her chest, trying to warm up, for the room was slightly chilly, and pondered what the next day could bring and what Sheldon's words had incited her to say. Worry. She did tend to worry so, but she knew it was pointless. What could she change after all? She shook her head at herself.

Sheldon, alone in his room, sat on the bed and slowly opened the cover. Finding the table of contents, he skimmed the page until he spotted Matthew. He flipped to the book and began reading. It was gripping and strange. Bits of it were familiar, like the Christmas story. He read through the famous Beatitudes and found the part Richelle had quoted. Its beauty was striking. It made so much sense and made everyday anxieties seem foolish and unreasonable. *Well,* Sheldon pondered, *they very well can be, but is this true? How do I know for sure?* Doubtful, his eyes flew over chapter seven. Confusion flooded him. Jesus was talking about narrow gates and trees and fruit and building houses; what did it all mean? He was sobered by the warnings he encountered, but why heed them if they weren't founded in reality. Was God real? Was Jesus? Questions poured into his mind; he reflected on the words before him. A lot of this was sensible advice, but there was so much figurative language, he just didn't understand. He rifled through the pages, and his eyes caught something that made him pause.

"But even the hairs of your head are numbered. Fear not, therefore; you are of more value than many sparrows. So everyone who acknowledges me before men, I also will acknowledge before my Father, who is in heaven, but whoever denies me before men, I will also deny before my Father who is in heaven" (Matt. 10:30–33).

He'd heard about heaven and hell. Eternal fire didn't sound very appealing. He slowly read over the words again, weighing them. Right before him he was told not to fear, and then that he was supposed to fear God, who could send his soul to hell? There was comfort and a warning . . . If you do not acknowledge me . . . Verse 39 troubled him; what did Jesus mean by saying whoever loses his life for Him will find it? How do you gain life by losing it? You're dead! Brows creased, Sheldon searched the pages for answers. Suddenly, a light dawned on him. Jesus was not talking about physical life, but spiritual, eternal.

There were many questions yet unanswered, but his eyes were heavy with sleep, and he had a headache that would only get worse. Sheldon closed the Book and put it on the bedside table, regretful that he didn't have more time. His mind full of everything he'd read, new ideas, doubts, he slid down under the blankets and flicked off the light. Laying there in the dark, he prayed, "Dear God, I don't know if you're real, but if you are, show me. Help me understand your words. I . . . I think I want to know what you mean. Maybe there's more to life than I thought." With a sigh, he rolled over on his side and tried to go to sleep.

"For the gate is narrow and the way is hard that leads to life, and those who find it are few." The words went round and round in his head, resounding like a drum.

Early the next morning, after a restless night, Sheldon crept down the stairs with the Bible tucked securely under his arm. No one was awake, and his straining ears caught no sound except for his own breathing and stealthy footsteps. The fire had died down to a few scattered, glowing coals so he arranged two small logs over them and blew steadily until it caught. He shut the door and opened the damper. Impatiently, he wrapped himself up in a throw blanket and settled down on the couch, curling up with the Bible. The minutes ticked away, and soon it was nearly seven. The sky grew pale as the sun began to awaken. Oblivious to the sunrise, Sheldon was utterly captivated by the words on the pages, drinking them in, getting a feel for the unfamiliar language and style. He was completely engrossed, but he still didn't know how to take these radical ideas; were they true or was this all some crazy kind of cult or something? His eyes blurred, and to his profound shock, he realized he was brought to tears by reading of the unjust, unexpected death of a man who'd lived two thousand years previous to himself. He shook his head at himself and dashed the tears away.

"Behold I am with you, even to the end of age." His grandmother had said words to a similar effect. She'd said Jesus had been with him throughout his life and protected him. Something snapped deep inside him and understanding flooded him; it was real! Jesus really had died and rose again. He had always been there, just like He'd promised! Sheldon knew in that moment that he would never be the same.

Her phone said it was 7:30, and her hand ran lightly along the banister as she hesitantly tiptoed down the carpeted steps. She hadn't heard anyone up, and so she pressed a hand to her mouth to keep a gasp from escaping as she came into the living room and found Sheldon lying on the couch, knees drawn up and clutching a large book to his chest. Richelle paused, but something in his unguarded sleeping face drew her nearer. There were tearstains on his pale cheeks, and a dusky shadow accented his jaw. But there was such peace in his features that she could almost feel it emulating from him. It hung in the air, thick, like a living, loving presence. His hand didn't quite cover the book, and her eyes lit up with joy as she saw what he'd been reading before he had fallen asleep. Richelle knelt beside the huddled figure and poured her heart out in earnest prayer.

Sheldon opened his eyes drowsily, his sleep disturbed by whispered words. A small head was bowed, hands clasped earnestly on the cushion, red hair spiraling over her arms. He was bewildered, yet didn't want to make any sudden moves and interrupt her. Not being able to keep from hearing, he caught a few coherent whispers and realized she was praying, for him. Fortunately he didn't have to say anything. As soon as she was silent, she hadn't even raised her head before he'd wrapped her in a tight hug.

"Oh!" she cried and strained closer, laughing. "Are you really my brother now?" she said against his neck.

"Yes!" They pulled apart and beamed at one another, Richelle wiping away happy tears. She sat beside him, and he began to tell her what had happened.

"You read all of Matthew? Let's read some of John together. You learn more about Jesus here." She flipped confidently to the book of John. "There's a more complete picture than in Matthew. I love John's Gospel." They began to read chapters out loud, and Sheldon found he understood it better than he had before, especially with Richelle trying to explain the figurative way Jesus had of speaking. He found it beautiful, and Richelle fell in love with the passages all over again; he was so enthusiastic and spellbound.

"Look! I questioned if this all were true, and it says right here that 'I am the way, the truth, and the life.' That's really cool."

"That is!" She smiled. "Because Jesus *is* truth, the creator of it, and cannot sin, which includes lying, everything he says is the whole truth. He is utterly trustworthy." He looked at her with eager eyes.

"And life? That means eternal life? I read in Matthew how if you lose your life for Christ, you'll find it." Richelle explained how the Christian's life was one of suffering, like the Lord's, and self-denial as they become conformed more and more to His image and gain eternal life by His side forever.

"The strange thing about this is, we can't do it." Sheldon looked confused.

"What?"

"He calls us to life because we're spiritually dead in our sin. He awakens us and gives us strength and faith to live a life pleasing to Him. And He promises to never leave us nor forsake us. So salvation is not to be earned. It's a gift. And we can't pay God back for it. He wants to be our refuge and fight our battles for us. Being a Christian is hard! We're not perfect, and we make mistakes. But we get back up and have faith that God will pull us through." She gazed contemplatively into the leaping flames. Sheldon mused over her words.

"That's amazing. So all He asks in return is our faith? Just to believe in him?"

"Yes, to have faith that He will fulfill His promises to us."

"Promises?"

"They're all throughout the Bible. One of the most beautiful ones to me is 'God who spared not His only Son, now much will He not also with Him freely give us all things?' All the things we need are ours in Christ and we don't have to go striving after things like kindness or patience because they're already ours. We have to have faith to believe that they are."

"So faith is obviously the key."

"Yeah," she said with a laugh. "Simple, but kind of difficult just 'cause we're human and we like to doubt."

"You can say that again."

"We like to doubt. Happy?" Sheldon made a face. "But anyways, God is amazing, He really is! He didn't have to save sinful people like us. Sin makes us God's enemies. That's who He laid down His life for, not His friends." Images of the scoffing crowd around the foot of the cross as Jesus died sprang up before his mind's eye. Richelle looked at him, her arms about her drawn up knees. "It's simply mind-blowing, trying to imagine a love like that!" He nodded.

"Yeah, I guess 'try' is a good word."

In the kitchen, he watched her make them some coffee and asked, "So why did you come downstairs?"

"Well." She placed her hands on the counter behind her and faced him. "I'd been laying awake for somewhere around an hour and couldn't go back to sleep for the life of me." He regarded her with his head to one side.

"Still worried, aren't you?" She shook loose hair out of her face, lips pressed together.

"No . . . I don't think so. I think I'll be fine. Not like we're going to be alone." Her smile was forced and didn't quite reach her eyes. Sheldon pulled open the fridge and handed her the cream.

"Would you like any toast?" She nodded and settled herself up on the counter. Four pieces of bread disappeared into the toaster. "The good thing is," he said, trying to be optimistic, "no day lasts forever. How long is he supposed to be staying?"

"Oh, who knows. He may decide to stay all day. I'll find something else to do if that's the case."

"Exactly. Sure you will. Clue and Uno love you, you know!" He winked at her, jumping away as she laughed and tried to poke him.

"Silly boy." She shook her head, but the smile remained.

Chapter 13
Family Relations

Tyson arrived at eleven, resolved to stay for at least a few hours. It was amazing the fortitude Richelle exhibited; for all the worry, now that Tyson was actually here, she didn't turn a hair. She was polite, but lacked the warmth that Sheldon loved so much about her. He saw the hard black eyes rove over her figure, shrouded in a loose creamy sweater dress. The utter lack of innocence and propriety in his lecherous gaze was revolting, and Sheldon nearly recoiled from the hand extended after he'd witnessed the way Tyson had looked at Richelle.

Tyson wore tight black jeans, and when he shrugged out of his leather jacket, he appeared to have forgotten to fasten pretty all the buttons on his shirt except the ones on the bottom. *At least it's staying on his body,* thought Sheldon sarcastically. In the thick of things moving away from the door, Sheldon lost his post by the girl's side, and he was repulsed to see Tyson's arm slip possessively about Richelle's slender waist. He said something in her ear that made her push him away, blushing angrily, but not before he'd ducked his head and brushed his mouth along her cheek. Furious, yet for her hosts' sake curbing her instinct to give him a well-deserved ringing slap, she dashed a hand over her cheek, indignation burning in her stormy eyes. This little scene happened so quickly that no one noticed it but for Sheldon, who was tagging along in the back. Tyson didn't seem to get the message that he wasn't wanted, and Sheldon reached out quickly and yanked Richelle forcibly back against himself.

"Leave her alone." The menace in his voice was clear even though he spoke in a whisper.

"The guy who ruins all the fun . . . or just wants to keep it all for himself. I see your game." Tyson smirked and moved on, drawing his uncle into conversation as if nothing had happened at all. Richelle wanted to run upstairs and cry; her pride and dignity were so outraged, but she lifted a slightly trembling chin and wouldn't give him victory over her. A hand pressed hers. Sheldon mouthed, "I'm sorry." He clearly felt responsible. She shook her head nearly imperceptibly and crossed her arms.

Sometime after dinner, Richelle decided to go out for a walk. Sheldon looked up laughing from a joke of Rick's and glanced around the room. Richelle was nowhere to be seen, and Tyson had excused himself a moment ago.

In the quiet away from the boisterous conversation, his ear caught the sounds of a commotion upstairs. Two at a time, he dashed up the steps and saw a sight that made his blood fairly boil. Tyson had cornered Richelle in the hall so she was unable to get away from him, and he had one hand clamped over her mouth and the other grasping her hair forcing her head back. She was struggling, but he was hurting her so she had to remain still. Whatever he was going to do to her, Sheldon didn't hang around to find out. Such a rush of anger surged through him, he was beside them and punched Tyson furiously right in the face before he realized he'd moved. The surprise wiped clean off his ugly mug, Tyson sprawled out on the floor.

"I said," Sheldon ground out from between clenched teeth, kicking Tyson as he struggled to rise, "leave her alone!"

His touch on her arm contrasted sharply with the rough treatment Richelle had received just a moment before, and she clung to him, terrified eyes on the figure prone on the floor, blood running from his nose. He spat out a contemptuous curse and leered at Richelle, who ignored him.

"That would've been more fun had not your knight in shining armor butted in," he spoke to her, ignoring Sheldon pointedly. Sheldon paused in the act of turning away.

"The black knights always lose. You should know that by now." He couldn't help the wicked gleam in his eyes and the smug tone. The front door slammed, and through the window he saw Richelle run down the street. Sheldon turned his attention back to Tyson. "Get up. I think your aunt and uncle are expecting you. And you've caused enough trouble for one day. You might wanna visit the bathroom before you get that all over the carpet, just saying." Tyson sneered, yet followed his advice; a bloody nose would call for an explanation of some sorts. Sheldon make sure Tyson returned with him to the living room and then waited for nearly ten minutes, judging from the old clock, before politely excusing himself.

He thought he knew just where he might find Richelle. Hastily tramping through snow, once again beneath those great forest trees, he spied footprints. She'd come this way.

The poor girl was huddled on a small boulder, her head in her arms, sobs shaking her slight body. He went and sat quietly beside her, not knowing what else to do. She lifted a face streaked with tears and buried it against his shirtfront, clutching the collar of his unzipped jacket in cold fingers. She felt his arms close protectively about her, and he began rocking her back and forth, not saying a word. Richelle leaned against him and let him shut everything out for a moment.

"You're so different from him." He ran his hand up and down her back.

"No matter."

"Yes!" She sat up. "He's horrible!" Sheldon tilted his head to better meet her eyes.

"Had my life taken a different route, who's to say I wouldn't be just like him?" Richelle knew he was right. Wearily, she dropped her face into her hands. Neither of them spoke.

"I wish he'd go home," she whispered.

"Yeah," he agreed heartily. "Let's not think about it, OK?"

"Easy for you to say," she said, more sharply than she'd intended. He exhaled softly, considering the affronted girl beside him.

"You're right. But thinking about it and getting madder over a wrong done to you won't make it go away. Trust me." His words were weighted, compassionate. She sniffed and wiped her nose.

"True. I don't want to be bitter. I just never ever want to see him again."

"Understandably." He stood and peered cautiously over the edge of the quarry. "Long way's down, huh."

"Yes. Don't fall over!" She grabbed at his arm anxiously. He laughed.

"I'm not going anywhere. Come on, let's go for a walk. Maybe stay out here for a while until we get so cold we *have* to go back to the house. Kill some time, whaddya say girl?" She looked up at him with a smile.

"I'm up for it, let's go!"

When they returned to the house, Tyson was leaving, just coming out the door.

"Oh, there you two are!" Mrs. Cohart sounded like she'd been wondering what on earth had happened. "Where have you been?" She continued without waiting to hear excuses, much to their relief. "Come say good-bye to Ty. He's got to go home."

Just like we're kids or something, Sheldon thought wryly. He warily held out his hand to Tyson, noticing satisfactorily how Richelle kept his body between her and Tyson.

"Nice to meet you," he lied with a condescending smirk, firmly shaking his clammy hand. Tyson inclined his head, shifted his attention to Richelle, and had the nerve to blow her a kiss. Sheldon bit his lip, bridling his temper, and then Tyson was in his car, revved the motor like the show-off he was, and roared off down the street. He heard a sigh of profound relief escape Richelle, and she turned and went inside without a backward glance. Mr. Cohart chatted with his wife as they closed the door, and Natalie followed

Richelle up to their room. Sheldon couldn't take anymore after hearing Mrs. Cohart tell her husband that Tyson was "a nice boy," only a "little rough around the edges." Both adults looked at each other in surprise as he strode up the stairs.

"Well." She pursed her lips and narrowed her eyes. "What's eating him?" Rick shrugged and poured himself another cup of coffee.

"Who knows? He'll be fine, Lilly. The kids seem a little off, probably too much exertion. They'll be OK in a little while." His wife dismissed it from her mind and took advantage of having her husband to herself, curling her hands around her cup as she sat beside him.

Natalie opened the door and snagged him as he went by.

"Get in here. We've got some stuff to talk about." Discomfited, he followed her into the room, appreciative that she didn't close the door all the way but left it open a crack. She pulled a beanbag off her bed and motioned for him to sit. Richelle looked moody and screwed up her nose as Natalie settled herself comfortably on her bed, obviously curious. "So," her eyes flicked from one person to the other, "what's up?" Awkward silence. Sheldon picked at a stray thread in the beanbag. "Come on, guys, I wasn't born yesterday. What's going on? Why did you leave? You were gone forever!" Suddenly, she checked herself and looked at them narrowly. Richelle put two and two together and decisively shook her head.

"No, no, it wasn't that." She blushed. Sheldon glanced furtively toward the door.

"Then what?" She was impatient. Sheldon met Richelle's eyes and then sighed as he began to speak.

"Let's just say that your cousin is highly inappropriate around your friend." Her eyes widened, and she looked at Richelle for confirmation.

"What?" She was incredulous.

"Oh, knock it off, Natalie. Anyone with eyes could see that something was going on. He's a pervert." He was disgusted.

"I had no idea . . ."

"I thought you weren't born yesterday," he smirked.

"Shel." Richelle's voice was quiet, but he acknowledged the warning. Natalie looked hurt, and he apologized, shamefaced.

"He hurt me." Richelle showed bruises on her arms that Sheldon hadn't noticed before, and he swore softly under his breath. "I don't know or want to think of what he might have done to me if Sheldon hadn't run upstairs and found us together." She twisted her hands together in her lap. Natalie looked at Sheldon admiringly.

"What did you do to him?" she asked eagerly.

"Punched him," he said simply.

"Good." She nodded emphatically. "I had no idea, Richelle. You should've told me!" she said gently, clearly mortified for her friend. "Mom and Dad wouldn't have dreamed of inviting him over if they knew."

"But he's their nephew! I just couldn't." Natalie understood.

"Well, trust me, he's not coming over again when you're here. I'm awfully sorry." Richelle smiled wanly at her, thankful for this assurance. Natalie began to chat of lighter things, diverting their minds with cheerful nonsense, and soon laughter rang through the house.

"See, Lilly dear, what did I tell you? They're just fine." Rick winked at his wife and squeezed her hand in his.

Chapter 14
Whisperings of New Beginnings

Sheldon enjoyed his stay at the Coharts' lovely home. But all good things must come to an end, and before he knew it, he was home, and with school starting back up in full swing, he and Richelle didn't get a chance to meet up right away. They met in the halls between classes, calling cheerful salutations to each other, sometimes sitting in class together, but no time for anything other than that. He'd bidden her good-bye at the train station when they returned and set out for home before her mother had come to pick her up. She'd been disappointed, but hadn't insisted he stay.

About a week had passed, and at the end of a particularly long day, Sheldon was riding the rickety old bus home when he got a text from Richelle inviting him over for dinner Friday. Delighted, he replied quickly, accepting the invitation and telling her he'd be most happy for a chance to check out the car as well.

The bus hissed ominously and sputtered to an abrupt halt; it was his new customer's house, what's-her-name's family. Clarisse, he'd found out. And he was most irritated when she ran her fingers lingeringly through his hair as she passed, a too sweet smirk; then he could breathe again; the bus groaned, gears ground, and they chugged off. Sheldon grimaced. She was infuriatingly relentless.

Friday, when school was out, Sheldon hunted through crowds of teenagers for a glimpse of Richelle. A slight frown pulled at his mouth. Suddenly, she was tugging on his sleeve.

"Come on, walk with me."

"Oh, there you are. Been looking for you."

"Sorry, my locker was jammed." Her lips were a thin line.

"On purpose?" he asked grimly.

"No, I don't think so. Why would it be? I've barely seen you enough to get labeled . . .," she broke off. "That came out wrong. Sorry."

"Naw, it's fine," he scoffed, kicking a loose pebble free from a sandy patch in the sidewalk. "I get what you're trying to say. Hmm, you're right," he said musingly.

"Coincidence." She changed the subject. "My parents are really looking forward to meeting you. Oh, my mom made lasagna, thought you'd like it."

"No, she didn't!" He was incredulous. "I simply adore lasagna." Richelle laughed.

"Never met someone who doesn't!" They walked in silence, the cold air discouraging further conversation, and they were grateful to arrive at a well-heated house. She opened the door, calling as she did, "Hey, you guys, we're home!"

There was a scuffle and a scraping of a chair's legs, and a sandy brown-haired kid rounded the corner, leaning casually against the wall, and regarded his sister and her friend frankly.

"Sheldon, this is Matt." Richelle puffed as she pulled off her boots, hopping on one foot. She grabbed Sheldon's hastily extended arm and saved herself from landing on the floor. Matt grinned, amused.

"Hi!" His affable face was open, and he held out a hand and grasped Sheldon's in a friendly grip. "Nice to finally meet you. I've only heard all about you ever since she met you." He jerked his thumb at his sister, who was hanging up their jackets. She crinkled up her nose at him playfully. "So you must be pretty awesome." Sheldon got a distinct sense that he enjoyed embarrassing his sister.

"Where's Mom and Dad, Matt?" She stepped around the boys and glanced into the kitchen.

"They aren't home yet. She went to pick Dad up from work. Other car is in the shop," he explained on the side to Sheldon.

"OK, they should be back soon though, right?"

"Yeah, yeah, in a bit." Matt lounged into the living room, throwing himself lackadaisically onto the leather couch. "Oh, gosh, am I glad it's Friday! No more school tomorrow!" He flung his arms over his head. "Freedom! But seriously," he rolled over on his stomach, "I couldn't stand another day just yet. Thank heavens for weekends." He sang out with a silly contagious smile. Sheldon grinned back at him, beginning to like him immensely, and sat on the love seat across from him. Richelle hesitated, not knowing where to sit, Matt taking up the entire couch and the love seat, well, love seats were kind of close quarters. She perched on the arm. Matt scowled at her reprovingly.

"Rik! You know what Mom says about sitting on the arms!" Hastily she slid down next to Sheldon and experienced a decided thrill to feel him against her, warm and firm. She was instantly embarrassed.

"Rik?" Sheldon looked at her with laughter in his blue eyes. "You didn't tell me about that one!" She blushed and stammered a bit before she responded.

"He's called me that since, well, ever since I can remember! Dad too. It's a pet name. Don't you start!" She poked his arm. He laughed.

"I won't." She didn't seem like a Rik to him. *Chelle fits her perfectly*, he thought. Matt propped his head up on his fist.

"So how was school? Everyone ready for a break?" He drew the word "break" out, somehow making it sound tantalizing. Sheldon folded his hands behind his neck.

"I've never been one to hate breaks."

"You'd be utterly inhuman if you did," Matt snorted. "Ah, hope the parents get home like now, before I perish of hunger." Sheldon looked at his sister and burst out laughing.

"A bit dramatic, isn't he?"

"He always is," Richelle said wryly. Her brother smirked, quite pleased with the effect he was having. He sat up, feet on the cushions. "You'd never believe how boring life would be around here without me." Richelle rolled her eyes.

"How about we substitute 'boring' for 'peaceful'. Then I would agree with you." Her eyes gleamed wickedly. "But I would miss you dreadfully, so don't go anywhere." He laughed.

"Hey, listen!" A car's motor purred and died in the driveway. "Oh, yay, they're home. Come on, you guys!" He bolted off the couch and went hurtling out of the room, yanking the door open and shouting something inarticulate.

"I wish I could borrow some of his energy sometimes," Richelle said affectionately. "It's endless." She stood up. "Come on, I want to introduce you." They followed Matt to the door at a more dignified rate, and soon there were handshakes and introductions all around, smiles and happy voices greeting Sheldon into their home.

Mrs. Callahan hurried into the kitchen to check on dinner, pulling her daughter along behind her, eager to talk to her. Of one accord, the guys headed out to the garage to see the car.

"He's so sweet, Richelle! Seems like a great friend. And very handsome." She looked slyly at the girl, knowing her daughter too well for her to be able to hide anything from her. "Don't tell me you don't agree with me." Richelle laughed and had to admit that she found him so. Her mother admired Sheldon greatly; Richelle having told her all about him and how he treated and protected her. "He's a good boy." Mrs. Callahan pulled open the oven and carefully moved aside the aluminum foil on the casserole dish. It was apparently done as she lifted it out with mitted hands. "We'll let it set for a little, and here, help me put this salad together."

She handed Richelle a serrated blade and a bell pepper as she diced a tomato. Working together, it was done in no time, and Mrs. Callahan took a pitcher of ice water out of the fridge and put it on the table. *She must have set it while Matt and I were at school,* thought Richelle. They put out a basket of Italian bread and a dish of butter and put the lasagna on hot cloths.

"All ready, Mom?"

"Yes, I don't think we're forgetting anything." She arranged a selection of dressings by the salad bowl and surveyed the effect. "You want to go get everybody?"

"Sure. We'll be inside in a minute." She hurriedly pulled on her coat and boots and stepped out into the cold.

They were in the garage, Sheldon walking around the car with her father, carefully scrutinizing it. Matt was looking as interested as he could, being as hungry as he was.

"I'm sorely tempted," Sheldon was saying, "I think I'll buy it. It's a nice car, and you're giving a great offer for it. And I really need a car." He ran a hand along the hood.

"And I really need to get rid of it!" Mr. Callahan laughed, clapping him companionably on the back. "Any time you want to come get it, let me know. I'll get you the registration papers. I could help you with all that if you would like me to." Richelle raised her eyebrows. He must really have taken a liking to her friend. Matt noticed her, and his face lit up with hope.

"Rik! Tell me dinner is ready!" She didn't have the heart to tease him and nodded. He was off like a shot.

"Hey, honey." Her dad pulled her into a side hug and gave the top of her head a quick kiss. "How was school?" He waited for her answer. "Oh, good. So it looks like I've got a buyer." He looked at Sheldon.

"I thought I heard as much." She smiled. Both guys were obviously pleased. "Hungry?"

"Starved," they said in unison, and laughed.

Dinner was delicious, and Mrs. Callahan beamed when he told her so. Richelle was glad that her family liked Sheldon; it would've been awful if they didn't. She shrugged and put a forkful of lasagna in her mouth. Who could not like him? He was honest, earnest, and on the whole, a most likable young man.

Sheldon found himself pulled in by Richelle's family, and her parents were wonderful people. They easily engaged him in conversation, and he heard himself telling them his plans of the near future, of getting an apartment in town as soon as he finished high school and getting away from his dad; he told them a little about him for something in their sympathetic understanding faces told him he would be accepted. Richelle simply couldn't believe what she heard her dad say next. He leaned back in his chair, chewing thoughtfully.

"You know, my boss has a little one-bedroom apartment above his garage, with a kitchen, bathroom, decent living space, and not at a bad price either." Sheldon lowered his fork, hanging on his every word. "It's going for five hundred a month. He knows people around here can't afford much more than that most of the time." He dug into the lasagna on his plate. "It's a sweet little place, and he's looking for someone to rent it, or so he told me." Sheldon stared at his plate, his mind working furiously. Could he afford it? He'd been saving for a long time; he had somewhere around fifteen grand in his savings account, but he'd need to get another job if he was going to get his own car and rent an apartment. Five hundred a month would quickly drain his resources, that much was obvious. But this sounded like a great opportunity.

"You don't suppose I could have his phone number? I will have to look into this for sure."

"Yeah, sure, you can. I'll get it for you after dinner. But look here, son, this is a lot to jump into. I'm sure you know what you can afford and all, and it's not my place to be even saying this." He felt his wife's detaining hand on his arm. "But shouldn't you pray about it?" Sheldon nodded slowly.

"You're right. But I still should notify him that I'm interested, don't you think?" He looked at the older man inquiringly.

"Yes, that's right. He will give you a few days to think about it and consider, you know."

"He will?" Clearly the boy had no idea about renting apartments.

"Well, yes," he checked himself and then said, "unless, of course, he already has someone else in line. Then it'll go to the one who decides fastest." Sheldon picked up his fork and cut a bite out of his piece of lasagna. Matt stretched and passed Richelle his plate for seconds.

"Ever feel like everything just comes together all at once?" Sheldon gave a dazed kind of laugh.

"Lot to handle, isn't it? Well, of course, it is!" Mrs. Callahan put a warm hand on his arm and smiled at him. "God will work things out for you, dear." He was surprised.

"Yes, I know He will." She'd called him dear? Was that something she called everybody? He loved these people; they were just the sort of parents he'd expected Richelle to have.

"I will talk to my boss about it and tell him you're interested and might need a few days."

"Thank you so much," Sheldon said sincerely.

He felt very connected to the Callahans and spent a wonderful day with them, enjoying talking to them immensely. Mr. Callahan dropped him off at the head of his street; Sheldon didn't want him to see what poverty he lived in. It was degrading. The older man didn't insist or ask questions, but merely complied to his wishes. Sheldon was surprised by the respectful manner he treated him, maybe not totally his equal, but that was understood, even expected. He was unused to getting other than professional respect. He'd also never had a casual relationship with any man; his father didn't count. He'd rather not know him anyways. But there was no condescending air about Mr. Callahan, either in his frank style of conversing or in his concern about him getting a better living situation. When he'd dropped him at the end of the street, he'd clasped his hand in a warm grip and told him to feel at home and stop by at the house any time.

Sheldon let himself in at the rickety door, loose on its rusty hinges.

"That you, boy?" a gruff voice shouted from deeper within the mess. The house was in horrible disrepair.

"Yeah, it's me." Backpack of homework on one arm, he moved guardedly into the house, suspicious. Dad nearly seemed to have forgotten of his existence since he never acknowledged his presence.

He stood unsteadily in the meager kitchen, lined face blanched, grizzled hair hanging in haggard deep-set eyes. "What's up?" The man stared at his son. "Look, if you're not going to talk, I'm going upstairs." He turned on his heel.

"Wait!" he choked, and Sheldon glanced back over his shoulder. Suddenly, his father clutched at his middle and retched into the sink. Uneasily, Sheldon saw it was mixed with a fair amount of blood. Gasping and reeling dizzily, his father wiped bloody vomit off his lips with a shaking hand. Sheldon pushed him into a chair.

"I . . . I don't feel well," he stammered in a whisper. Wide eyes followed the boy as he cleared all the bottles off the surfaces into a waste bin. Even the full ones. Angrily, he would've started to his feet had not a wave of dizziness overwhelmed him. "What are you doing?" he managed to spit out. Sheldon didn't even look at him or pause in what he was doing.

"Something you should've done years ago."

The sick man felt his muscles tense and barely made it to the sink. There was more blood. Sheldon realized something wasn't right. He kept throwing up until nothing but fluids were coming. It was obvious he was unwell, but his face, devoid of any hint of color, didn't tell of fever. Exhausted, he stumbled to his seat, holding his throbbing head.

"How much did you drink?" There was no emotion in Sheldon's voice. His father shook his head. "How much?"

"I didn't."

"Didn't drink?" He crossed his arms over his chest, scoffing, unbelief coloring his tones.

"I swear," he said hoarsely. "Something's wrong." Sheldon gave a snort of laughter, humorless.

"Well, I figured that out."

"No," he moaned. "My head aches so, I can't see right. I feel so awful."

"Hangover. You should know what those feel like by now."

"Sheldon!" He froze. He hadn't heard his dad use his name for years. "Call. Emergency." His hand fell listlessly off his lap, dangling over the side of the old chair. "Hospital." Sheldon stared at him for a moment and decided he'd better call 911. He dialed quickly and held his cell phone to his ear. Hastily, he gave the operator his information and paced up and down the small living room waiting for the ambulance to arrive.

"Are they coming?" his father called hoarsely from the kitchen. Sheldon replied without turning his head in his direction.

"Yeah. Didn't you hear me talking?" There was no response but coughing. Sheldon sat on the edge of the couch, the cushions ripped and the stuffing coming out, yellowed with age. He waited not even five minutes, chin propped on one fist, before he heard the sirens down the street. The open door let cold air into the little house, but Sheldon didn't care and stood on the top step watching the emergency vehicles pull up.

There seemed to be a million people, and Sheldon gave the details of what had happened in a few words while paramedics rushed his father out and into the back of the ambulance on a stretcher. He was told to climb in beside him, and before he knew it, the sirens were going off seemingly right in his ear, and they were on their way to the hospital. The ambulance lurched over the potholes dotting the old dirt road. Sheldon looked at the guy holding an oxygen mask to his father's face and got a cheery smile.

"He's gonna be fine, kid. What's your name?"

"Sheldon."

"Sheldon. I'd say nice to meet you if we were in a more pleasant circumstance! I'm Mike. Looks like your dad is in for a little stay at the hospital, huh?" Sheldon nodded, appreciative for the man's attempt at conversation, but he didn't feel much like talking. "You doing OK?" Mike shot him a quick glance as he ran some vitals on the prone man in the stretcher. Sheldon shrugged.

"Yeah, I'm fine. Didn't think I'd be riding in an ambulance when I woke up this morning."

"Yeah, I'll bet you didn't. But I wouldn't worry too much, your dad is in good hands." He smiled encouragingly. Sheldon inclined his head in acknowledgment and was glad when Mike lapsed into silence as he worked.

In the ER, Sheldon didn't know what he was feeling. He stared into space, his mind a blank. The doctor had come out moments before, telling him in gentle tones his father had Alcoholic Hepatitis. He explained that they would need to run some tests and scans, and he was going to have to perform a liver biopsy in order to confirm a clinical diagnosis.

"Son, your father's health is precarious, and this is serious. Depending on the test results . . ." He paused. Sheldon's intent gaze told him he should say the worst. "Depending on the results," he said again slowly, "we may have to operate. It is likely he will have chronic liver failure. In that case, it is detrimental that he has a liver transplant. Please understand that any surgery is risky."

"I understand."

"Yes. I'm sorry, son. It's a lot to take in. He's staying the night, so don't worry about anything." He laid a sympathetic hand on Sheldon's shoulder then pulled open the door and disappeared behind it.

After an indefinite period of time, Sheldon rose to his feet and strode out of the room.

The parking lot was a lot bigger than it had seemed earlier that day, and Sheldon struck out across it, tracing the sidewalk along the edges. He found the chill air reviving after the closeness of the hospital and its chemical scent. It was a long walk back to the house, but even as he grumbled over the inconvenience, part of him was grateful for the time to think, forced upon him as it was. There was simply nothing else to do but think things over, for he was alone with only his thoughts to keep him company. He was tired, and as he faced the facts with a shaky indrawn breath, he found his emotions were churning about inside him. He shook his head and squinted down the road in front of him. Things really were a mess. "God, I don't know what to do." He closed his eyes, his feet keeping up a steady but automatic rhythm over the asphalt pavement. He felt a presence, like someone was walking beside him, and he turned his head quickly to glance over his shoulder. There was no one there, however, and he shook his head and laughed at himself a little. He was getting a bit jumpy. But he still felt it. After his initial alarm, he realized it was a comforting kind of presence, and there was a deep sense of peace about it that he recognized. He was never totally alone. Even as he walked along the city sidewalks, no other human about, his solitude was not complete, for he knew God was watching over him no matter what was happening in his life. There was a great comfort in that for Sheldon. So he talked to God about everything that had happened that day. At first he felt a little silly; after all, he was talking out loud under his breath, and there was no one to be seen should someone come up behind him. He was skeptical. No one wants to be taken for being stark-raving mad, but after a bit, it began to feel natural. And furthermore, everyone knows that talking with someone makes the tedious things in life go faster.

When he got home it was after dark and late. Sheldon bolted the door and took a loaf of bread and some peanut butter and jelly up to his room to make himself a sandwich. The kitchen was a chaotic mess, and there was still bloody vomit in the sink, where his father had never rinsed it down the drain. Sheldon was too tired and emotionally drained to deal with it and wanted to be in a relatively clean place to eat his supper. He put the food on the dresser and sat wearily on his sagging mattress, dropping his head into his hands. He let out a long breath and pulled his phone out of his backpack, plugging it in to charge on his bedside table. It was blinking. As he had expected, it was a text from Richelle, wondering where he'd been all day. He ignored it and methodically made his sandwich. After he ate, Sheldon showered and gratefully crawled between his sheets, pulling them up to his chin with one hand and picking up his phone with the other. Quickly, he sent her a reply, sketching a simple outline of the day's experiences with a concise and clear choice of words. The result sounded rather impersonal, but he didn't feel like he wanted to unleash the full vent of his emotions. *Anyways,* he thought, *what is the use?* His pillow bunched up comfortably into his shoulder as he nestled down under the blankets, the room dark. Sheldon blinked as his eyes slowly became accustomed to the absence of light. He was just getting ready to slip away into a cozy state of unconsciousness when his phone rang, jerking him out of sleep with a sickening jolt of adrenaline.

"Hi?" he mumbled.

"Sheldon! Hi! It's Richelle. I got your text. I'm so sorry. How are you doing?"

"Oh, hey, Chelle. I'm doing OK, I guess. It's just a weird feeling somehow, you know?"

"I'll bet. Is your dad going to be OK? You said he'd probably have to have surgery."

"Yeah, probably. He's at the hospital tonight. Obviously!" He gave a short laugh. "I don't really know what to say. It's a lot to take in. But he's in good hands, and I know God is in control." He heard her sigh on the other line.

"Yes, I understand. You're right. But hey, I want you to know something. Anything we can do for you, please let us know! I . . . I wanna be here for you, you know that." Sheldon smiled. She was such a sweet caring girl.

"I'll do that, Chelle. You're a good friend. I got to go, girl. I had to walk home from the hospital, and I'm toast."

"OK. You get some sleep, all right? Can I tell my family what happened so they can pray for you and your dad?"

"Of course, you can! OK, good night, Chelle."

Richelle wished she could hug him. But she wasn't with him. She replied affectionately, "Good night, Shel."

Despite the chaos of the next few weeks, the Callahans were adamant he spend as much time away from home as possible, and he became more or less a part of their family.

His father was back at the house now with a nurse coming over every day to administer his medications, and he got plenty of state care besides. The biopsy had been successful, and he was, as his condition was seriously advanced, scheduled for a liver transplant in March, which was as soon as they could get him in. His alcohol intake had decreased significantly, but he still managed to get a drink or two when he was alone and Sheldon was away. Buddies.

His nurse could tell by only looking at him, and she was very vocal in her disappointment.

"Do you want to live or not?" She'd ask, rattling his medicines about, lips tightly pressed together. She was a tall, vivacious woman with wings of shining black hair that she always kept swept up in a bun at the nape of her neck. Sheldon's father had taken a liking to her, which wasn't highly unusual with him. But at least he treated her as the lady she was, because her mannerisms demanded respect.

"I can't believe it's already halfway through February!" Richelle remarked as she and Sheldon sat doing homework together one afternoon. His pen scribbled furiously before he replied.

"Yes, hmm," he said, clearly preoccupied.

She flashed an affectionate glance at the blond head bent studiously over his page. Smiling, she tried to refocus her attention on her homework, but it was hopelessly tedious. She was daydreaming when Sheldon pushed aside his completed English assignment.

"The longer you stare out the window, the longer you're going to have to sit here." His amused remark broke through the pleasant haze enveloping her mind. She snapped out of her reverie.

"True. But you know how I despise chemistry!" He didn't reply, but slid another sheaf of papers across the table toward himself. Matt joined them with a silent nod.

It was nearly six o'clock when they finished and quite ready for supper.

Carrying a heaping plate to the table, Matt asked Sheldon if he'd like to spend the night. The simple question recalled a myriad of childhood memories to his mind, and he hesitated a heartbeat too long in replying.

"Sheldon?" Matt gave his shoulder a friendly punch.

"Sure, I'd love to. Dad will be fine." His voice trailed off as he pulled out his chair and seated himself.

He felt someone cautiously kick him beneath the table in the middle of the meal, the talk flying from mouth to mouth. He was quieter than he usually was. Richelle's eyes were full of questions.

"Are you all right?" Her eyes were so expressive that he could almost hear her voice. Funny, he'd never noticed how clearly she was able to communicate without words. He screwed up his mouth and gave a slight affirmative inclination of his head.

Around eleven, Matt headed up to his room, and Sheldon followed Mrs. Callahan in search of a sleeping bag.

"How's your father doing, Sheldon? Is there something on your mind? You don't seem entirely yourself tonight!" He passed a hand over his eyes with a sigh. She looked at him searchingly and then sat down on the floor and patted the place beside her. He slid down. "Tell me, honey." She tilted her head to one side expectantly, her eyes warm and compassionate.

"Oh, I don't know. It's a lot of things, I guess." He looked uncertain. "Stress from school and then dad. I . . . I guess I never expected anything really bad to happen to him, and the doctor told me there is a possibility he might not make it. From the funny way he said it, it's probably a high possibility. I don't feel like it's all real, if you know what I mean." Mrs. Callahan drew him close and tucked his head beneath her chin, gently stroking his blond hair. "You guys are so kind to me. Why?"

"Well, I . . ." She paused and shrugged a little. Her hand continued through his hair. "We love you. You're a sweet boy, and you're different. And because we are called to love, Sheldon, whether we feel like it or not. You're one of us." She shook him gently. "And you're a brother to the kids. Why, just the other day, Matt told me how great it is to have a big brother around. And you're like a son to Evan and me." She pressed a kiss to his hair. "We love you. And we want to help in any way we can." He blinked.

"God's been so good to me." He gave her a quick hug and pulled away..

"Now," she said brusquely, wiping her cheeks, "since you're my boy, you'll have to call me mom."

"Mom," he said slowly as if he was tasting the word on his tongue. "I haven't called anyone mom for almost ten years." For a heavy moment, she wished she hadn't been so hasty. Then he smiled, nodding his head vigorously as he stood, giving her a hand to help her up.

"Oh, Matt is going to wonder what on earth happened to you. Tell him I had you crawl up there to find a sleeping bag." Yanking open what he'd thought was a cupboard in an odd place, she revealed a low crawl space storage and handed him the sleeping bag.

"Well, good night then." He gave a crooked smile. "Mom."

"Good night, dear." And she kissed him on the cheek, just like she always did with her own children. She watched him go, her heart heavy for him even while she rejoiced in a new-found son.

Matt's vivid imagination made him an interesting conversant although his intense habit of exhausting each subject in careful exploration of its properties soon took its toll on Sheldon's patience, frayed as it was.

"Look, can't we talk about something else now?" His delicate insinuations had gone unnoticed for several moments. Matt stopped jabbering and laughed.

"What, you don't like my opinions on political upheaval?" Even in the dark room, it was clear he wasn't insulted in the least.

"Not at this time of night, I don't," Sheldon snorted and flipped over onto his back.

"Whatcha wanna talk about then?"

"Maybe how soft floorboards are."

"Hmm, tired and cranky, are we?"

"Tired, yes, cranky, no. But that could change!" he added quickly.

"OK, OK, hey, it's cool to have you over, bro."

"Oh yeah?" Sheldon looked up at the ceiling.

"Yeah." Matt cleared his throat. "Well, we should try and sleep. Night."

"Mhm. Night, Matt." He removed his arms from behind his head and thrust them into the warmth of the sleeping bag, burrowing down inside it.

Chapter 15
Settling in the Midst of Chaos

Sheldon pulled the Honda into the long driveway, his tires crunching over icy gravel. He'd called Mr. Callahan's boss and finally got an appointment to see the apartment. Understanding that Alvin Smith was a busy man, he'd patiently waited for weeks. And he struggled to mask his annoyance when a woman, presumably Smith's wife, opened the door at his knock.

"Hello, hello, you must be our prospective renter. I'll be right with you, just let me grab my coat." The door shut in his face, and he allowed himself a grimace. Obviously, Smith wasn't in a hurry to get the apartment rented. He scuffed his sneaker against the snowy welcome mat.

"Right this way, young man." She closed the door snugly behind herself and hurried across the graveled round driveway to the garage. Off to the side of the building, a short steep flight of steps ran along the wall up to the apartment. The woman explained that the long wait had been due to the unfinished kitchen. "Alvin didn't expect anyone to be interested right away when he put the ad out. We are sorry if we've caused any inconvenience."

"Oh, not at all." He moved about the tiny kitchen and poked his head into the bedroom. There was a full-sized bed and a set of drawers. A small night stand was severely cramped against the light green wall.

"It's five hundred a month. Heat and water are separate," Mrs. Smith replied in response to his inquiry. "We'll give you a week to consider." He raked a hasty hand through his hair.

"I've given it a lot of thought, and I don't think I'll get a better situation. I love it. It's a very nice apartment." She beamed with pleasure. "I think I'll take it." He gave a decisive curt nod. Chattering away, she gave him a file of documents to sign. Sheldon quickly read through the forms and asked when he could move in.

"As soon as you need to. You'll have to bring your own blankets, towels, and that sort of thing, but everything else is here permanently. Just a few things you need to understand. No loud parties. You can have them, but we don't want to hear anything, and you're responsible if anything happens. No destroying my furniture, and you need to keep everything neat. Is that clear?"

"Yes, ma'am. Of course. You don't have to worry about partying." Her skeptical look indicated he had yet to earn her trust. He jotted down his signature on the dotted lines and handed the sheets of paper to the woman.

"Well, thank you very much. We'll see you in a bit. Hopefully, you don't have much trouble moving in." He agreed with her, thanking her for her time as he followed her down the precarious steps.

"So yeah, I got the apartment the other day!" He hunched his shoulder to steady the phone and began shoving his belongings into boxes and bags. "I know, I'm ecstatic, signed all the papers and I'm starting to pack up stuff I don't need right now." He listened for a moment, rolling up posters from his walls and stowing the tubes snugly in the bottom of a box. "Tell your dad I can't thank him enough for making me aware of this opportunity. Hang on one sec, gotta take some stuff out to my car." He slipped his phone into a pocket and lugged the boxes into a stack and perilously threaded his way downstairs and to his waiting car.

"Hello? Yeah, I'm here. I'm just about ready for trip one." He dashed up the stairwell. "So how's the fam? Haven't seen you guys in a few days, things have just been so busy lately." He laughed. "Oh, good, glad to hear it. Tell Mom my dad is hanging in there. He's having surgery in two days. She wanted to know."

Richelle talked while he emptied his drawers and took down his mother's picture. Tenderly he wrapped it in tissue paper and an extravagant amount of bubble wrap.

"You and Matt wanna come help me settle in?" She was more than willing. "Cool! I'll pick you guys up in, say what, an hour? I wanna get everything over there first." He cleared out his safe behind the picture and tucked the wad of bills into a pocket in a luggage bag. "OK, awesome, I'll be there. And yeah, I'm going to be officially moved in tomorrow. Yeah, yeah, I know it's Sunday, but Dad's going in Monday, and I've got to be there. It's only right. I don't know what might happen, and I don't want to wait 'til Tuesday. Can't have the stress of moving hanging over me on top of everything else, Chelle." She saw the logic in his thinking. "Well, I'll be over in a few. Got to go, the car is full. See you soon!"

He carried box after box up the narrow stairs, piling them all on the floor in the little bedroom. On his second trip, he swung by the bank and deposited all his money into his savings. It was an addition of a little over a thousand dollars. He didn't make bank runs very often and enjoyed the drama caused by the great wad of cash and checks as the clerks sorted them out. Anyways, he liked seeing the big numbers on his bank receipts. The winter had been good, the frequent storms bringing in a fairly steady income.

Richelle and Matt were waiting for him when he pulled up, but he popped in to cheerfully announce to their mother that she could expect another for dinner.

Each carrying boxes, they emptied Sheldon's car in one trip, and he let them in at the door to his apartment.

"This is beautiful, Shel!" Richelle looked around, the packages filling her arms forgotten momentarily.

"I know, it's perfect." He dumped his armload carefully on the floor.

"Nice bed." Matt was jealous. Sheldon grinned.

"I'd prefer a nice one if I gotta pay so much to sleep in it," he said. Richelle flipped open a box. She peeped inside dubiously.

"You didn't fold anything? Are these even clean?" She lifted out a T-shirt with her fingertips and examined it dubiously.

"Sure they are. I didn't bother folding them. They would've gotten all messed up anyways." She shook her head forlornly and snapped the wrinkles out of the shirt, folded it up neatly, and tucked it away into the dresser. The guys disappeared into the minuscule bathroom with a box of various toiletries.

"You use Axe?" Matt's unbelieving laugh rang out. Sheldon's reply was too low to be coherent. Richelle reached the bottom of her box and lifted out a clumsy mass of bubble wrap.

"What on earth?" She shot a surreptitious glance at the open bathroom door. "This is ridiculous . . ." She'd reached the tissue paper. Finally tearing off the rest of it, she turned the frame over and caught her breath. Sheldon emerged for another box and caught her red-handed.

"What are you doing?" She looked up at him guiltily, the picture clutched to her chest. He squatted on his heels beside her. "That's my mom. I wanted you to see her picture." She pulled the frame away from her body and studied it.

"She's gorgeous."

"Yes, yes, she was," he said in subdued tones. "And she was a great mom." Richelle looked at him closely and then back at the photo.

"You look very much like her, you know?"

"Hmm, I know I do. Not quite *just* like her though."

"Close enough." She laughed. "You could be twins!" He gave a lopsided smile, and his eyebrows quirked. He took the picture from her and leaned it against the wall on top of his dresser.

"Gonna have to hang it up. It's not home without her." He traced his finger over her hair beneath the glass.

"Eh, what's next?" He met her eyes for a moment, not able to keep a sigh from escaping his lips. They opened another box.

He didn't have many things to unpack, and they were easily done within two hours even at their slow pace.

Sheldon looked around the rooms.

"Well, thanks, guys! That took way faster than I thought it was going to. Got a few things at the house that I kinda need, but it's gonna be great to have my own place tomorrow." His grin, though tired, was infectious. "Come on, let's run over to your place and get some food."

"Sheldon," Richelle said as she hesitatingly stepped after him on the old staircase, "Mom wants you to eat with us, anytime you want to. She said there's no need for you to buy food when you're so close to our home."

"Aww, she did, did she? I don't know, I couldn't pull from you like that! But I still will come over when I can. I just don't want to be dependent." He turned red in the dim garage.

"I see."

"No, no, I don't mean it like that. It's just . . . Well, I appreciate it, Chelle. I really do. But when you grow up, you can't depend on other people to provide for you. It's presumptuous, and I don't want to take advantage of your parents. They'd understand. Of course, I'll come over as much as I can, like usual. You're family to me, but I can't just drop in to eat your food. How is that right?" She looked at him, Matt glancing from one to the other nervously.

"Richelle," he said suddenly. They both looked at him as if they'd forgotten he was there. "Sheldon's a guy. We're like that." He lifted his hands, palms up. "We gotta get out there and fend for ourselves. It's part of the freedom, and it's just what it means to be a guy, and, heck, it's growing up too. I get what he means. Don't worry, Shel, Mom will understand completely." Sheldon gave him a grateful smile and put a hand on his shoulder as he ducked into the driver's seat.

Richelle understood as much as she was able to. Some part of her was still offended at his refusal. She didn't want him to grow up; she wanted to feel like she could reach him, and when he was vulnerable, she felt control over how things went; she felt needed, and if he grew more distant—she was fearful of the future. She

141

loved him, but if he pulled away, how could he ever learn to love her? And she wouldn't see him much when they graduated high school; what about college? What then?

"Hey." His touch on her shoulder sent electric thrills over her skin and only added to her confusion. "I'm sorry if I offended you, Richelle. It couldn't have been further from my intentions. It won't be any different than it is now. Really, it won't."

Even as he said it, he wondered. He'd have to get more work, and work would pull from leisure time. But he didn't think she needed to hear that now. He'd hurt her somehow and wanted to make up. She cracked a weak smile. The attempt was admirable, considering the chaos of her emotions.

A silent drive ensued; then the initial awkwardness wore off, and Matt made an attempt at conversation.

"So how's the car?"

"Car? Oh yeah, it's fine. Drives great, very happy with it." Sheldon rolled the words out hurriedly. He was hungry and looking forward to dinner and time to relax before he had to head back to the house. Matt grunted and gave up. They were nearly home anyways.

Richelle tried not to let her emotions ruin the evening, but every time Sheldon spoke to her, she could sense the tenseness, see it in his face, and it hurt her knowing that she was causing him pain. She was to blame; it was all her fault, and she wished she could push everything aside and enjoy having him over for the little while he'd still be there before he left. She'd messed everything up by being so stubborn in refusing to put her scattered feelings aside. She shook her head, exasperated with herself, and started the dishwasher. "It's fine," she told herself as she wiped off a counter. "You're just totally overreacting. Grow up!" She put forth a brave front until he left.

"Bye, guys, see you soon. Bye, Chelle." He shut the door, and she could hear his firm footsteps receding into the night. Just like that, he was gone.

Richelle shut her door and leaned against it heavily. Then she took out her journal and began to write furiously, chewing on her pen between thoughts. When she had finished, she felt much better, and her outlook on life had improved vastly. She let herself fall back on her bed and released a puff of pent-up air.

Tomorrow was Sunday, and she'd see him again; she was glad he'd taken to attending church with her family. She got off her bed and went to her closet, pushing back clothes to try to find something to wear. She pulled out a few dresses and finally decided on the turquoise; it was new and had never been worn.

A knock sounded on her door. Frantically, she wondered if she'd done anything stupid to draw unnecessary attention to herself that night. The door opened, and her mom came into the room. Mrs. Callahan stood for an instant and then sat cozily on the bed.

"Pretty dress. I've never seen you wear it."

"I bought it a few weeks ago and forgot I had it." She rummaged in her jewelry case and pulled out a necklace and earrings to match and laid them on her dresser top.

"Richelle, what on earth is the matter with you?" She saw the pained expression flit across her daughter's face, and then it was gone, and she compressed her lips as she saw a smooth mask slip into place. "What's going on between you two?"

"Two? What are you talking about?"

"Don't feign innocence with me, young lady. I can tell when people are feeling out of sorts, and you acted very strangely toward one another tonight. I've never known you to be so wound up!" Richelle swallowed uncomfortably and found great interest in the carpet's design. Her mother got up and put her arms around her. "Can you tell me?" she asked gently. Richelle hugged her tightly and searched for words.

"Mom, I'm just so silly. I told him about you wanting him to eat here all the time and not have to worry about food, and when he refused, I took offense. And he was so sweet about it, so careful to explain himself. I feel so immature, but I don't want him to . . . I don't want things to ever change between us, like, I don't want him to put our friendship on the back burner." She took a breath. "I know he has to grow up and all, but . . ."

"You're afraid of what will happen when he moves? Honey, you can't hold him back. You don't want to control him, do you?" Richelle shook her head.

"You be constant. There's no reason why he would want to leave, Chelle. We're like family to him. Just keep being yourself around him. If you're so emotional, he's going to sense a need there, and if anything scares him off, it'll be that. He doesn't need anyone draining him, Richelle. He needs someone steady. And you're his friend. Be that for him! His life is a roller coaster right now, you can't do that to him. He needs you to be constant because everything is so uncertain for him right now. He's changing residence, starting his own life, he's on his own primarily, and that's huge for anyone. But with his dad, Richelle, love is unconditional. You think you love him, then sacrifice what you're feeling. It will only harm him. Be yourself." She squeezed her daughter close.

"Be faithful to your friends, honey. One day you might find yourself in need of one, and they'll treat you like you treated them. Now, you get some sleep. Tomorrow is church, and he always comes over for the day. Pull yourself together, sweetie." She took her by the shoulders and locked eyes earnestly.

"Thanks, Mom," Richelle said and was glad when her mother left her alone; she needed to ponder her words. She knew her motives were selfish. Her mom was right.

She pulled her shirt slowly over her head and removed the rest of her clothes and pulled a nightie on. Her bed pillowed her body in a soft embrace, but it took her hours to fall asleep.

Sunday dawned; the sun was warm, and the snow showed promising signs of an early melt. But it being March, that was a highly unlikely course of events.

Sheldon pulled on the clothes he'd set aside for his last day at the house, and after brushing his teeth and hair, he shaved and threw everything into a bag. He slammed the car door and gripped the wheel as an intense yawn stretched the muscles in his face, still trying to wake up. Slipping a pair of Aviators on as protection against the bright morning sun, he drove to church.

He easily found a parking space and walked inside the building, downstairs where they served coffee and doughnuts. He hadn't bothered with breakfast. Helping himself to a steaming cup and grabbing a glazed chocolate doughnut, he seated himself on a couch and crossed his legs, one ankle across the opposite knee. A few people greeted him cheerfully, filling cups with the dark brown brew America ran on.

He'd made a few good acquaintances in the few weeks he'd been coming and found he really liked the church as a body. He found the preaching fascinating. And he knew he'd grown leaps and bounds in his faith by absorbing the spiritual food offered. He chewed contentedly and thought about nothing in particular.

"Hi, Sheldon." He looked up and nearly choked on his coffee.

"Hi. Wow," was all he could manage. She was beautiful, sheathed in turquoise, her hair in flames against the vibrant color. The dress came to just above her knees, and her little silver heels showed off her pretty feet to perfection. Admiration was written all over his face, and she blushed.

"You like it?"

"Like it? You look great! I love that blue on you, your hair looks amazing with it." She sat beside him, positively glowing.

"They have chocolate doughnuts?" she asked as the last morsel disappeared into his mouth.

"It depends. I'll go see if there's any left. Want a coffee?"

"Yes, please." He acted so disconcerted; he'd never offered to get her a coffee.

"Three sugars, right?" She nodded and watched him go up to the counter, feeling pleasantly surprised.

"Where's everybody else?" he asked, carefully passing her coffee and her doughnut. His fingers brushed hers, and suddenly, he felt shy but quickly mastered himself.

"They're all in Sunday school. It's already started. You weren't in the high school room, so I figured you might be here."

"We're gonna be late!" He shot a glance at her brimming cup.

"It's all right. You know how much they talk beforehand."

"Yeah, true. Hey. I just wanted to apologize for yesterday."

"Oh no, Shel, if anyone needs to apologize, it's me."

"I should've chosen my words differently."

"Look, we both know I seriously overreacted. Please, I'm sorry. Forgive me!" She looked intently into his eyes, her own pleading.

"Of course, I forgive you! You're my best friend." Relief flooded through her.

"Yes, and I don't want it ever to change." She was so vehement it threw him.

"Why on earth would it?" He drained his cup and balanced it on one knee. "Keep the trust, that's all, Chelle." His face was serious. "Because without trust, everything falls apart." He offered her his hand, and as she stood up, he suddenly realized she was an awfully pretty girl. Impulsively, he gave her a whirl, and she gasped, knocking into him.

"Sheldon!" she giggled, failing to reprove him. He grinned roguishly back at her and tossed their empty cups into the trash can. They walked to their class and sat on a couch by the door.

"I don't think this is the best time to ask, but do you like dancing?" he leaned his head close and whispered. She couldn't help the thrill she felt.

"Yes. Why?" she whispered back.

"The senior prom is coming up. Would you go with me if no one else asks you?" She stared at him, eyes sparkling.

"Are you asking me to the dance?" A few kids stole glanced over their shoulders, but her attention was zoned in on his response.

"Well, yes, I suppose I am." His nonchalant attitude couldn't hide the hopeful anticipation in his eyes.

"Yes!" she burst out in a fierce whisper. He raised his eyebrows.

"Yes?"

"Yes, yes, yes! It'll be loads of fun." She looked around the room. "What an odd place to ask!" Her giggle was contagious, and he bit his tongue to keep from laughing out loud.

"It is, rather. We'd better pay attention now. Thanks." She let herself get lost in his blue eyes.

"No, thank you. I didn't think you danced and was resolved to stay home." For all his efforts to hide his smile by biting it out of existence, his eyes danced merrily.

"Gosh, I hope I get more out of the sermon!" He laughed as the class broke up. "I didn't even catch the text. At least I got my prom date though." She smiled back at him and gathered up her coat and pocket book.

"At least." And she stuck out her tongue.

"Come on, silly." He took her arm on the stairwell; her heels made walking precarious, and there was a crowd.

A moment later they slipped into their pew beside Matt.

"What on earth were you two gabbing about back there? I bet you didn't hear a word Jack was saying!" Richelle froze and stole a nervous glance at her father; he was deep in conversation with the man in the row behind theirs and hadn't heard Matt.

"We were talking about graduation. Of sorts." Sheldon tacked on quickly at her scowl. Her forehead smoothed, and she smiled innocently up at her brother, settling her purse by her feet.

"Why don't you just tell me it's none of my business?" He feigned irritation. "Fine, fine, keep your secrets." He flipped through his bulletin casually.

"Ah, you don't fool me. But thanks, we'll do that." Sheldon couldn't help the smirk as they rose for the call to worship.

Underneath his nonchalant facade, Sheldon couldn't hide that he was deeply worried. He'd been diverting his mind with nearly everything he could, trying to convince himself everything was going to be fine, but in the end, he knew his father might very well die, and he didn't know how he could reconcile himself to the knowledge of the possibility. He bowed his head and prayed that the surgery would be successful and his father would heal quickly. Then, he paused. He'd never ever prayed for his father before. He closed his eyes and knew God had truly done a great work in him. The hate had disappeared. And somehow, he was able to put his past behind him and not count the many wrongs done against him by his father. He'd forgiven him. He sat in the pew beside his best friend, utterly blown away by the power of the Lord who had rescued him.

Sheldon threw his keys on the table and sat down despondently. Now that he was alone, he couldn't push away the thoughts that crowded him. He sighed and dropped his head into his hands. Tomorrow was going to be a rough day. He shrugged and walked to his bed. Sleep was evasive. Bits and pieces of the day he'd spent at the Callahans' flew through his head, but his thoughts kept returning to his father. There were a lot of prayers going up that night. Exhausted, Sheldon got little sleep. The morning came too soon.

He dragged himself out of bed with the bleak sun, checking the time. He had to be at the hospital at ten. And he was bringing his father. He was miffed when he found he had not gone shopping, and there wasn't a scrap of food in the place. Grumbling grouchily, he rubbed the sleep out of his eyes and brushed his teeth, pulling on a pair of jeans. He roared down the road, hightailing it for the grocery store. Disheveled hair standing on end in careless disarray, he tore through the aisles throwing boxes of cereal and various foods into his cart and added juice, milk, eggs, cheese, and butter. Consulting his wristwatch at the checkout counter, he figured he barely had enough time to put everything away, grab a bowl of cereal, and pick up his dad.
"Hey, Dad. You ready for this?" Sheldon waited for him to put on his boots.
"It's gotta be done." He forced open the old door and stalked down the path to the driveway. Rotting leaves clung to the wet muddy pavement, slush melting in ugly brown puddles. Sheldon heaved a deep breath and followed him to the car. The man didn't speak to him the whole trip. When they arrived at the hospital, he sat hunched in chair in the surgeon's waiting room while Sheldon spoke to the receptionist.
"You can sit over there. A nurse will be with you in a moment," she said in a hushed voice.

"Thanks." He sat across from his father, hands clasped between his knees.

The wait seemed to take forever. Really it was only about fifteen minutes before the door swung open and a nurse clad in purple scrubs with a clipboard in hand called his name.

"You'll be fine, Dad. I'll stay here." Chett Trindell turned and looked down at his son.

"Go home." And he walked away. Sheldon gritted his teeth but stayed where he was. Why did he always have to hurt everybody? Why couldn't he ever say anything nice, even just for once? The receptionist cast a sympathetic look his way.

"You don't have to stay here. The surgery is about an hour, and he'll be under anesthetic for a while. We'll call you when he wakes up, if you like," she said in hushed tones after he'd been sitting for nearly ten minutes. He shook his head and stayed where he was.

"Thanks, but I'll stay." She continued typing, and silence descended over the room.

Time dragged agonizingly by until the surgeon came out to tell him that the surgery had gone well and that his father was sleeping.

"We'll let you know how things turn out, son. This stage is highly critical, but he'll be fine if he gets through tonight. Things are looking good so far!" He gave a tired smile. Sheldon stood up, wincing slightly. Pins and needles shot up and down his legs.

"Can I see him? Real quick?" The man regarded him, deciding, and then jerked his head.

"Come on, I'll show you. Just a minute though."

"Thanks." Sheldon followed his white lab coat down the hall to a recovery room. The lights were dimmed, and their eyes took a second to adjust. His father was lying in a small bed, sheets smoothed up over his hefty body. His face was ghastly, and he had lines and wires attaching him to machines. Sheldon stepped over and looked at him quietly. He looked different when he slept, younger, even now. He stood in silence a moment then motioned to the doctor, and followed him back into the waiting room.

"We'll call you when anything further occurs. Take it easy." he said as he turned and hurried away.

"Thanks, I will." Sheldon picked up his jacket and left, hurrying to the elevator. On the ground floor, he emerged into the parking lot and sucked air into his lungs hungrily. He was glad to get out of the hospital. He jumped into his car and decided to get lunch at his favorite restaurant.

He ordered a steak dinner and fiddled with his utensils. The food would be a long time coming. Waiting seemed to be a new hobby lately. Waiting for apartments, waiting at hospitals, waiting for food . . . he was bored.

Surprised, he found that he was trembling slightly, and his face felt flushed. Quickly, he gulped his glass of water. He heaved a sigh, wondering if this was what stress did to people or if he was really coming down with a cold or a virus of some sort. Time would soon tell.

Draining his refilled ice water, he took out his phone. Knowing Richelle would be in school, he sent Mrs. Callahan the particulars of the surgery. He slouched in the leather seat and impatiently drummed his fingers on the yellow-stained wood of the table. The cars zipping by down the road provided a diversion, and he began to look around and notice the other people in the restaurant. There were quite a few; he'd just been so absorbed in himself that he hadn't even noticed the underlying hum of voices.

By this time, his food arrived, and he dug ravenously into golden mounds of fluffy mashed potatoes smothered in gravy and a thick juicy steak flanked by green florets of broccoli. His stomach filled steadily, and he was feeling much better when his plate was clean.

Outside, the sky was bleak and colorless. Checking the weather report, he found his hunch to be correct; they would be getting snow tonight. And he had some shoveling to do. He sat in his car and looked through the details. It would be coming in around midnight and continue into the early morning. Exasperated, he huffed and backed out of the parking space. He despised being out and about at half past four in the morning, but it couldn't be helped, and he needed the money. *The worst is school days though,* he thought dismally. When all he wanted to do was fall into bed and crash, he had to chug coffee and go to school.

"Early night tonight," he muttered out loud to no one.

The snow had been riding the wind in light flurries when he woke up; it was dry but had accumulated during the early hours. He didn't feel quite up to snuff, but he had ignored his protesting body and headed into the wintry cold, shovel over one broad shoulder. The work had gone quickly; he was relieved it wasn't wet, heavy stuff, and he'd been able to return to the apartment for a piece of toast and a coffee before he left for school.

Now it was lunch break, and he shuffled into the mess hall, late. He sat on the floor in a corner, not feeling up to more than picking at the unappetizing cafeteria food. The few hours remaining loomed ominously ahead. He wished he could go home and sleep until tomorrow! His head on his up-drawn knees, he closed his eyes in a futile attempt to shut out the loud buzz of voices. They were grating on his frazzled nerves and began to nearly cause physical pain. A headache set in.

"Hi, Sheldon. Where's your friend?" The effort to raise his eyes to the speaker's face was dizzying, and he found it difficult to focus. He mumbled something unintelligible and dropped his head wearily. Clarisse pulled out a chair from a neighboring table and dragged it over to where he sat alone. For some reason he didn't care; he let her torment him all she wanted. "I didn't see you yesterday. How come you weren't here?"

"Dad's in the hospital," he managed to get out. She tilted her head to one side, earrings jangling as they hit against her cheek.

"That's too bad. Poor old guy." Her tone was careless. "Must be nice to get the house to yourself." He should've been shocked at her callousness, but he felt oddly numb and disinclined to correct her or stand up for his father. She could think what she liked. He shrugged. "You might get lost in there all alone. Want a little company?" She laid a caressing hand on his knee.

"I don't need company," he said roughly, flinching away. Her face tightened, and the sensual smile froze on her parted lips. "We've already been over this."

"Gah, you'll be just like your father." She sprang out of the chair and faced him so close that he could feel the warmth of her body. "And one day you'll want company. Trust me." She turned away, simpering.

Her words stung him more then they should've; her prediction that he would be just like his father hit his core and shook him deeply. What if she was right? He'd heard of kids growing up in homes just like his, who shed away from alcohol like it was the plague. But how many of these people had turned to the bottle, embracing all that they had hated? He shuddered. A cold breath of fear shivered up his spine, and he couldn't shake it. What if he was no different from his father, deep down inside? No, he told himself feebly. He was making himself a new life, striking out in a different direction. There would be no set of footprints following his father's across the sands of time. But the uneasy sense of fear did not dissipate, and he found he wasn't convinced.

Chapter 16

Pain of a Different Kind

Richelle was vastly relieved when school was out and burst out of the classroom into a hall crowded with teens pushing and shoving for the exit. Suddenly, she thought she heard her name called out over the din and hesitated, unsure if it was only her imagination. But there it came again, and she saw Sheldon making his way unsteadily toward her. Two bright spots reddened his white face, and his eyes were unnaturally bright. He was trembling and appeared to be having a difficult time walking.

"Sheldon! What is the matter?" He reached her and staggered against the wall, his breath coming in ragged gasps. "You look awful!" He coughed, moaning as it tore through his burning throat.

"I can't drive." His voice was husky.

"My word, Shel, this is really sudden! Hang on." He looked as if he might fall. She knew she'd never get him on his feet again. "Lean against the wall." She stood next to him, her mind racing. "I'll have my mom pick me up at your place."

"It's illegal. I'm not twenty-one," he whispered hoarsely, raising his head and meeting her eyes for a split second.

"Hush, I can drive. You are in no condition to attempt it. I'll be careful. Come on." She sent her mom a hasty text and pulled him away from the wall. "Lean on me, quick! Careful, careful." Stumbling through the halls, Sheldon barely having the strength to stay erect and place one foot in front of the other, they made it to the parking lot. He was much heavier than she'd anticipated and was nearly a dead weight, which only made things worse. People were everywhere, cars coming and going; it was utter chaos. She found his car and dragged them both toward it.

She fell into the driver's seat, gasping heavily and dragging great breaths into her straining lungs. Sheldon's eyes were closed, but he looked so terrible that she was frightened. He should never have come to school after the snow; she knew that between the stress of his father and shoveling, he'd worked himself into a vulnerable state of exhaustion. Because of this, he'd fallen prey to a fast-moving virus.

She reached across his inanimate form and buckled his seat belt. She strapped herself in and started the engine. Sheldon's head tossed back and forth feverishly. Anxiously, she maneuvered her way down to the road and picked up speed, casting worried glances at the boy beside her. Silently she prayed that they'd make it without mishap to his apartment. Driving carefully, they arrived safely, and Richelle pulled up to the building as close as she dared. Her heart thumping wildly in her chest, she sprang out and ran to his door, bracing herself for his weight as she tried to help him out.

"Sheldon, work with me!" she cried in despair after several vain attempts to pull him out of his seat. But he was nearly delirious and quickly losing all remnants of strength. Trying a new tacit, she swung his legs out first and held him under the arms, endeavoring to haul him up. It worked, to a degree, his weight sagging against her, and she almost lost her balance. Struggling, she got him standing and draped one of his arms over her shoulders, hanging on to his waist for dear life. She supported them both against the garage and pulled open the side door. Seeing the stairs almost made her cry. How could she even hope to get him up them? It was impossible. A wave of despair swept over her, and she sank down on a dusty old box, holding him awkwardly half on and half off her lap. Sweat trickled down the back of her neck, and she felt her energy draining away.

"What on earth is going on?" Mrs. Callahan stood in the doorway, bewilderment etched into her face.

"Oh, Mom! I've never been more glad to see you in my life!" Sheldon began to slip. Instantly, her mother took stock of the situation and rushed forward, lending her support.

"Let's get him up those stairs." It was a difficult struggle, but they managed.

Mrs. Callahan wiped her brow and picked up Sheldon's legs, pulling off his boots as she laid them across his bed. "The poor boy, he's burning up!" She smoothed his hair away from his damp forehead. "We've got to get him out of these clothes and into something more comfortable."

Richelle ran over to the dresser and pulled out his pajamas and a clean pair of socks. Mrs. Callahan indicated the door with a speaking glance as she took them.

"Go on, hurry up before he's too delirious to work with me."

Richelle scuffed her booted foot along the rug, doubtful as to whether her mother could handle him on her own.

"I'll manage." She lowered her voice so he wouldn't hear. "He'd be mortified if he knew you'd helped him get undressed." Richelle couldn't argue with that and went into the kitchen and wandered around aimlessly, wishing she could help but rather relieved her mother had insisted she'd leave. Quietly she creaked down the stairs and clicked the side door shut; they'd forgotten about it in the rush of getting the sick boy up the stairs and into bed. When she returned, she heard her mother calling her.

"Yeah?"

"He's soaking wet. Can you grab me a bowl of warm soapy water and something to wipe him down with?"

"OK sure, give me a second." She flung open cupboards and found a bowl that was big enough and filled it in the sink, slipping a small cake of soap beneath the surface of the water. She snagged a washcloth and knocked on the bedroom door.

"Come on in."

Sheldon was propped up against the cushions, shirtless, but apparently lacking the strength to speak. His hollow eyes stared out of his sickly wan face, dark smudges like bruises standing out starkly in contrast with his pale skin. He looked awful, and she couldn't take her eyes off the woeful figure as Mrs. Callahan took the bowl out of her hands.

"Sheldon, honey, lean against Richelle, OK? I'm going to wipe you off so you can rest better." Richelle sat on the edge of his bed, embarrassed for him, but he seemed too ill to care. Exhausted, he leaned into her, his bare skin hot. Shivers swept over him as the washcloth smoothed over his back, and Mrs. Callahan clucked her tongue.

"I do believe you're going to get the chills, but you're covered in sweat, and I have to clean you off." He coughed harshly, and Richelle could hear his teeth chattering close to her ear.

"You nearly done, Mom? He's freezing!" Her mother dried him off quickly with a T-shirt. Sheldon's miserable eyes followed her across the room as she picked up his pajama shirt off the ground where it had fallen.

"Here we are, honey. You'll feel a lot better now, I promise." She slipped the cotton folds over his disheveled head and tucked his arms into the long sleeves.

With a sympathetic smile at her poor friend, Richelle gently pulled the cushions out from behind him and helped him lie down with his head on one pillow. She smoothed back his hair and his eyes closed at the soft touch of her fingertips on his skin. She moved closer, kneeling beside the bed, and continued stroking his hair.

"Poor thing," she said, and his mouth quivered slightly in a small smile, and he opened his eyes. "Yes, you are a poor thing. If you only knew what a fright you gave me. There's no telling what might have happened to you if you hadn't found me before I went home." She threaded a fair lock through her fingers. "Your hair is so soft." He emitted a weak breath of air that sounded mildly bemused.

Mrs. Callahan had cleaned up the mess she'd made of his room and came to the door to speak softly with her daughter. Richelle looked up from stroking Sheldon's hair.

"I need to run back to the house to get a few things, and I'm going to get him some soup and some clear liquids. Anyways, I want you to stay with him in case anything happens. He has a fever, and it needs to break. It probably will tonight, but in the meantime, we want to get it up as high as we can to burn it off. He'll sleep for a while now. I hope it's restful . . . he's going to have the chills, and then a moment later, he'll be burning up. No matter how bad he looks, do not let him kick off the blankets. They have to stay on, it'll help break his fever. I'll be back in an hour or so. Remember, the blankets stay on. Richelle," She leaned on the doorknob and looked her daughter in the eyes, "don't keep the poor boy awake!" She turned away, and Richelle could hear her rapid footsteps descending the stairs.

Sheldon had slipped into a deep exhausted sleep, and Richelle tucked his blankets up to his chin, smoothing them neatly. Having nowhere else to sit, she walked around the bed and scrambled up onto the other side, gingerly settling herself against the overstuffed pillows jammed up by the headboard.

She studied him while he slept. His forehead was creased slightly, and his lips were tight. It wasn't a peaceful sleep, and he tossed fretfully. Richelle's nerves were set on edge, hoping he wouldn't roll off the bed, and even made a lunge for him once, but he righted himself in the nick of time. After a while, he seemed to settle down, turned on his side hugging the blankets to him. His quiet breathing reassured the girl beside him, and she muted the volume on her phone and played a few games. An untroubled half hour ensued, and Richelle was really absorbed in the moment when a sudden movement from Sheldon caused her to fall to her death in Temple Run. She was almost annoyed until she saw he'd pulled the blankets over his head and was quaking beneath them, sending tremors through the bed-frame. The chills, how she hated them!

Richelle hurried into the minute living room and snagged a heavy afghan off the arm of the couch and drew it over top of

157

his shivering body. Nothing seemed to make him warm, and she had a wild idea of slipping in beside him and holding him until the shivering dissipated. She rolled her eyes and snorted at herself. Then as suddenly as they had come, the chills were gone, only to be replaced with a burning heat that urged him to straightaway shove off all the blankets. Richelle pulled them back over his chest. He pushed them away. This continued; Richelle grasped the blankets in both hands, but the fever raging throughout his body gave him a nearly unnatural strength, and she had to try something different. So she kept batting his clutching hands away. Before long, his poor body began to shake again, and he woke up in a cold sweat, eyes wild and pained as cough after cough tore through his throat, leaving him sucking in droughts of air. It made an odd-sounding croaking whistle as it rushed into his lungs.

"Oh, Sheldon," she whispered as he flopped back on his pillow, his energy spent. She tucked the blankets snugly around him, rocking back on her heels.

"I'm hot." His voice creaked strangely in his ravaged throat.

"I know you are, but you must keep the blankets on, Shel. You've got a fever." She laid a cool hand on his forehead and was unnerved by the crackling heat of the skin. "Wow, a really high one at that! It's gotta go down!"

"But I'm so hot!" He sounded almost childish, his head tossing restlessly on the dampening pillow.

"I know you are, I do, but if you keep them on, your fever will break." He turned on his side facing her, seeking relief.

"I'm so sick. Thank you—don't know what I would've done . . ."

"Hush now." She laid a finger to his dry lips. "Oh, I'll be right back, got to get you a drink." Soon she was back with a glass of water and propped him up with one arm behind his head and held it to his mouth with the other hand as he eagerly drank it dry.

"That's better," he sighed gratefully and laid back, wincing as he restrained a cough. "I can't believe that all happened so fast." Richelle nodded in agreement.

"It is strange, but not really all that much. I'm actually not very surprised." He raised his eyebrows, looking at her with unfocused eyes heavy with sleep. "You're driving yourself into the ground, Shel. And with things the way they are with your dad . . ." She shook her head. "Are you feeling any better? I know you're exhausted, but any difference?"

"I don't think so. I don't think I'll make it to school tomorrow." She was shocked.

"Wait a sec, you're not going anywhere! You're not stirring from this bed for at least three days. Your health takes precedence over school, and I'm going to drop in every day to make sure you're doing all right. Shel, you have to give yourself a break." A whisper of a smile touched his lips.

"I thought you'd say as much." He shut his eyes and stretched his legs out and then curled up in a ball hugging the blankets. Richelle brushed a hand over his hair, and he sighed.

"Please, I like it," he said as she pulled her hand away. She shrugged and reclined beside him. *As long as he's relaxed,* she thought to herself.

The sensation of his hair running through her fingertips made her begin to feel sleepy; the sound of his steady breathing was soothing. Her eyelids drooped, and she laid her head against his shoulder, still smoothing his hair. He opened his eyes as he felt the heavier contact and glanced back over his shoulder, seeing her red head. Twisting an arm about, he touched a ruddy lock and wound it around his finger. Moments later, fatigue swept over him, and he succumbed, his eyes drifting shut as he gave in to the sweet call of sleep.

The sound of rustling grocery bags and thumping and jangling awoke her; she distinguished the sounds of cans and bottles. She sat up groggily; her neck had a cramp where she'd slept against Sheldon's none-too-soft shoulder. The creaking bed sounded loud in ears used to the silence, and she froze, casting anxious glances at Sheldon's quiet form, not wanted to be guilty of waking him. She couldn't see his face, but he didn't move, and she slowly crawled down to the end of the bed and hopped off, padding out to the kitchen, a yawn stretching her jaw.

"Hi, Mom," she mumbled. Mrs. Callahan shot her glance as she took a bottle of juice from a bag.

"You look like you just woke up! Did you take a nap?" She arranged the groceries in his refrigerator.

"Kind of, I didn't realize how tired I was. Nodded off, I guess."

"I just hope you don't catch whatever Sheldon has." She laid a heating pad on the counter and dug in a tote bag, taking out bottles of medicine, throat spray, icy-hot, boxes of herbal teas, and a stack of clean washcloths. Richelle turned her mouth down and shrugged.

"I could," she said pessimistically. Her mother laughed at her, neatly folding the tote bag into a little square.

"How's he doing? Anything happen while I was gone?"

"He's doing OK. He had the chills and got really hot, and we had a regular tussle over the blankets, but I explained everything to him when he finally woke up. Poor thing. He talked a little, and he's sleeping well now. Can you believe, he wanted to go to school tomorrow?" She was still incredulous.

"He's a committed young man. I like that. Very driven."

"Yes, yes, he is," Richelle mused. Mrs. Callahan looked at her quickly.

"Richelle, I want to ask you something. Is it OK just being friends with him?" Her daughter stared at her in surprise.

"Of course, it is! Just because I—" She stopped, confused, her cheeks reddening.

"I mean to say," her mother tried again, "does it give you pain to feel differently for him than he does for you?" An uncomfortable expression flitted over her face.

"Mom. Really, I don't want to talk about this. It isn't fair. Who cares how I feel? It only matters that I am the friend he needs. And I'll be what he needs me to be." Her sacrificial attitude made her mother secretly proud of her.

"Just be careful. I know it's hard." Richelle found great interest in the random boxes of cereal thrown about on the table. Obviously, the conversation had outlived itself.

Sheldon awoke to the sound of voices and couldn't help listening in. The short dialogue left him in a muddle; he didn't know what to think. Richelle liked him? It was as if he'd heard something never meant for him, and he had a strange discorporate sensation of having violated her privacy and wished he could unhear it somehow. His emotions were in turmoil, and he couldn't decide if he was disappointed or pleased. His mind was too tired to want to think about anything, and he tried to set it aside for another time.

He coughed and wished Richelle had left him a glass of water to relieve his dry throat. It hurt to swallow. He pushed himself up on one elbow, and a rush of dizziness overwhelmed him, and black spots danced before his eyes. His pupils dilated as he strove to see, but it was as if he was peering down a tiny tube from a great distance. He dropped back on the bed, knowing it was stupid to try to get up for he'd only fall. Although he still felt wasted from sickness and lack of energy, he couldn't go back to sleep. Too many thoughts swirled through his mind, and despite the vertigo, he didn't feel so ill as he had before. This was probably because he was in bed, but it made all the difference in the world.

The door cracked open, and someone peeped in at him. Owlishly, he tried to distinguish who, blinking as he forced his eyes into focus, but the door eased shut. A little miffed, he stared up at the ceiling.

Seconds later, Mrs. Callahan came in with a mug of tea and asked him how he was feeling. He pulled himself into a sitting position carefully lest the dizziness should attack him and replied that he felt a little better. She set the mug on a plate and placed it in his lap.

"There, I made you some peppermint tea, drink up. I think I'm going to stay with you just for tonight, to keep you company and make sure you're all right." Taking a sip, he glanced at her in surprise.

"What? Oh no, you don't have to do that. I'll be fine."

"How do you know? You might start throwing up, and what would you do then?"

"I never throw up."

"Well, I'm staying," she said with a hint affectionate stubbornness. He yawned and straightened his shoulders. The tea was too hot for to be drank comfortably, and he let the mug warm his hands. He felt a chill race down his spine at the contact. "Do you feel up to watching a movie? Or would you rather try to get some more sleep?"

"I don't think I could sleep right now."

"You and Richelle can watch something on Netflix. Would you like anything to eat? I brought soup and fruit if you'd like a frappe."

"Eh, thanks, but I'd rather not. Maybe later though." He gave her a crooked smile. She fluffed up his pillows, and settling him comfortably, she went to get Richelle and told her about her idea.

The girl went down to Sheldon's car and fished her laptop out of her backpack.

"Hey, did you sleep OK?" she asked him, sitting on the edge of the bed and scooting back beside him. For a second, he wondered vaguely how she'd speak to him if she knew what he'd overheard. Suddenly, he felt a little awkward with the knowledge she felt more than friendship for him.

"Mhm," he said, clearing his throat. She opened the laptop, and her fingers flew over the keys punching in passwords as she logged in.

"Let's see . . ." She pulled up Netflix and scrolled through a page. "Here, how about you pick?" She slid the laptop over to him. He scanned through a few pages but didn't see anything he was inclined to watch.

"Meh, this is all junk," he muttered.

"Yeah, most of it is. But we'll find something!" she said confidently. He leaned his head back on the pillows and took a few deep breaths. "You OK?"

"I'll be fine. Give me a sec." She scrutinized the screen.

"Hey, let's watch this one," she indicated.

"What, *Kate and Leopold*?" He couldn't be less enthusiastic. She laughed at him.

"Why not? It's slower paced." She grinned convincingly. He had to smile at her dancing eyes.

"All right, fine. Whatever." He scooted lower, snuggling into the blankets.

"Isn't this just deliciously cheesy?" Richelle giggled partway through the movie. Sheldon snorted. Despite himself, he kind of liked it, but he'd have died before he admitted it.

"Where's your mom?"

"Shhh!" The most silly grin was pasted on her face. It was rather awkward to be watching a couple kiss sitting next to the girl who liked him, and he fidgeted uncomfortably.

"She went home to make dinner."

Sheldon yanked out the overstuffed pillows propping him up, and turned on his side with a sigh. The volume sounded loud and hurt his head. Reaching out a hand, he turned it down a notch and pillowed his head on his arm, drowsily watching the figures dance on the screen.

When he awoke, everything was quiet; the room was darkened, the shades pulled down halfway. He felt like a person caught in someone else's house. Cautiously, he swung his legs over the side of the bed and eased to his feet. He felt a wave of oncoming dizziness, but it passed when he put his head down, and he padded in his socks out to the kitchen, leaning against the wall as he went.

There were bottles of various medicines neatly arranged on his counter, and the refrigerator had several things inside he hadn't bought. Mrs. Callahan's generosity was touching.

The hot water felt wonderful coursing over his achy body; his senses were heightened, and at first the water drumming onto his skin was nearly painful, but he'd soon accustomed himself to it. He was greatly relieved when he stepped out of the shower, though perhaps a little shakily, and rubbed himself all over with a rough towel. His back hurt, and his neck was decidedly cramped from sleeping in the wrong position. He wrapped the damp towel about his waist and headed through the apartment to his bedroom.

The laundry needed to be done, as he was pulling on the only other pair of pajama pants he owned. Utterly spent from his exertions, he could barely get back into bed and shut his eyes as he fought to control his rapidly beating heart and slow his breathing. At least he felt all right as long as he was lying down. With the dizziness and weakness he was experiencing, he knew he wouldn't be able to walk about for at least a few days.

He emerged around nine o'clock to use the bathroom and found Mrs. Callahan ensconced on the couch, curled up with a book. She looked pleasantly cozy and asked him how he was doing. He made a face and told her he'd be with her in a minute.

She made room for him on the couch, and he sat down unsteadily, faint dark spots obscuring his vision.

"Hi, Mom," he said when he'd recovered. She smiled at the familiar affectionate term.

"Hi! Sick of being sick yet?" A rueful look flashed into his eyes.

"Yeah, but I'm rather enjoying the attention or I would be if I didn't feel so out of it most of the time."

"You always see the bright side in everything, don't you?" She hugged him.

"Well, maybe not the bright side, but I try to see the best in things, I guess." A cold breeze clung to the ground, and he drew his feet up, clasping his hands around his knees.

"It is a little chilly in here, isn't it? I think it's better that it's on the cooler side though. Germs still stick around more where there's warmth," she remarked.

Sheldon had set the thermostat at sixty degrees when he'd left for school that morning, and no one had touched it for it remained where he'd left it.

"I'm going to turn it up to sixty-five. There's no use freezing to death. I get cold really easy anyways." Carefully he turned it up a notch with a gloomy thought to his heating bill as he did so. He was glad for all the snow, even if he had got sick because of it, for he needed the money.

"Hungry?"

"Hmm, yeah, I am." He sat at the tiny kitchen table as she rummaged in the fridge for the soup she'd brought.

"I couldn't bring myself to buy you any canned soup, so I made up some chicken noodle. Hope you like it."

"I'm sure I will. I love your cooking."

"You are a flatterer, aren't you?" He grinned sleepily.

"But it's true!" She set the little pan on the stove and turned the burner on high, stirring it about with a wooden spoon.

Sheldon rested peacefully on a full stomach, peacefully enough, for he awoke numerous times either in a sweat or in various stages of freezing. Mrs. Callahan checked on him throughout the night, taking her role as nurse seriously.

A cold light shining in through the windowpanes gradually wore into his subconscious, and he opened his eyes slowly, his bed warm in the cool room. He pushed aside the blankets and gasped as his body adjusted to the change in temperature, gooseflesh prickling up his arms. Even after hours of sleep, his headache remained, and his throat hurt so he was loathe to even attempt swallowing. He shuffled out to put on some water for tea, hoping to soothe it with the hot beverage.

Mrs. Callahan was up tidying the living room where she'd slept, and he croaked a good morning. A frappe was in the blender, and he put on the kettle.

"Morning, Sheldon. I made that for you. It's light and good for your stomach." She indicated the full blender. "I have to go home when you've finished. Would you like me to drop Richelle off after school?" Seeing his skeptical look, she suggested he text her if he'd rather not.

His legs trembled a little as he sat down, the spineless, rubbery feeling unpleasant and unpredictable. He ate the frappe with a spoon, every bite measured, not trusting his fingers to have the strength to grasp the brimful glass. The simple combination of strawberries and bananas tasted delicious, but it was nearly room temperature by the time he finished. He was hustled back into bed which Mrs. Callahan had straightened and folded the blankets neatly back.

"You have hardly any strength. Don't do anything stupid while I'm gone." He smiled at her motherly caring and took his steaming cup of tea from her, leaning back into the yielding comfort of the cushions. "You all set?"

"Yes, I think so. Thanks so much for everything, Mom. I can't thank you enough." She patted his hand.

"It's the least I can do. Well, good-bye, Sheldon. I'll be by sometime to check in on you. Take it easy and stay in bed!"

The engine started up, and he heard it meld into the steady stream of vehicles and become indistinguishable.

The tea receded lower and lower, and soon the cup was set on the bedside table, and Sheldon was so woozy he had to take a nap.

Richelle was worried about Sheldon and had a difficult time paying attention in class. She hoped he was doing better than the previous day. Another uneventful day might have passed had she not needed to use the bathroom after lunch.

She pumped soapy foam from the dispenser, and rubbed it over her hands. She was rinsing the suds down the drain when the door eased open and a girl with shoulder-length bleach blonde hair sauntered in. It shut with a muffled bang behind her, and she stared at Richelle, almost sizing her up so it seemed, out of pale blue eyes that were traced with a shocking amount of heavy black eyeliner. Red lips split into a garish grin.

"Well, hello, hello," she said. Richelle stared back, wringing her hands and wiping them on a paper towel, perplexed. "How's our friend?"

"I'm sorry, but I have no idea who or what you're talking about. Now if you'll excuse me, I have a class to get to." She reached for the door.

"Oh, I think you do," the girl said easily. "Sheldon? I do believe you know who I'm talking about." She leaned against the wall with a satisfactory smirk as Richelle stopped in her tracks.

"Sheldon has no friends. Why don't you be honest and just say you're enemies?" She desperately wished she was back in class.

"Oh, my dear girl, I am being honest. Of course, he didn't tell you about me. Should I be jealous?" She giggled in a familiar way that turned everything sour. "Has he kissed you yet? You could agree with me that it is a most thrilling experience." Her eyes were wide and innocent as if she was sharing a cherished secret. Clarisse saw the undisguised confusion in the other girl's eyes and felt a surge of triumph. "Oh, I'm sorry," she said slowly, her voice fairly dripping with perfectly affected sympathy. "I don't suppose you're used to sharing your boyfriend, but you'd best know the worst." She leaned closer and dropped her voice to lend a little drama to her deceit. "Sheldon gets any girl he wants, and he uses the same story with every new one. Didn't you tell me he has no friends?" She shook her head sorrowfully, and suddenly, Sheldon's tale seemed phony; had she been led on, had she placed her trust in a boy just as bad as Tyson? Richelle was horrified. "But he's stuck by me since eighth grade." A dreamy smile touched her red lips as if she was lost in memories of sweet bygone days. "He once told me it's because I'm not jealous when he has a little fun with the other girls. I'm Clarisse, by the way."

"Richelle," she replied automatically, swallowing back the bile that rose in her throat. It's an awful thing to have your carefully constructed dreams crushed by a few words, leaving your world poisoned.

"Ah. Richelle. I suppose he'll be angry with me for telling you he's only playing you, but I couldn't bear seeing you hurt. Poor thing!" Clarisse laid her hand on her arm and left, thoroughly satisfied with the successful execution of her venomous plan.

Her hand had been cold, but Richelle had hardly felt it. Her skin was lifeless; all the warmth had gone from it long ago, leaving her face white. She felt hollow and emptied of every beautiful hope she'd ever dared harbor. She stood rooted to the ground. Memories flashed through her mind, and the tears welled unbidden in her eyes, blurring her vision. Clenching her fists so her nails dug into the flesh of her palms, she drove them away, steeling herself for the inevitable remainder of the school day. She strode purposely down the hall, heels clicking. Bitter anger encompassed her heart, leaving her emotionless and numb, and she took notes robotically, the hard seat which usually was a cause of complaint going unnoticed.

She was standing on the entrance steps of the large brick building scanning the road for any car that might be her mother's when she got the text. It was her mom telling her she was going to drop her off at Sheldon's place. Richelle ground her teeth and, with fingers trembling with furious outrage, sent a curt negative response. She didn't want to see Sheldon for a long, long time, never mind being forced to face him. The thought of spending hours with him like she had only the day before turned her stomach. The phone buzzed, and she read her mom's reply.

"Why ever not?"

"Had a bad day at school." It was the truth. She couldn't remember a worse day at any school she'd ever attended.

Ten minutes later, she was sitting in the passenger seat, sullen and disinclined to any form of conversation.

"Whatever is the matter, darling?" Her mother was concerned. She'd never seen her daughter like this. She stared unseeing at the dashboard. This was shock, anger. Her mom narrowed her eyes. "Did you have any trouble with some boy today?" She waited anxiously for her answer. It came in the form of a slight decisive turn of the head, a negative. Mrs. Callahan could see she was too upset to push her for details. She was confident the story would come out sooner or later. "Are you sure seeing your best friend wouldn't cheer you up, maybe a little?" Richelle's face worked in an effort to control the rush of indignant rage that swelled up without warning in her breast.

"No!" she spat out in a strangled voice, leaving no doubt in her mother's mind that it had something to do with Sheldon. What had that poor unfortunate boy done now? Never had she seen such a reaction in her daughter.

She dropped Richelle off and went to go pick up Matt, who attended a private school because of a preference over public. Richelle enclosed herself in her bedroom and didn't come out for hours; she needed to be alone. She threw herself across her bed and sobbed as if her heart would break. By and by, the anger had drained out of her, washed away by her tears, and she cried for the hurt, the aching void left behind and for a lost friendship.

Sheldon was watching Studio C videos on YouTube when he heard determined footsteps marching up the stairs. One set, so he derived from this that Richelle hadn't come. He wondered why. A brusque rap on his door, and he called out admittance. He looked up uncertainly at Mrs. Callahan.

"Is something wrong?" he asked, surprised by the tensity in the lines of her face. She came into the room, regarding him with keen eyes. The mattress creaked as she sat on its edge.

"Tell me something, Sheldon." The woman seemed to be having difficulty phrasing her words. Sheldon looked at her encouragingly, curious as to what she had to say. "You've somehow hurt Richelle deeply." Even as she said it, she felt a pang for disclosing her daughter's feelings without her consent. "She didn't want to see you and said she'd had a bad day at school. Do you have any idea what is going on?" His blank face communicated his bafflement.

"Not a clue! We had a great time yesterday. Well, I mean she did. She was herself, but I haven't talked to her since. I can't imagine what happened. I mean I didn't talk much, because I couldn't, but I thought she understood that. Really, Mom, are you sure she said it was specifically anything to do with me? Because I'm positive I haven't done anything." He picked up his water glass and swished some of the thirst-quenching liquid down his dry burning throat. He winced as he swallowed.

"Not exactly." She relayed the short dialogue they had had. Sheldon was clearly as puzzled as her.

"I don't know what to say!" he said helplessly, raising his palms. "I don't understand!"

"Well, I apologize for coming in here to accuse you." He laughed despite the troubling situation.

"Oh, not at all. I totally understand. You are her mother after all." He ducked his head, remembering how his own mother had always defended him and stood by him through the thick and thin of his childhood. Mrs. Callahan brushed a hand over the top of his head and went into the kitchen to get him something to eat.

She straightened his room as he ate the rich beef stew, letting the broth trickle down his throat. It felt so good.

"You're feeling better, aren't you?"

"Yes, a little. Can you tell?"

"You took forever with your breakfast. But then again, you'd ventured out of bed."

"Yeah, but I do feel better. We'll see what happens when I take a shower tonight." He told her how weak he'd been the night before.

"Wrap up in a towel and sit on the toilet for a few minutes. Things won't be so bad then. Trust me, that's happened to me many times. The rest gives your body time to recuperate." She gathered up his dirty laundry and packed it into an empty box left over from moving. "I'll get this done and bring it over sometime soon. You'll be OK tomorrow, all right enough to walk around and heat up your soup. You can call me if you need anything, OK?" She lifted the box and turned the doorknob. "I'll try to get these back to you tonight. Bye now!"

Not once during the entire week he was ill did Richelle stop in to see him or reply to any of his texts. Sheldon had quit texting her after three or four messages in which he expressed his bafflement and apologized for whatever it was he had done. He experienced more pain from her unexplained deliberate silence than that which he suffered from his illness. He found himself slipping into bitterness and the old familiar hatred tugged at him. Hours and days ticked by in monotonous procession, and he thought about the friendship they had shared and went over and over every scenario on his mind but couldn't imagine what had gone wrong. There was no logical explanation. Disbelief, despair, and anger each vied for the upper hand, but somehow, he felt a strange peace in the midst of the chaos.

His father was recovering from the surgery nicely, and the doctors said he was home now, with state care coming in every day. It was one less thing to worry about, but Sheldon still came by to visit him sometimes, just to check in on him.

Sheldon struggled. It was a battle for him, the loneliness swept in like a storm at sudden moments when he had thought he was fine. Originally, he'd accepted it, as much as he could with no explanation whatsoever, and thought he had moved on. But the peace he had experienced came and went like sands shifting with the tide. He found he couldn't get over it, the loss of his friend. It was as if his mind was a broken record, constantly going over and over the memories they had made together. She had been more a part of his life than he'd realized. But people never seem to know what they had until it's gone, be that a thing or a person, and Sheldon felt Richelle's absence keenly. He had no one to confide in, no one to tell the little details and silly moments of his life to, the moments no one would ever see. Little things, like nearly dropping a razor down the toilet in his groggy morning haze before his mind was clear or the big things. Like the way God had spoken to him through a verse, a scrap of a song on the radio. Something he had learned that excited and intrigued him. His life seemed purposeless somehow, with no one to share it. He tried to tell himself he was OK, and that after all, he was used to living totally on his own and having not a soul care if he awoke in the morning or not, but it was useless. He'd tasted the way life was supposed to be, known the touch and laughter of a friend, and he couldn't ever go back now. He knew what it was like to be alone and had no desire to live that way again. If he had a choice, he would never know the ache of loneliness again, but the decision didn't appear to lie in his hands. There was nothing he could do or say to change things.

Sometimes, he caught himself daydreaming in class, and when he came to himself, he would be gazing at Richelle's auburn head, and a time or two, she had glanced up to find his eyes on her, and his heart flipped inside his chest with a sudden hope that was agonizing, but she had severed the contact instantly. It felt like a piece of his soul died every time it happened.

And the nights were the worst. He could make it through a day and come out in one piece, the pain of the rift between he and his best and only friend forgotten for a few blessed hours; then reality would come crashing back full force when his mind wandered free with nothing to keep it busy. Sheldon hated nights when he wasn't tired enough to fall asleep as soon as he crawled into bed. "It isn't fair," he told himself, and the tears would come. Tired and alone, he didn't feel very much like fighting them, but as the days slipped into weeks, there was no change in Richelle toward him, and the tears of sorrow and confusion began to be tainted more and more with anger and the pain of bitterness.

Time is said to heal all wounds. True or untrue as that may be, it did seem to deaden the pain, a little. His anger dissipated slowly and left only sorrow and hurt behind where there had been a bitterness that bordered on hate. Sheldon felt numb, but there was still a void in his heart that Richelle had filled; the hunger for companionship had been sated with her presence in his life. Now that she was gone . . . He had Matt as a friend, but it was not the same. There didn't seem to be anyone who could take her place.

Chapter 17

Taking the Leap

The April rains drummed down on the car's roof and soaked through his hoodie as Sheldon ran for the shelter of the school, his feet pelting over the pavement along with the fat raindrops.

The teacher shot him a reproving glare, and several heads turned as the door creaked open and he slid into a chair. He was late for class, but as he always said, better late than never. He chewed on the end of his pen waiting for noteworthy material.

An auburn head was bent studiously over her notebook, but she didn't fool him. She was more aware of his presence than of any other person in the room. His cheeks burned with a misplaced sense of shame. He turned his head away from her and bent his gaze to the blank sheet of paper on the desk before him. Unlike the previous day, his emotions warred within him, and he desperately wondered if he would ever heal.

Sheldon took to avoiding her as much as possible if only to protect his aching heart, but it was challenging when they were in the same building and attending many of the same classes. Sometimes, he would feel the weight of her gaze on him, and once he looked up, meeting her eyes for a split second before she returned her attention to the teacher. Richelle couldn't deny the shiver of pleasure that raced over her skin at this form of contact.

He'd looked so pained. *Served him right,* she thought, squaring her shoulders, and it was as if icy fingers gripped her heart, smothering any thaw that might have occurred when the spring in his eyes came against the winter of hurt pride consuming her.

One day, the cafeteria had served up hot dogs, and the kid in line ahead of him splattered ketchup all over Sheldon's shirtfront.

"Oh, sorry . . . here." He dabbed at the mess with a useless napkin, spreading it around and only making matters worse.

"It's all right." He stepped out of the line and headed for the bathroom, curbing his temper, for he had reason to believe it wasn't entirely an accident. Most things usually weren't.

The school had consolidated space and incorporated a gym locker in the bathroom, the result being a huge maze of corridors and rows of lockers lining the walls. Sheldon threaded his way to the sink and yanked the sticky shirt gingerly over his head. He managed to avoid his hair and crumpled it into the sink. He hoped the hand soap would save the T-shirt from an ugly orange stain. He was standing there scrunching it about in the soapy water, stripped down to his jeans, when he caught a movement behind him reflected in the mirror. Mildly, he glanced over his shoulder and froze.

Clarisse leaned one hip against the wall, pale eyes looking him over with a disconcertingly bold expression. Utterly shocked, he gaped at her, his wrists submerged in the water.

"What the heck are you doing in here? Get out!" he commanded.

"Following you, of course." She sidled over, running cool fingertips along the bare skin of his back. He faced her, red.

"You're going to get in trouble. You'd better leave."

"What will you say?"

He raised his brows. "The truth of course!"

She smiled, revealing pointed teeth. "You will, will you? We'll have to stretch the truth a little then, won't we?" Quickly she raised up on her tiptoes, steadying herself with one hand flat on his chest and brushed her lips across his mouth before he had the chance to jerk away. "Things look a little different for you now, don't they?" she said smugly. "Who's going to believe you when you say I came in here and kissed you? Sounds highly unbelievable." He dashed a hand across his mouth, wiping the red lipstick away, and angrily wrung out his shirt, the tips of his ears flaming.

"Leave me alone." She followed on his heels to his locker and pushed herself in front of him, blocking his way.

"No. I won't leave you alone." She looked tearful, and her voice took on a soft wheedling note. "Not even when all your so-called friends desert you. I'll always be here." He didn't pull away as she took his hand in both of hers, such a crushing weight of hopeless despair crashed over him. He had been deserted. Her hands slid over his skin, and she nestled her head comfortably on his shoulder. He closed his arms about her numbly, and she felt his cheek on her hair. Hungrily, she raised her warm red mouth to his. He lowered his head and felt her hot breath on his face, and only a soft warning whispering deep in his soul caused him to hesitate. He pulled back, and his arms dropped to his sides.

"Please go away. You don't understand." Fire flashed through her eyes as he turned to his locker, fumbling with the combination. He whipped a hoodie over his head, shoving his arms through the sleeves.

"No, you're the one who doesn't," she said, trying to conceal her anger. "You're burning all your bridges, and you don't realize how alone you are." He astounded her completely by breaking into a sudden smile.

"Clarisse, I am never alone, and there is not a moment in my life where I ever will be. There's nothing you can say to change that I have a Friend." He shoved the damp shirt inside the locker, and the door slammed with a metallic clang.

"But she isn't your friend. I mean, look at the way she's treating you!"

"I wasn't talking about her." He strode back to the cafeteria. She was clearly confused and hung back as he grabbed a plate.

Richelle had noticed when they walked in, and the sight of Sheldon with that girl and the smile on his face cut deep, too deep for her own comfort, especially when she was always telling herself she didn't care. She pushed her fork around her plate and furtively watched him out of the corner of her eye as he took a seat at the table across from hers. Clarisse made as if to seat herself beside him, but his arm draped across the back of the chair prevented her. He twisted in his seat and stared her down. She tossed her head, and her heels clicked as she moved to another table.

The girl observing this exchange was puzzled. Girlfriend? It was highly unlikely, given the behavior displayed. If anything, Sheldon seemed disgusted with her. *But then again, they probably just acted the whole thing out to deceive me,* she thought, crumpling her paper cup. But if that was the case, it didn't explain his reddened cheeks and downcast eyes. If it had been acted out for her benefit, Sheldon would've looked at her to see how successful the performance had been, if she'd taken the bait, so to speak. Not once did he so much as glance in her direction during the remainder of lunch.

Richelle watched him and Clarisse for weeks. The girl was barely tolerated, and Sheldon clearly wasn't "sticking by" her.

After school one day, she managed to catch up with Clarisse on the way out the door and walked beside her, the other girl's fast pace making speech difficult.

"So, I think you didn't tell me the truth all those weeks ago." Clarisse smirked.

"Believe what you like. Obviously, your relationship with him hasn't been the same." Richelle grabbed her arm and forced her to halt.

"You lied! You're not his girlfriend. Anyone can see that!"

"Well, explain to me why he brought me into the guy's bathroom and kissed me. He can kiss like no one else." She was infuriating. "My lips were sore for days." Richelle chose to disregard this colorful bit of information.

"He'd never bring a girl into the bathroom." Clarisse stopped dead and brought her face close to Richelle's, her words a hiss.

"If you're so sure of him, why don't you ask him?" She pushed her. "Ask him if he wasn't there when we kissed, ask him where we were. Ask!" She shoved Richelle out of her way and hurried onto her bus.

The girl stood rooted to the spot, her breast heaving. What should she do? Did she believe it? Had she ruined a friendship with Sheldon forever? He and Matt were still great friends; he'd had Sheldon over a few times to hang out at the house but had taken to going in Sheldon's direction because of the strain between he and Richelle. Richelle felt a pang of regret but couldn't put aside her wounded pride to heal the rift. She was the one wronged and wasn't about to go crawling to anybody.

Easter came and went; Sheldon had gone up and spent the weekend with his grandmother. She'd been delighted to have him and had invited a family from her church over for Easter dinner.

The service was beautiful, reminding Sheldon of his suffering King who had laid down His life for him that he might have eternal fellowship with the Father, proving Himself to be a never-failing Friend. One who had conquered death and would never leave him, he thought, as they sang the triumphant words: "Up from the grave he arose, with a mighty triumph o'er his foes. He arose a victor from the dark domain and he lives forever with his saints to reign."

It had been a refreshing time, and he'd refocused on Christ as his all-in-all, giving his cares into more capable hands than his own. He was confident that God had a purpose in this muddled mess he'd somehow made of his friendship with Richelle.

His grandmother noticed he didn't mention the girl's name, and there were no more late-night conversations. Wisely, she kept her disappointment to herself. God would raise up a companion for her dear grandson; she knew He would. "But oh, Lord, must it be so painful for him?" she asked.

The weekend of good food and better company was all too short, and she waved good-bye as his navy-colored car cruised out of sight.

"God be with you, my dear boy." The wind snatched the words from her mouth, and they were gone as if she'd never spoken them. But her prayer rang on, and always would.

Sheldon was a sensitive young man, with a keen observance of the dispositions and behavioral patterns in other people. So it came as no surprise when he soon sensed a change in Richelle's attitude toward him. Her manner had undergone a thaw of sorts, and she no longer looked away as quickly as she had before when he caught and held her gaze with his own. But she still evaded him and refused to speak a word. He couldn't legitimately accuse her of being stubborn without first labeling himself a hypocrite. He hadn't even tried the easy route and texted her. And he wouldn't do that. No, it just wasn't his style.

There wasn't a trace of snow to be seen anywhere, and with the return of spring came the flowers. So long desired after the long, cold bleak months of winter, they bloomed like so many bright flames of color in brown gardens and among the young spears of fresh green grass. Crocuses and daffodils, snowdrops and tiny purple violets filled hearts with the old joy of beauty and life, fresh every year after the dead of winter. The temperatures were climbing with little leaps and bounds, and the sun shone down lazily; warm breezes filled the air. Spring was here to stay.

It was on one such day, Saturday to be exact, that Sheldon set out for a walk. This was not just because of a whim created by a desire to be out in the beautiful sunny weather, but he'd been playing with an idea for days and had finally decided to go through with it. The air was pure, and he drew it into his lungs vigorously; it was like breathing in new life. He'd thrown open all the windows in his apartment to let the clean, warm air sweep away the stale.

His pace slackened as he drew near the Callahans' house, and he stopped, one hand on the white picket fence surrounding the property. He hadn't been here in over a month. It was a strange feeling, looking up at a house he'd frequented every day and to feel like an unwanted imposer. Shrugging away the thought and the hurt that threatened to drown him once more, he strode purposely up to the front door and had his fist raised to knock when a flash of white in the garden caught his attention. He stepped away from the door, captivated.

She was a dream, a soft white dress clinging to the slender curves of her body as she walked over to the huge old maple and settled herself lightly on the wide wooden swing that hung from a thick limb. The new leaves hid her from view, and her back was turned to him so she couldn't possibly see him, not until he stepped out from behind the tree trunk. The craggy old bark beneath his hand reassured him that it was real; he was not staring at a vision. She was really not more than three feet away from him, and yes, those beautiful green eyes were raised to his in unguarded surprise. Her hair made red splashes of color as it cascaded down her back, contrasting with the creamy white of her dress. He was speechless and found his mouth had gone suddenly dry. Richelle was so shocked to look up and see him standing before her that she spoke first, not realizing she'd opened her mouth until she heard her own voice.

"Sheldon! What are you doing here?" Her tone was incredulous. He winced, and the power of speech returned and with it the purpose for his coming.

"I came to see you—Richelle. I can't stand this any longer! I don't understand what has come between us. Please, please tell me so I can make things right again somehow!" He took her hands in both of his, pleading with her desperately. They were cold. She caught her breath as he knelt in front of her, his grip strong, eyes intense. She didn't have the willpower to pull away. "Tell me!" He shook her gently although every muscle in his body was tense.

"I . . . I." She couldn't meet his gaze and blushed furiously.

"What is it, Chelle? I thought you valued our friendship! I'll do anything to make it the way it was." He was so intense. Were those tears in his eyes?

"Clarisse, told me . . ." She broke off, frightened by the sudden flinty set of his face. He let go his hold on her hands and leaned back against the tree, his eyes hooded and dark in the shade.

"Clarisse. Of course," he muttered under his breath. "What did she tell you?" His voice was hard. Haltingly, she repeated the charges Clarisse had leveled against him: how he was her boyfriend, how he was a notorious girl chaser, how he used the same pitiful ploy to lure girls into his clutches so he could use them as he pleased, and how Clarisse had told her this to save her from being hurt.

He was absolutely furious, his face crimson. She could hear the struggle for control in each trembling breath he drew.

"You believed this absurd pack of lies? Why?" he barked. She shed away, and his voice softened. "I'm sorry, Chelle. But you know me. My character should have withstood her deceit. How could she dupe you so easily?" Then suddenly, he checked himself. He knew why. What person, girl or not, likes to be told the one they love is only out to play with them and drop them when they get what they wanted? Richelle was an emotional mess anyways, defenseless against a ploy with a drift like Clarisse's.

"I'm so sorry, Sheldon!" He could hear the tears in her voice before they began to fall. "I'm an awful friend. I'm so sorry I doubted you! Won't you ever forgive me?" Her hands twisted over and over in her lap, the words dissolving into hiccupping sobs at the end. For a second he was tempted to make her pay for the pain she'd caused him. He hesitated and then moved over and sat on the swing beside her, cupping a warm hand over her knee.

"Hey, of course I forgive you! You're my best friend, and things were miserable without you." He closed his eyes and sent a silent prayer of thanks as he gently wiped away her tears and cradled her head against his chest. He looked over her head, clenching his jaw as he thought about what he would do when he saw Clarisse that coming Monday. She was a poisonous little viper and would be getting a piece of his mind. Richelle pulled away. He turned toward her and instantly saw from her expression that she hadn't disclosed everything. He crossed his arms, tilting his head toward her. She bit her lip nervously, clutching the rope with a clammy hand.

"She said you'd kissed her." If he had been shot, he couldn't have exploded off the swing any faster. It rocked crazily, and Richelle clung tight to steady herself.

"And?" His voice grated on her ears. He stood stock-still with his back to her.

"You forced her into the guy's bathroom." She heard the pent-up groan of rage, and he whirled.

"Do you want to know what happened?" he nearly shouted, eyes blazing in his white face. "Do you want to? Well, I'll damn well tell you. She followed me and forced herself on me. She's been trying to ever since I met the little freak." The words came out hard and contemptuous. "She's revolting, disgusting, and I can't stand the sight of her. And no, she barely touched my mouth, but it still feels like a violation. You know what that feels like, Richelle Callahan. She and Tyson would make a brilliant match," he spat out, fists clenched. Richelle threw caution to the wind and went to him, laying a hand on his arm.

"Careful, Sheldon, careful." She turned his face so he was looking at her. "Don't let the hate win." The muscles in his face softened, and suddenly, he wrapped his arms tight around her.

"Life is a mess without you." he whispered into her hair. She leaned into him, her heart beating so she was sure he'd hear it. She loved being in his arms; he was so strong, and the feeling he awoke in her was dangerous and so unknown that sometimes it frightened her, but not today. She gloried in the sensation, delighting in the strength of his arms, the whispering of his breath in her hair, feeling his chest rise and fall in constant cadence. He squeezed her and pulled back, looking at the ground, feeling almost embarrassed.

"I'm so glad we're friends again! Don't let Clarisse torment you. Gosh, does she have a thing or two coming her way! I . . ." His blue eyes flickered up for an instant and then stopped, riveted on her face. At the abrupt silence, she raised her eyes and met his gaze, her expression quizzical. Slowly, he reached out his hand and touched her cheek, fingers just brushing her skin. Her breath caught in her throat, and then he couldn't deny the ache in her eyes and moved swiftly close to her. With both hands, he cupped her chin, and tilting her face up to his, he kissed her, drinking her in like the sweetest wine in the world. The sun dimmed; there was a roaring in her ears, and her mouth was on fire, his lips burning on hers, intoxicating. Never had she imagined such passion, and she fell into his arms when he let her go, his breath coming quick and hard. She trembled as his arms enclosed her, lips stinging from his kiss. His heart was beating so close to hers that she could feel it, fast and rhythmic in his chest. His hands tangled in her hair, forcing her head back, his mouth on hers, insistent, passionate kisses, his breath on her face hot and sweet. Somehow, she found herself in his lap with her arms around his neck, his hands guiding her head through the motions suited to the whims of his mouth, tipped one way then the other.

And then the fire was gone, and the lights flickered on. Sheldon gasped, deep, shuddering breaths tearing through his lungs. He held her, his body tense, pulse hammering, every fiber of his being throbbing in time. He groaned and strained her to him, feeling the angles and curves of her body against his own. For a moment, he was quiet, tracing her features with one gentle finger, memorizing them: the line of her brow, her nose, cheekbones, her chin, and slowly, tenderly, her mouth. Richelle pulled his face down to hers and slowly began exploring his mouth with her own, warmth flooding her as he responded, and he kissed her desperately, faster and faster. She began to cry, her tears dampening his cheeks. He kissed them away, knowing she was so full of joy that she was ready to burst. He let her go as she struggled out of his arms. She was suddenly afraid; his passion was so wild and reckless that she was both lured and frightened by it.

"I was so blind, Chelle. It took almost losing you to make me see that . . . Well," he laced his fingers through hers, "we could be so much more." Sheldon wiped a tear off her cheek, and took her into his arms. She abandoned her fear and let him gather her up, her face buried in his sweatshirt, breathing in the masculine scent of his body. Sheldon held her for what seemed like an eternity, running one hand soothingly up and down her back. It was a comforting sensation, and she reached up and cradled his head in her hands, kissing his hair.

He moved his hands swiftly to her shoulders, heat sweeping over them in a wave, his warm mouth on her throat, fingers caressing the little hollow of her collarbone. He buried his face in her breast, his breath warm against her skin through the soft material of the dress. Her arms wrapped around him, and she leaned her head against his, whispering sweet nothings in his ear.

Chapter 18

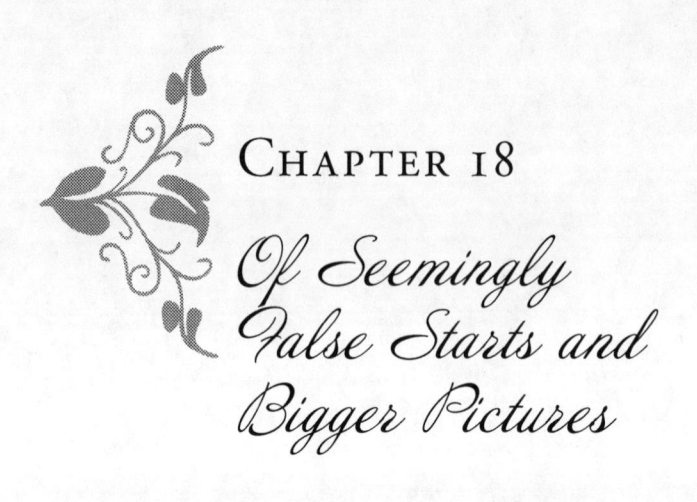

Of Seemingly False Starts and Bigger Pictures

Sunday, Mr. and Mrs. Callahan were dumbfounded to see Sheldon slide into the pew beside their daughter. He hadn't sat with them for months, never talking to Richelle when he greeted all the other members of the family, and yet there he was, holding her hymnal between them and exchanging companionable whispers back and forth. They looked at each other questioningly, but one knew as much about it as did the other. Matt beamed with obvious pleasure; it was good to have the family back together and at peace once more.

Mrs. Callahan couldn't hold back her curiosity any longer by the time they were settled about the table for a chicken dinner. Sheldon looked at Richelle with a grin that lit up his handsome face and made his eyes sparkle.

"Well, we had an awful misunderstanding, people spreading nasty rumors about me and we fell apart. None of it was true." He speared a green bean and crunched into it. "Yesterday, I couldn't stand the tension any longer, and I missed everything: you guys, having Chelle's friendship, and being able to come over without a moment's notice, so I came and apologized. We talked everything over and made up." He felt Richelle's elbow in his side and thought he could guess what she was thinking. He reached under the table for her hand.

"Oh, that's wonderful. I'm so glad!" Mrs. Callahan said, her husband nodding in agreement.

"Glad to hear you guys worked things out. We all missed you. Goes to show how others suffer for our choices." He cast his eye at his daughter, who studied her plate, knowing full well just how right he was.

When no one was watching, Sheldon leaned over and whispered in her ear, "Made up *and* out!" She choked and nearly upset her water.

"Wow, careful there, Rik!" Her father steadied the glass.

Cheerful banter passed back and forth as they finished up lunch and cleared off the table.

The day wore on into the late afternoon, and Richelle's parents meandered upstairs for their Sunday nap, and after a while, Matt reluctantly trudged up to his room to work on a history assignment that was due on Monday.

Alone together with Sheldon, Richelle felt suddenly awkward and shy, remembering the things that had passed between them only the day before. She dropped her gaze to the ground, and a flush stole into her cheeks as he got up from his easy chair and crossed over to her.

"Hey," he murmured, easing down beside her. Her heart raced as he traced her fingers with his, and took her hand in a firm grip. "Wanna go for a walk? We could get ice cream!" he said in a wheedling tone. As if she needed persuading! She smiled and met his eager gaze.

"Let's!"

"Isn't this weather beautiful?" It was warm; there was no need for even a light sweater, cottony clouds drifting lazily across the brilliant blue sky.

"Oh yes. I love the springtime. It's hard to imagine only a month or so ago, there was still snow," she said.

"Hmm, although not a month ago. 'Or so' was more to the point," he laughed. "Do ya think it's weird for a guy to like flowers?" He picked a violet and twirled it between his fingers. She watched him hold it to his nose, a playful question in his eyes.

"No, not at all. Not enough of you guys have your appreciation for beauty." He knew she meant the beauty of nature that so often went unnoticed, but he held light fingertips up to her face.

"I'm glad of that. Because if they did, I wouldn't have even had a chance." He tucked the tiny flower behind her ear, and they lost themselves in each other's eyes for a long moment before resuming walking.

The little ice cream shoppe at the end of the street was a popular place, but there were only a few customers so late in the afternoon. They ordered sundaes and sat side by side on the tall old-fashioned stools to enjoy them.

"Maraschino cherries." He prodded the little garnish to the side of his dish with is long-handled spoon. "You like them?" he asked incredulously as she scooped up hers with a bit of ice cream and popped it in her mouth. She nodded emphatically, and he dropped the undesired bleached cherry onto her ice cream with a face that communicated his obvious distaste. Her eyes sparkled merrily as the second cherry disappeared closely in the wake of the first. "Never could make myself like those things." The fluffy whipped cream and luscious rich mocha ice cream melted on his tongue.

"More for me then. We should get these more often." He grinned at her mock seriousness.

"I take it that you don't object to dates where ice cream is included?"

"No, never. I could never turn down one of these." She licked her spoon.

"What if I decided not to take you for ice cream? What then?" he flirted shamelessly. The playfulness receded partway from her face.

"I wouldn't care, I just love being with you. You know that." A chocolate smudge on her lip made her look so adorable he felt a sudden urge to kiss her.

"Well, it wouldn't do for you to starve. Yeah, everything seems better when we're together. Why didn't we figure this out sooner?" She propped her chin against her fist.

"We? My dear boy, you are most mistaken. You're the thickheaded one!" she laughed.

"Well, I figured that out. I have a confession to make." She was curious. "Do you remember back in March when I got sick? The very first day?"

"Of course, I do."

For several reasons, he knew. It was the end of their friendship as they had known it and the beginning of a lot of pain. But yes, good had come out of it.

"You know that conversation you had with your mom out in the kitchen when you thought I was sleeping?" She blushed pink.

"No! You were awake? You knew?" she questioned incredulously.

"Not for certain, but a lot of things made sense. I couldn't come up with any other logical conclusion from what I'd heard than to believe you liked me."

"You were the same though! Oh gosh, I can't believe you knew! We watched that ridiculous movie and you knew I liked you!" She hid her face in her hands and laughed helplessly. Sheldon dug deeper into his sundae, grinning.

"How long did you like me before I came round?" he asked, his gaze intent on her face.

"Goodness. Don't you laugh at me!" The innocent look in his eyes wasn't reassuring. "The moment I met you." Sheldon whistled.

"Am I one clueless guy or what?"

"Yes, yes, you are! What about you?"

"What? When did I start liking you? I don't know," he said musingly, staring at the revolving ceiling fan. "I suppose it was kind of gradual. I realized you were crazy beautiful after a while, actually, when you came in that Sunday I asked you to the prom.

I think. But who knows how long I would've held out, well, procrastinated if I hadn't known my feelings were returned. I noticed more and more what a treasure you are and how you're beautiful inside as well as out." He shrugged and ate a spoonful of melting ice cream. "And when everything fell apart, I couldn't believe how much I missed you. Gosh, it was like having a piece of my heart ripped out, and I didn't know how to fix it. Guess I got desperate." She smiled at him.

"Did you plan on reducing me to a puddle of tears and kissing me?"

"Goodness no! I just wanted your friendship back. The last thing on my mind was . . ." He stopped and handed her a napkin. "Wipe that off before I'm tempted beyond what I can bear." The chocolate smudge was gone. "That's better. Now finish that up or I'll have wasted money on you!" She laughed.

"Look who's talking! Speaking of being reduced to puddles!" Sheldon grinned at her teasing tone.

"Now it's just a milk shake of sorts." They discarded spoons and drank the remainder of the sundaes.

The doorbells jangled cheerfully as they stepped out on the sidewalk. A leisurely pace took them to the park in the center of the little sleepy town. There was a large pond at the edge, mostly obscured from the road by a rise in the surrounding landscape. It was a pretty spot with trees growing in thick profusion down to the water, where they gave way to last year's rushes and the beginnings of green water grasses. Most of the flowers grew wild down there, but the sidewalk was ranked with rows of flowering ornamental trees whose pink and white blossoms filled the air with their sweet perfume. Spring flowers bloomed in carefully tended beds. Sheldon and Richelle walked through the park down to the pond and sat on a wrought iron bench to listen to the sounds of nature. Frogs and birds were in full chorus, and somewhere in the forest across the water, a woodpecker drummed for his supper in a hollow old tree.

"It's hard to believe the world is full of chaos and disorder in a place like this," Richelle said quietly.

"Hmm," he agreed, content to sit and take in the tranquil beauty. "It's so powerful. God feels so near when things are like this."

"He does. But He's never gone. He's just as near when life is a mess, although we have a hard time believing that sometimes."

Sheldon slouched on the bench, digging his hands deep into his pockets. *How can anyone not love him,* Richelle thought, looking down at him. He met her eyes and smiled, leaning his head affectionately into her shoulder. Her fingers always had a soothing effect on him when she ran them through his hair.

"I want to talk about a few things," he said quietly.

"What is it?" She paused, resting her hand on the top of his head. Sheldon shrugged and sat up straight.

"I just think we need to talk about everything that happened . . . I don't know, just what we both were feeling. What we went through." He swallowed. "We need to be able to trust each other if we're gonna make this work. You know . . ." And he threaded his fingers through hers. "You and me."

"You mean what happened because of Clarisse?" Sheldon nodded. Richelle took a deep breath and let it out slowly. "You don't trust me even though we figured everything out?" Her eyes looked hurt.

"Chelle, don't make it sound like that!" he cried, squeezing her hand tightly. "But you know we both suffered. And I was hurt probably more than you were, not meaning to sound stuck up or anything, but it's true. You thought I'd . . . well, messed with you I guess you could say, and tell me if I'm wrong, but I'll bet you were kinda angry."

"I was," she said simply. "And hurt, and I felt betrayed and used. To be honest, I didn't feel like I could ever trust anyone ever again, because I loved you so much, and I thought you just walked all over me . . . It was awful. But," she smiled up at him, "I was all wrong! None of what I felt matters because I misjudged you and you never betrayed my trust." Sheldon held up his hand.

"See, that right there is what I want to talk about, really, the fact that you misjudged me. I'm sorry, but I can't totally wrap my mind around that! Yeah, I get everything you were feeling and understand the betrayal thing and all, but what I don't understand is why you didn't talk to me about it! We were best friends one minute and the next arch enemies!" Richelle looked out over the still waters of the pond, trying to make order of her thoughts.

"Well," she said finally, "I thought everything I knew about you was a lie. I couldn't reconcile the person I knew you as with the person Clarisse said you were. I was too angry and prideful to be vulnerable to talk with you about it, I guess, because I knew I would believe what you told me. I didn't want you to hurt me." She looked at him, the line of her mouth tight. He reached out and rubbed his thumb along her cheek.

"OK, I think I get you now."

She smiled at him and said tentatively, "You mentioned suffering more than I did. Is that because . . . because I was the only friend you had and you felt I treated you like everyone else had? In the past?" Sheldon looked down at his hands.

"Yes," he said ponderingly. "Part of it for sure. Think how you would feel if you'd waited years for someone to care enough for you to be your friend and you shared your life with them, only to have them walk out with no explanation at all when you had completely believed they would never hurt you . . . because you thought they were different. I think you would experience a little pain, don't you? I couldn't believe it, Chelle. Really couldn't. It was so hard. Especially when I realized I loved you . . . I couldn't believe I'd somehow lost you." He told her of his conflicting emotions when he could care less and then how he would be lost in the depths of despair. He told her the dark thoughts that had haunted him, the anger that had blinded him, the sorrow, the loneliness, the pain . . . all of it.

"Oh, Shel." She heaved a deep sigh when he ceased speaking. "I can never say I'm sorry enough times. I can't fix what I've done! I wish . . . I wish I could go back and do everything differently!" she cried vehemently. He laughed softly under his breath and passed an arm around her shoulders.

"Knowing you would change it if you could is enough. No, you can't change what happened, but we're trying to undo the damage that's been done to both of us. And hey, we were both to blame. We were both stupid and stubborn! But it doesn't matter now. We've got each other, and we'll get through this. It won't take so very long." He squeezed Richelle gently to him, and she leaned her head on his shoulder.

"I'm glad about this, if I can say that," she said quietly. Sheldon looked down at her in surprise, his eyebrows shooting up.

"Why on earth would you ever say that?" he exclaimed.

"Well, think about it. If this had never happened, we would never have grown closer together in this way, well, maybe not never, but you know. Our friendship is deeper because of the pain we went through than it was before. And also, we're more than just friends." Sheldon regarded her, his face thoughtful.

"There's a little bit of good in every bad thing that happens, isn't there?" he mused, tucking a stray lock behind her ear.

"There seems to be." They hugged each other tightly for a moment; then Richelle straightened up.

"Come on, we'd best be getting back home before someone misses us and wonders where we went," she grumbled.

"Who cares? Let's stay here forever." He laughed and grabbed for her hand.

"Can't do that, you silly. Come on." He looped her arm through his, and they walked up the embankment.

He stayed late that night, catching up and making up for the time he'd lost with the family. They were all watching a movie—all but Mr. Callahan, who didn't feel like it and had retreated to his study. They ate bowls of popcorn and worked through a plate of chocolate chip cookies Mrs. Callahan had made to celebrate Sheldon's "homecoming," as she termed it.

"Want us to pause it?" Matt asked as Sheldon got up and tried to creep unnoticed out of the room.

"No, that's fine. I'll be back in a minute." Instead of running up to the bathroom like they had expected him to, he sidestepped the stairs and walked over to Mr. Callahan's study, rapping softly on the heavy oak door. He was nervous but felt he needed to do this.

Evan looked up as he entered, his reading glasses perched on the bridge of his nose.

"Sheldon! Hi, son, didn't expect to see you, you're not my wife!" He chuckled and indicated a deep leather chair. "What can I do for you?" He steepled his fingers and regarded the young man inquiringly. Sheldon cleared his throat.

"Well, sir, I would like . . . it's about . . . you see . . ." Evan grinned and relaxed back into his seat, arms crossed over his broad chest.

"Yes?" He drummed his fingers on the arm of the chair, amused. Being a father, he thought he could predict which direction this was headed in. Or perhaps it was because he remembered a similar speech from his own high school years. Sheldon tried again.

"You see, sir, it's about Richelle." The words were out, and there was no going back now. "I've never asked anyone for a thing like this, so I guess I don't know how, but I'd like to date her, and I don't feel free to unless I have your permission." He held his breath. There wasn't a hint of moisture in his mouth; it seemed to have all gone to the palms of his hands. He wiped them on his jeans. Mr. Callahan looked at the nervous, hopeful young man sitting before him, anxious and sweaty, and took pity on him. There was no point in prolonging his misery. He removed his glasses methodically.

"Sheldon, I admire you greatly. You're an upright young man, and I know you well enough to be sure Richelle will be safe with you. Don't take offense if I say it like that, for I know dating someone, being attracted to someone, sometimes can be really tricky. It's difficult! She's my daughter, and I love her very much, and I demand you show her the respect she deserves and never ever put her in a situation where she might compromise. I'm giving you my permission, young man. Just be careful and be wise. Pray about this. And, Sheldon," he said warningly to bring the boy's attention back down to earth and keep his head from shooting up in the clouds for a moment more, "I need to ask you something. Do you intend to marry my daughter if you are led to believe she is the right one for you?" Sheldon met his eyes squarely.

"Sir, I'd never ask you if I wanted to date her for the sake of dating. I wouldn't treat her like that. She has feelings, and I won't take advantage of her in that way. I know her as a friend, but I guess there's only so much I can learn about her in that role." Her father looked at him thoughtfully for a moment and held out his hand.

"I have to say I was waiting for this and have given it a lot of thought and prayer. Treat her like a lady, Sheldon." He shook his hand and chuckled to himself when he was gone, remembering the boy's dazed expression.

"Where have you been?" Richelle asked him softly as he sat beside her.

"I'll tell you later," came his whispered reply, full of suppressed excitement. They looked at each other in the dim room lit by the TV screen, and he brushed a stray lock around her ear, smiling so much like a kid on Christmas that she thought she'd burst if she had to wait a second longer.

"What?" His eyes glinted as he shook his head, refusing to tell her, his white teeth flashing in the dark room. She could hardly wait 'til the credits began rolling by and tried to pull him out into the hall. He held up a detaining finger, leaving her chewing the inside of her cheek impatiently as he said good-bye to her mother and brother. His hand plucked at her sleeve, and he moved out to the door, yanking on his sneakers as she hovered next to him.

"Come on, gotta tell you something."

She walked beside him out to his car. He stood and stared at her, his gaze tender, and she found herself smiling back at him with no idea what they were grinning about.

"So I talked to your dad, and guess what?" He grabbed her around the waist and spun her around. "He gave me permission to date you!"

"He did?" she squealed, happy face illuminated by the pale moonlight.

"Yeah, he did! Gosh, I was so nervous he'd say no!" He put his hands on her arms and looked happily down into her upturned face. They sat together on the back of his car and talked it over.

"This seems strange, doesn't it?" she asked shyly, letting him hold her hand.

"Hmm, it is though. We don't see each other for weeks and weeks and then bam! We're dating!" Neither of them said anything and looked up at the velvety night sky with its millions of tiny pinpricks of light. "Nothing like a starry night sky," he remarked. He rubbed her am. "Hey, I should be going. We've got school tomorrow and I've got to work. I'm going to have to apply for another job, no more snow you know." He sighed and ran a hand through his hair. "It's hard supporting yourself. But I'm getting along fine."

"OK." He met her eyes and suddenly tipped her face up to his with a hand on the back of her neck.

"Good night," he murmured, touching his lips lightly to hers. "You taste sweet!" He gave a breathy laugh and kissed her deeper. She was still for a long moment, and then gently pushed him away with a self-conscious glance toward the house.

"Shel, what if someone's watching?" The look on his face indicated he could care less if the whole world were watching. He captured her hands in his and stole one more kiss. They slid off, and Sheldon walked round to the driver's side.

"See you tomorrow, Chelle." And he ducked inside. Richelle stood there in the cool night air hugging herself as the car's taillights faded out of sight.

Mondays were always hectic with a new week starting up or so it seemed to Richelle. She stuck to Sheldon like glue as much as she was able to.

Clarisse saw them scribbling notes to each other as they sat together, and the smiles they shared made her furious. Despite all her efforts, the opposite of all she'd been working toward had occurred; they were faster friends than they had been before. And from the looks of it, they were more than just friends. *They must have figured things out,* she thought peevishly.

There was no doubt in her mind that they had when she felt someone take firm hold of her arm and yank her about-face. Sheldon glared down at her with a fire in the set of his face that did not bode well for her. She couldn't even squeak in protest as he roughly led her away from the crowded center of the school, heading down a flight of stairs dragging her behind him.

Not a soul was in the basketball court when he rammed the doors open and shoved her through. The sound of them slamming shut echoed through the empty court, and to Clarisse, it sounded like the gavel striking as she was found guilty and sentenced to her doom.

He turned slowly and faced her, fists dug into his pockets, his eyes black with anger. She tried, but there was nothing to swallow. Frightened? For the first time in a long time, all confidence had fled. Sheldon took a heavy step toward her, dark eyes menacing in the dim light. She backed away.

"How dare you." Anger hissed in the suddenly close air. "How dare you pull a stunt like that on me." The muscles in his jaw clenched, and he advanced. Clarisse scuttled backward, but she moved too fast, and her high heels slipped on the polished floor, and she tripped. Terrified at what he would do in his anger, she began levering herself across the floor with her hands, anything to get away from a punishment justly deserved. He began shouting, his voice gravelly with emotion, magnified by the empty space and coming at the girl seemingly on all sides, echoing inside her head until it drowned out everything, leaving her face to face with her fear. Suddenly, his hand came up violently as if to strike, and she cowered with her arms over her head. Perhaps something in her prone posture struck a chord in him, perhaps not, but after a suspenseful minute of shaking in fear, nothing happened. Cautiously, she lowered an elbow and peeped up from behind it. He was still standing just over her, staring at his upraised hand, face blank. Hastily he shoved it into his pocket and shot her a withering glare.

"Everything about you sickens me." He looked like he wanted to say something else, but his face twisted and he spat on the ground, spinning on his heel, leaving her lying there.

Richelle snuck out of the house late in the afternoon and walked at a fast clip so she was out of sight of anyone at the house. She was worried; she sensed a marked reserve in Sheldon's behavior and his treatment of her. Something was up, and she had every intention of finding out what. A cool breeze snapped her shirt close to her, the loose ends flapping around. It might have been chilly had the sun not been so warm. She was a little out of breath when she walked up the driveway. His car was pulled up close to the garage; obviously, he had to be home. She pulled open the side door and tramped up the rickety wooden stairs.

Sheldon had just finished his homework and was sacked out on the couch. He was depressed and inclined to brood. Finals were fast approaching. Things were crazy with work, and he was having second thoughts about everything, or so it seemed. His head fell into his hands, and he stared darkly at the grain in the wooden floorboards.

A knock at the door shattered his introspection, and his head came up with a jerk. He didn't make a sound, hoping whoever it was would just go away. The door creaked hesitantly open, and a face peered into the room cautiously. Richelle. Everything in him shrank away; he had no desire to talk. He cursed himself silently for leaving the door unlocked. He always locked it!

"Shel, why didn't you answer?" She didn't wait to hear his response and came into the room, kicking off her shoes. His eyes followed her as she walked over to him, but he didn't speak. "Won't you tell me what's going on? Can't we talk about this?" she asked anxiously.

He sighed and severed eye contact. Instantly, she sat beside him, her weight on the little couch causing him to slide into her. He moved over so he wouldn't touch her.

"Shel?" He looked at her, misery etched all over his face. "What on earth is the matter?"

"Richelle, I . . ." He paused. "I don't think we're gonna work." Her eyes widened. "You're not safe with me," he whispered, bowing his head.

"Of course I'm safe with you!" she ejaculated, putting a hand on his knee.

"No, no, you're not! You don't understand. Everyone was right, Chelle. I'm no different than my father!" She reached out and turned his face to look at her.

"Of course, you are. Don't say such things. You are not your father, Sheldon."

He told her what he'd done when he met with Clarisse. She leaned forward, her intense eyes forcing him to meet her gaze.

"Tell me something. Did you hit her?" Confused, he admitted he had not. "From what I've heard of your father, he would've done more than slap her once. Shel, you've got to look at the big picture here!"

"What big picture? This is the whole damn big picture. I'm going to be abusive if you stay with me," he said in despair.

"Hey, cut that out! Stop it, Sheldon!" He looked at her in surprise as she shook him. His eyes slid to the floor as she continued. "You are your own individual person, Shel. You're not the sum of your genes. Who your parents are does not make you who *you* are. Look at me!" She almost pleaded. "You're a new person, Sheldon. You're Christ's. We move on. You can't be held in fear and be so self-focused. You freak out when you almost do something you attribute to your dad! You're a different person, you're you! No one can tell you who you are because you make that yourself. And your identity is in Christ, what He thinks of you, not what other people think. Not even yourself." She paused for a moment. "Look, I'm not excusing your anger. You're responsible for what you did, but you didn't hit her. You didn't allow your anger to get the better of you."

"But it's the thought that counts, right? Chelle, I was so angry. I wanted to hurt her."

"But you didn't. You need to confess this to Jesus, ask His forgiveness, and, Sheldon, move on! Don't dwell in the past of what might have been!" They sat in silence. Sheldon replayed everything she'd said, mulling it over. She was right! He was caught in self-pity. He looked at the girl thoughtfully.

"Do you remember when we first met, how I told you I felt different around you?" She nodded. "How I said when you were with me I felt like I could be free? I still feel that way," he said slowly. "You help me keep perspective." He turned her face toward him with a single finger on her chin. She smiled tremulously.

"It's not me, Shel."

"I know, but you're a candle in the dark. If it weren't for all the time and counsel you're invested in me, I wouldn't be where I am today. You know it's true. You're such a blessing to me."

"I'm glad for that." She relaxed against him as he folded her in his arms.

Chapter 19

The Big Night

Sheldon was pleased with the way the interview with his boss went. He wanted a few more hours a week or he would've had to apply for another part-time job. His boss was perfectly happy to accommodate him and raised his salary along with bumping him up to full time. Sheldon was rather burned out between finals and the late-nights working after school, any time he could fit in. He had bills to pay as well as rent; food wasn't all that cheap, and he didn't want to break into his savings when it wasn't necessary. Less than a week, and he'd finish high school. It was a strange thought to not have to go to school every morning. He took a few days off from work to study. He felt pretty confident he'd pass the exams but would rather be safe than sorry. So he was cooped up hours into the nights, reading, taking notes, drinking quarts of coffee and tea just to stay awake. Cramming mode was on. There was a mutual understanding between him and Richelle, and they didn't see each other the whole week of finals. He didn't give it much thought until they bumped into each other in the hall, and he could see from the look in her eyes that she missed his company.

"We'll make up, Chelle, I promise. Good luck on your finals!" he said before he dashed away.

The whole populace seemed to relax, and you could almost smell the relief in the air when finals were over. Of course, with prom coming up, it wasn't entirely over, and parents took their daughters dress shopping and to salons; hair stylists racked up the cash. And of course, the night of the prom, well, the entire day, they made a killing. Holidays of any sort were always good for business.

Richelle was ecstatic over her dress, but she was stubbornly insistent that Sheldon wouldn't see it even on the hanger before the big night. He found her stubbornness adorable and told her so. But she wouldn't let him see the dress.

Sheldon took out his tux and felt extremely glad he only had to get it pressed after all those months in the back of his closet. He didn't want to drop a hefty sum for a rental. He rang up his grandmother for a little chat and told her that her prediction had come true. She was pleasantly surprised to hear that he and Richelle were dating and insisted on hearing the whole story. So the whole tale tumbled out.

"You know I have to meet her. She must be an extraordinary girl, Shel," she exclaimed when he'd finished.

"Oh, she is, Grammy, she is." She could hear from his voice he was grinning from ear to ear.

At last, the day arrived and such a flurry of preparation! The little town came alive for once; the streets thronged with people, mostly teens hurrying here and there. Beauty parlors were packed. Richelle was thankful she'd scheduled an appointment weeks in advance. Otherwise, she'd never have gotten in.

Sheldon, on the other hand, was mostly bored the whole day until he had to get ready to go. Had to because he couldn't put it off any more without being late to pick Richelle up. Before too long, he pulled into her driveway and killed the motor. He stiffly extracted himself out of the car, making sure he didn't forget the bouquet of soft pink rosebuds he'd bought for Richelle and anxiously checked his suit over for any creases that might have appeared on its starched surface. He cut a dashing figure, and Evan whistled as he held open the door.

"That's one snazzy tux you've got there!" he said teasingly. "Rik is almost ready. I'll run up and tell her you're here. Come on in." Sheldon hastily stepped inside and watched Mr. Callahan march up the stairs. He heard him knock on her door, and his exclamation of obvious admiration made tingles of nervous anticipation race up and down his spine from his head to his toes. He fiddled with his buttons and wondered what he would do if she didn't like roses.

There was a swish of satin skirts and the sight of her standing at the head of the stairway took his breath away. She was stunningly resplendent in a minty green gown. The light sparkled off the rhinestones worked over the bodice, and a few twinkled in the long skirt. An intricate mass of auburn curls were swept up on top of her head, and glittering emerald earrings swung as she started eagerly toward him, the green intensifying her beautiful eyes. A matching necklace clung to her throat above the sweetheart cut of her gown, her pink lips curving into a shy smile that didn't even try to hide her delight in seeing him.

"My gosh. You're beautiful!"

"Do you like it? I hoped you would!" She turned slowly around for his approval. "Isn't it pretty? I had to get it. And your tux, I do adore it! It's even better than in the pictures!"

"It's absolutely gorgeous. You do, do you?" He looked at her, taken in by her beauty. "Wait, it needs something more." He pulled a rosebud out of its neighbors and nicked off most of the slender stem. It nestled in her lustrous curls.

"Hey, you two wanna take some pictures before you leave?" Her dad grinned at them, camera slung over his arm. It would've been difficult to refuse him.

"Oh yes! Under the tree in the garden?"

"Yeah, that would be nice. You sentimental thing, you!"Sheldon whispered to her as they trooped out into the garden. It was beautiful outside, so alive and green. He couldn't help flashing back to another day when he saw her settled on the same old swing and stood gazing at her raptly before he moved up just behind her, his hand over hers on the thick twisted rope. A tiny curl had escaped at the back of her neck; her perfume wafted up to him. He almost forgot to smile as Evan's finger clicked down, and the picture was taken. Apparently, the older man had a secret passion for photography, for he knew some great poses and almost made them late as he took shot after shot, insisting each time for "one more." He'd even made them hold each other as if they were dancing.

"You know what I think?" Sheldon said as he handed her into the car and shut the door. She watched him walk round to his side, wondering. "Your dad is a hopeless romantic. He must have taken fifty pictures!" he exclaimed as he pulled the seat belt across his chest and secured it.

"Fifty?" She laughed. "Maybe twenty. You do love to exaggerate."

"Same difference." He laughed.

"Come on, Shel, we're going to be late!"

"I know, I know! I can't begin to tell you how beautiful you are in that dress." She flushed with pleasure.

"You're not so bad looking yourself," she replied bashfully, and he grinned at her.

"Thanks for the compliment. I'm speechless." They laughed.

Disco balls hung from the ceiling, reflecting colored lights and shooting checkered patterns over the dancer's faces. A live cover band provided the music.

"Quite good, aren't they?" Sheldon shouted over the din. He'd plied her with all sorts of sweets and desserts before the dancing and felt very much at ease as couples began moving into position.

"Yes, I like it!" Richelle said breathlessly. His hand hovered at the curve of her waist, just touching her, and he took her hand in his other confidently. She was astonished. "You know how to dance?" He shrugged, ungraceful in the moment.

"Well, I didn't want to be unprepared. Last hurrah of my high school days, you know." He was just chattering to cover up his embarrassment and divert her.

"You took lessons?" It was really more a statement than a question. He glanced around the room vaguely, his face green then blue in the flashing colored lights. She couldn't help a foolish silly smile. "You're going to have to teach me if we're going to be legitimately dancing." Swaying couples weaved around them, postures intimate and nearly passing as embracing. Sheldon instructed her in the proper stance and slowly led her out onto the floor. She found he was a sure and firm leader as he guiding her through the steps.

"You're catching on fast!" he said encouragingly as she began to follow his lead with more semblance of her natural grace. She gained confidence quickly, and soon, they were waltzing across the dance floor, admittedly with a fair amount of bungled mistakes, but they got better as the night wore on.

"This is so much fun!" she exclaimed.

"Yes, it is. Are you thirsty?" He glanced at the refreshment table, longing to dip into the huge crystal punch bowl. She nodded and hooked her pinkie through his as he maneuvered through the crowd toward it.

They leaned back against the wall, grateful for the solid firm support as they sipped the fizzy punch, observing the activity on the dance floor. Sheldon watched one guy spin his girlfriend around much too fast and thanked his lucky stars the material was fitted just tight enough to prevent a sudden unseemly flare out. Or maybe she would've deserved the humiliation for having worn such a flimsy, skimpy creation in the first place. He liked the rustling noise Richelle's silky gown made when she moved and found new appreciation for its beauty and modesty. He took her empty disposable glass and chucked it into the trash, taking her hand as they began dancing once more.

So many bodies made the air hot and close, and after a few thrilling whirls around the room, her heavier sweeping dress made Richelle long for a breeze of fresh cool air. The experience of dancing with Sheldon was more exhilarating than she'd dreamed it would be, but after a bit, he noticed the way her eyes kept sliding away from his to gaze yearningly at the door. Gradually, he drifted toward it with a purpose, his hand firm on her waist.

"Come on, let's get out of here for a while." He grasped her hand, and no one noticed them ease out the door. Richelle in tow, he dashed up the stairs and made for the red illuminated exit sign. "There, ever so much better out here, isn't it? Can you breathe now?" He could see her teeth gleam in a smile as his eyes slowly adjusted to the dark.

"Yes," she said, taking a deep breath. "It's so hot in there!"

"Yeah, tell me about it. Hey, I got an idea, come on,"

"Where are we going?"

"You'll see when we get there," He said with a laugh and set off across the parking lot, directing their steps up a gentle rise and into the woods surrounding the campus. He didn't speak until the buildings disappeared behind them, swallowed up by the tall trees. Richelle walked close to him, hanging on his arm as she tripped carefully after him, hefting up her generous skirts with one hand.

"Ah, here's the path. Don't worry. We'll be there soon." He tried to set a vigorous pace, but her little silver heels were less suited to hiking than his shoes were, and he slowed to an even walk.

"Just around the bend now," he spoke eagerly. "I found this place years ago when I was a little kid. I've never seen anyone up here before, and I doubt if any of the kids know about it." The faint trail wound around and ended on the top of a grassy hill overlooking the town. It was like something out of a painting, stretched before them as a canvas, lights twinkling like so many candles. "See, over there's the school, and see that tall spire?" He pointed. "That's the church. When it's light out, you can identify many of the buildings."

"It's so pretty!" she said, listening to the wind soughing softly in the trees crowning the hill. With a contented sigh, Sheldon flopped down in the long springy grass and tipped his head back to look up at her as she stood uncertainly.

"Come on, sit down," he admonished.

"Oh, but I couldn't. I'd stain my dress," she objected. Sheldon slipped out of his jacket, spreading it out on the ground.

"There." He patted it invitingly. She folded her skirts about her protectively and sat beside him.

"What a night!" he started out conversationally. "You were perfect." His smile was irresistibly sweet.

"No," she said. "I just had an excellent instructor." He nearly snorted but drew a caressing hand over the side of her head as she nestled up to him. He pulled her close to him and gently pressed a kiss in her silky curls. She slid her arms around his neck, her skin smooth and warm, her perfume rich, floral, and heady. Perhaps it went to his head, but her soft lips were being kissed gently, the intoxicating sweetness closing her eyes without her being conscious of having done so. "Shel!" she whispered earnestly and then gave in to the passion welling up within her breast. He was taken aback at first and then responded wholeheartedly, returning her kiss for kiss. She leaned against him, running her hand up and down his back, cradled close to his chest, loving the rapid beat of his heart.

"I wish we could stay here like this forever," he murmured into her hair. She held him tighter.

The cool night breeze sent a chill over her bare arms, and she tucked her hands in between their warm bodies. Her skin was cold as he touched her lightly, and he wrapped his arms closer about her. "Do you want to go back down?" She shook her head decisively.

"Oh no. I'm fine. Please, I don't want to go," she spoke imploringly and he couldn't have refused even if he had been so inclined.

"Me neither. But aren't you cold?" She turned her back to his comforting firm body and pulled his arms snugly around her waist, leaning back to plant a soft kiss on his cheek.

"I want to stay here with you." He didn't argue anymore and nuzzled into her neck.

The necklace's delicate clasp was undone, and it lay forgotten in the grass as he became more adventurous. Not a breath of air escaped her lips as he slid the thin straps off her shoulders with heavy hands, and his hot mouth was on her neck, the moment intense as she felt frozen in time, oblivious to anything other than the sensation of his closeness and his caressing hands on her shoulders. She felt so small next to him as he gripped her arms and kissed her mouth with an urgency so firm and demanding, she knew his lips would leave bruises. Not that the thought so much as crossed her mind as she was drowning in his earnest passion. She felt like a leaf swept along by a swift current, powerless.

"Shel," she managed to get a word in edgewise, "Shel!" She turned and buried her face in his neck. "I love you." He sat perfectly still. Gently he stroked the velvety skin of her shoulders, running his thumbs slowly up and down, up and down. His voice came calmly, to his surprise given the raging inferno within.

"You mean the world to me. I wouldn't have it any other way." She pulled back, and he gazed into the liquid depths of her stormy green eyes, their color barely discernible in the glow of the early summer moon. Her eyelashes fluttered as he traced his finger down her sweet little nose. He loved her nose, straight and fine, the nostrils wide and sensitive. He kissed the very tip, and she giggled, quickly kissing him back.

He lay back on the grass with a sigh, elbows cocked up at the sky, careless of his white shirt. She looked at him with a glowing affection.

"Do you think they're still dancing down there?" Her face was turned toward the twinkling lights far below, but he detected a slight wistful note in her voice.

"Why not dance up here?" He was on his feet before she had time to react and held out his hand to help her up. She carefully smoothed her skirts, rhinestones glittering in the pale moonlight. Slowly, he guided her once more through the steps of the waltz, and then they were flying, faster and faster, their delighted laughter echoing across the wooded valley. Breathless, she leaned against him, the adrenaline leaving her drowsy, energy depleted.

"I don't think I could do that again! It must be so late! Everyone is probably going home now." She laid her head on his chest and rested her hands on his shirtfront, the fingertips of one hand hooked over the edge of his breast pocket as they swayed in time to the rustle of the leaves in the breeze. His hands rounded her waist, and she felt his hair brush her forehead as he let his head rest affectionately on hers.

"If they're dancing like this, they either left a long time ago or are still at it. I could do this all night. Waltzing actually takes effort."

She didn't reply and after a while began to lean further and further, and when he caught her from toppling over, he figured if he waited any longer he'd have to carry her back to the car.

"Hey, wakey wakey." His breath stirred the wispy hair over her ears, and she opened her eyes sleepily, holding on to him as she stepped away to keep her balance. "We gotta go home, Chelle." He bent and retrieved his jacket and would've missed her emeralds if their sparkle hadn't caught his eye.

It was midnight; the parking lot had a stray car or two here and there, a few couples loitering around with no thought of leaving in the near future. Richelle sank into the passenger seat, her body aching with exhaustion, but she was blissfully happy.

Sheldon kept yawning as he drove, eyelids drooping in a valiant effort to keep awake; even in this state, they were safe, for not many people were out at such a late hour, and Sheldon was alert in a blurry sort of way. The moon shone silvery on the road, on the houses, and the streetlamps were yellow pools of light as they wove through the streets to Richelle's house.

He threw the Honda in park and relaxed in the seat, letting out a long sigh.

"Tired?" He looked up, blond hair fanning over half of his handsome face.

"Yes, but every moment was so worth it." He let go of the steering wheel and traced the curve of her cheek.

"I had a wonderful night with you, thank you."

"Welcome, Chelle. Thank you. You made everything perfect." She smiled at him, her fingers twining through his over the console.

He walked with her to the front door and held back as she went up the steps. She paused with her hand on the doorknob.

"Good night, Sheldon," she said, suddenly bashful, but she didn't move. There was a question quavering in her eyes that he couldn't say no to, and in a second, he was beside her, drawing her into a close embrace with his cheek pressed against hers.

"Good night." She didn't resist his kiss and was left aching for more when he walked back down the path and drove away. Wearily, she turned the handle and shuffled into the dark, quiet house.

Not a soul was awake, and she pulled off her heels, tired feet sinking luxuriously into the carpet as she tiptoed up the stairs to her room.

Her arm at an awkward angle, she fiddled with an elusive zipper, managing to snag it in groping fingertips, and the gown sank to the floor as she allowed it to slip off her tired body. The scent of Sheldon's masculine cologne clung to her skin, drifting up to her, evasive and tantalizing. She let down her hair, ruddy curls tumbling past her slender shoulders nearly to her waist. She pulled on a T-shirt and sweat pants and was asleep before her head touched the pillow.

Chapter 20

Burning Summer's Heat

Life was strangely different with no school, less demanding, and Sheldon found himself with more time on his hands. He took a full work week, his shift stretching from eight to four, sometimes working weekends, but even then, he still managed to have time to pursue his goals. He hadn't really given his goals much thought; things had been so hectic over the past few months that he just hadn't had the time to consider. Honestly, any thought of future-orientated plans hadn't even crossed his mind. Now he had to figure some things out.

He was sitting outside at a picnic table eating lunch at work and fell to daydreaming. There were so many things he didn't know, so many concepts foreign to him; he wanted to learn more about the God he served, more about the Christian life. There was a vast wealth of knowledge written by so many saints over the ages, it was staggering. *Where to begin?? I guess it doesn't it really matter, as long as I start somewhere,* he thought, chewing on a piece of cold pizza.

So newly settled in an apartment aptly suited to his needs, he didn't feel inclined to strike out on his own anywhere just yet. He didn't want to move away from his little family that had tucked him under their wing, or his grandmother. And Richelle, he knew he'd pine for her if he had to move away from her. She was the light in his small world, and he loved her with every fiber of his being. Moving was not an option at this time in his life, but traveling, now, there was a thought, which required money. He pushed the wishful thought on the back burner for later.

His work got him by; it wasn't the greatest. He didn't mind it but couldn't see himself working in a grocery store for the rest of his days. There had to be something he was interested in. But he couldn't think of anything he'd love doing, a dream job had never occurred to him in survival mode. He was a fighter; he'd do whatever was necessary to stay alive and wasn't one to look for the path of least resistance. Sure, some people had jobs they loved doing, but somebody had to do the mundane things in life; it just wasn't for everybody. He bit off the last bite of crust and rolled up the brown paper bag, standing and crumpling it into a trash can.

College? He'd decided to take a gap year and work, maybe not even go, for way up here, everyone was a nobody. No one was a somebody; no one from this tiny town in the middle of nowhere had ever made it to somewhere. Life went on, college degree or not. *Anyways,* he thought as he took the place of another guy behind a register, *I just didn't have the money to put myself through college.* It was astronomical.

He flashed a smile at a customer and gave her a pleasant greeting as he automatically reached for the first item on the conveyor belt. The woman's weekly groceries were quickly passed through his expert hands to the bagger. Sheldon shot him a disapproving glare as he began to put a head of lettuce in with dish detergent and bathroom spray.

"Hey, you wanna keep everything in categories," he explained in low tones so the boy wouldn't be unnecessarily humiliated. "Keep cleaners by themselves, and produce should go into a separate bag. And cans go with cans," he added in for good measure. Who knows what the loaf of bread would have suffered if he hadn't intervened for its precarious and uncertain welfare.

Kids these days! he thought with a roll of the eyes, *would they ever learn?* He rang up the sale and inserted the lady's check into his machine, which ate it up and spat it back out duly stamped all over. He handed her the receipt, and she lugged her full cart away as he turned to the next person in line.

The hours ticked by, broken by runs to the coffee machine for quick spurts of liquid energy. Some days were downright enjoyable if your bagger was talkative, and he'd made a few fun acquaintances this way. He and one guy, Josh, were even so far as to consider the other a tentative friend.

He was an amiable young man in his very early twenties, two or three years older than Sheldon. He was a good worker and worked a few jobs, but he was always promptly on time. His sunny smile lit up everyone's day, and he had expressive brown eyes that could speak for themselves. Sheldon always looked around for his dark close-cropped curly head bent over his rack of plastic bags when he came in. The boy worked irregular hours, more often than not arriving within a few hours of Sheldon leaving. He told him once he worked for a landscape company besides this job. He said he loved being out of doors, but it was hard work.

"Makes this look downright pathetic," he joked, hefting a full pack of soda around to the back of a topped-off cart. Eventually, Sheldon learned he supported himself and his ailing mother, along with his younger sister. "She should be getting a job here soon," he said cheerily, wishing a customer a good day. "She's just terrified of the whole thing, but she gets it. She wants to work here so she'll be with me some of the time. Don't suppose you could look out for her sometimes?" He was jamming boxes of pasta into a bag and didn't look up as he asked the question.

"If she gets the job, sure, I'll do that for you."

"Thanks, pal," Josh said, thankfulness ringing in his tone. "She's just so shy. If she knew she had someone watching her back, it would mean a lot to both of us."

"Yeah, I get you." Sheldon leaned his hip against the counter, glad for a rest when no one made a beeline for their register. He looked contemplatively at the older boy. "You should come over sometime and hang out if you'd like." Josh grinned.

"Really, that would be cool. If I ever get a chance, I'll let you know. You're a cool guy," he remarked as someone else came to take his place, and he moved away with a cheerful wave.

Sheldon wasn't so sure about that but was glad his invitation had been accepted. Josh was an interesting person, and there was a certain quality to him that Sheldon felt akin to. He wasn't afraid to work, that one. He'd do what he had to to support his loved ones, his family. What a precious thing a family was! You didn't know what a blessing it was to even have one until yours was taken from you, leaving you no better off than an orphan.

He worked overtime, and the sun was a dull orange sphere burning on the edge of the horizon when he trudged up the stairs and unlocked his door, chucking his keys carelessly on the table. The air was heavy and hot, giving full credit to the humid month of July. He flipped on his AC until and went to take a cool shower.

The living room was a few degrees cooler when he came out, clad in a loose pair of cotton shorts. He rifled through a short stack of DVDs he'd rented from the library and inserted one into the reader, sacking out on the couch in front of the wide-screen TV. He was ready to do something mindless and be entertained. Two hours of high-speed suspense and action ensued, and then he poked around in his scantily supplied fridge for supper. There was cheese, so he made a grilled cheese sandwich. A puddle of ketchup on the corner of the plate, and dinner was served.

He felt sorry for his phone as he texted Richelle with greasy fingers, but he could always wipe the screen clean. As always, she was overjoyed to hear from him. Work demanded much of his time, and he rarely texted her to extent anymore. She asked him if he was alone. He blinked, and his thumbs flew in response. Who would he be with anyways? The phone buzzed in a video call invite. A smile lurked about the corners of his mouth as he accepted, and her pretty face appeared on the little screen.

"Hey!" she said, tucking her long hair behind her ears, earrings sparkling.

"Hey, you! What's up?"

"Oh, nothing much. Just finished dinner. I'm up in my room now. Wanted to see you. How was work?" He grinned.

"Meh. Nothing out of the ordinary. Oh, wait, did I tell you about Josh?"

"Josh?" She looked confused. "No, you didn't. Is he someone at work?"

"Yup, he is. He's the nicest guy ever, and we're kinda sorta friends. You might get to meet him soon." He told her the little he knew about his background and about the conversation they'd had. "I think you'd really like him. Might start up a gang of our own friends if his sister is as cool as he is." He grinned.

"Oh, he has a sister? That's cool! I'd love to meet them, Shel. Josh sounds great. I'm glad you've made a friend at work." She smiled into the camera, making it appear like she was looking right into his eyes. It was a little unnerving.

"Yeah, me too." He lay on his stomach and propped his chin upon his fist. "You know, I've never seen him around. I'll bet they're new to town. Well, relatively new."

"How long has he been working with you?"

"Oh, maybe two months. You loving this weather?" He changed the subject, grinning as she stuck out her tongue as if it was ninety-five degrees in the room.

"It's getting just brutal. New Hampshire was supposed to be cold!" she exclaimed, flopping onto her bed and back into the cushions. "We're going to have to go to the beach soon. I haven't been to the ocean up here, and it's half an hour away!"

"No! You're not serious!" She nodded vigorously, eyebrows raised in acknowledgment of the inexcusable pitifulness of her deprived existence. "Wow, name the day and the hour, my dear, I'll have to take you. Hey, don't suppose you like water parks?"

"Water parks? Oh, I adore them!" He propped the phone against the armrest and laughed.

"Look at that, we've got two potential dates!" They both had great big silly grins glued on their faces. "It would be an all day thing, but it sure would be a blast." He had a sudden inspiration.

"Hey, what do you say we get together with Natalie again, have her come down and I invite Josh?" Her face lit up.

"That's a great idea! What about his sister too?"

"Oh, I don't know. I thought about, well, what would we do about Matt? I've only got so much room in my car, ya know, girl?" She screwed up her nose.

"Yeah, you're right. He'd never forgive us if we left him behind. Talk to Josh about it. See what he thinks!"

"Yeah, I'll put it out there. Just so he has time to think about it. Wonder if he works Sundays," he mused, chewing on his thumb. Richelle was clearly happy.

"Natalie will be ecstatic! Oh, did I tell you, I told her we've been dating, and she said she predicted it ever since I first told her about you. I was crazy about you." She laughed.

"What's with the past tense?" he teased, unable to turn down the opportunity. She made a face.

"Was, am, will, always will, it's all the same." He snickered.

"I'm glad you're so attached."

"If I was sitting there, I'd smack you."

"Oh, I know you would. So I'm taking full advantage of your absence." His eyes danced wickedly.

"Oh, you're bad. What am I supposed to do with you?" He laughed as she rolled her eyes.

"Anything you'd like. Just don't be too cruel."

"Are you always so flirty or are you just tired and silly?"

"You tell me."

"You're impossible," she shot back, but they both knew she was loving every minute of it. He sighed.

"Yeah, I'm really tired. What's new? It's been a long week. Tomorrow, I think I'm working at three or something like that. Till late. And I never work Sundays. I get to sleep in tomorrow!" He touched his fist to the screen in an imitation of a fist bump.

"Sleep, glorious sleep!" she crowed, laughing. He grinned, turning over on his back, holding the phone over his head. Richelle couldn't help blushing when she saw he wasn't wearing a shirt.

"You doing anything tomorrow?" A thrill flashed through her.

"You know how Saturdays are. I'm always free after lunch. Mom and I are usually done cleaning the house then, and we all hang out and do whatever." He saw the expectancy written all over her face.

"Well, I was thinking." He played with his earring. "I've got a few hours tomorrow. Want to hang out and drive around, maybe go somewhere together?" Her beautiful smile flooded in like a sunrise.

"Absolutely! Of course, I do!"

"Sweet! Can't wait to see my girl again." This tone of voice was for her ears alone, and she loved it.

"Can't wait to see you," she replied softly. How did she manage to make her words sound like a caress?

He yearned to have her with him and gazed at her raptly. She was so beautiful. Her auburn ringlets, tumbling in spirals over her shoulders, her green eyes, changing like the sea, her sweet full lips, that adorable chin, the dimples when she smiled like she was now—why she was the most beautiful girl he'd ever seen! It was a beauty deeper than her rosy skin too. Sometimes, he forgot himself and called her his little treasure because she meant so much to him. The longer he knew her, the deeper he grew to love her, and he cherished the moments they spent together, whether alone or with her dear family.

They talked for hours until the lighting became bad, and Richelle couldn't really see him very well. By then they'd exhausted all conversation and wished each other a good night.

They'd arranged for him to come over for lunch and then go out after. She couldn't wait. Dates with Sheldon were always so much fun, even if they just sat in the park and talked, it didn't matter. Just being with him made all the difference. It had been too long since they'd seen each other last. She'd been finishing her driving lessons and had a driver's test at the end of the month. Only a few short weeks, and she could have her license! It would be good to be able to drive without waiting for her parents to decide they wanted to go places. And of course, Sheldon had been working like a maniac since they'd finished school, and it would be nice to be able to go see him without him having to drive to get her.

She sighed and flipped through her music library, playing an old country artist. When she'd finished picking up the few items strewn around the floor, she took a volume from her bookcase and became absorbed in a fantasy world of knights and ladies, good and evil, usurpers and magicians, love and betrayal.

Sheldon puttered around the cluttered apartment. Busy weeks had had their toll on the upkeep of the place, and it was in sad disorder. Luckily for the state of things, Sheldon was no slob and hated messes nearly as much as having to clean up after a week's worth of them. It's amazing how quickly things disintegrate into sorry confusion when you're caught up in other things. He ran a sink full of soapy hot water and dumped the dishes in. The broom poked into dusty corners and collected a dirt pile of astonishing size. After giving the counters a good wipe down, his little apartment was looking vastly improved. Sheldon did up the dishes and toweled them dry before he stowed them away in the cupboards. His bedroom and the living room were in need of a little tidying, and soon, he was curled up on the couch with a book by a well-known pastor named Tim Keller. His straightforward style made difficult concepts easier to grasp, and Sheldon was fascinated by the treasures he uncovered in the man's inspired works.

The sun sank deeper, and the distant mountains swallowed the smoldering orb in a dusky embrace. The shadows grew longer in the dark room, and yellow lamplight pooled over the page he was reading.

Sheldon retired at ten and lay awake with a heart full of amazement and gratitude. He could sense his faith growing deeper. Life was good. Just to know he was held in the palm of the God who'd made him . . . who'd never let him go . . . His eyelids drifted shut, and his chest rose up and down in a constant rhythm.

"Anywhere in particular you'd like to go?" he questioned as they walked up from the backyard through the garden. The day had dawned blistering hot, and their shirts already stuck to their backs.

"I haven't given it much thought," she admitted, running her hand around the dry basin of the birdbath as they passed. "I don't care as long as your AC is on!"

"Yeah, it is a hot one!" He squinted in the glare of the sun reflecting off the shiny paint of his car. "Here, hop in, I'll blast the AC." The inside of the car felt like that of an oven, and instantly, her sweaty clothes adhered to the leather seat. Relief came quickly, cool air blowing out over their hot faces. They cruised around town for a bit, and then Sheldon headed for the open country on a sudden whim.

"Where are we going?" He glanced over innocently and then returned his attention to the road. Heat waves rolled off it, shimmering in the sun. It was brutal out.

"Oh, I just had an idea. It's too hot to go traipsing about town."

"You and your ideas," She shook her head. Sheldon was subject to sudden attacks of caprice; he was rather impulsive. Richelle had come to accept this aspect of his character, strange because he was so steady in other respects. But his best ideas were the product of a sudden impulse, and she'd learned by now he wouldn't tell her where he was taking her until they arrived. He seemed immensely pleased with himself, and his Aviators couldn't hide the elated cast of his features. She toyed with the radio and finally settled on a good station.

"Oh, I like this song!" His teeth flashed between his widespread lips.

"Mhm, I can tell. Is there a song you *don't* like?" he teased, poking her playfully in the ribs. She giggled and squirmed away.

"Well, yeah! Stop it, stop it, that tickles!"

He loved it when she dissolved into helpless laughter. It didn't occur often, and he didn't want to stop but figured he could wait unless he wanted them both to die in a car accident.

"You always pick the worst times," she sniffed, running her hand over her nose.

"Don't I always." It was probably a good thing. "Oh, I remembered from a previous conversation involving cliff gliding that you're not afraid of heights?" She flipped her ponytail over her shoulder, staring at him intensely, but she was unable to perceive his expression through his tinted shades.

"No, not very. Just don't ask me to entrust life and limb to a little rope dangling over a sheer cliff, and I'll be just dandy." Her dry humor made him laugh.

"I won't ever ask to you do that, rest assured. I'm with you on this one. Couldn't pay me! I've seen some crazy things on TV, some people are insane. You wouldn't believe the risks they take!"

"Oh, I know! They're so daredevil it's unnerving. They think they're invincible or something. People never think the horror stories they hear might be a possibility in their own lives. But things can happen so quick, there's just so many things that could go wrong!" He nodded and bit his bottom lip as he pulled to the side of the lonely road. "Where are we?" she asked as he unbuckled his seat belt and propped the door open with one flip-flop shod foot.

"Come on!" He looked like a grinning bug in those glasses, an adorable one at that. With a smothered laugh, she followed suit and stood behind him, pulling her tank top down over the top of her jean shorts. They crossed the road, not a car in sight, and plunged into the sparse forest. Gradually, a dull roar fell on their ears; the roar of a river or a waterfall, Richelle realized. She looked at Sheldon quizzically. "You and I are going for a little swim, girly."

"But, but, in these clothes?" she sputtered. He gave her a look which indicated that she'd asked a stupid question and the answer should be obvious.

It was a tumbling wide waterfall, cascading over a long sloping drop, spray shimmering in a hundred rainbows. The water poured into a deep green pool cupped in a small natural excavation in the sandy cliffs before it sped off in its course down the river. The little spot was obscured from view until you were directly upon it, and the beauty of it was stunning, the sheer walls of rock plunging down into the foaming green water. The play of colors in the waterfall were mesmerizing. Sheldon touched her shoulder.

"You coming it? Dunno about you, but I'm hot!"

"We both know that, Sheldon," she teased. He shook his head, stripping off his shirt and throwing it in a heap along with his shades and car keys, chucking his flip-flops after. She was hesitant. "Don't tell me you're scared." He crossed his arms, chewing his lip in excited anticipation, as well as impatience.

"Is it very deep?"

"Nah, maybe twenty feet at the most, straight drop where we're standing. Over there," he pointed "is a shelf you can sit on and climb out back up here. It's perfectly safe, Chelle. I'm right here." He shifted from one barefoot to the other on the rocky burning sand. She kicked off her flip-flops and pulled out her ponytail, hair loose and free. "Ready?" His face was alive with excitement, and he took her hand as he stepped to the edge of the pool. He jumped before she had quite prepared herself. The rush of air as they fell, Sheldon's whoop of pure glee, then the brisk cool water closing over her head. She let go of his hand, opening her eyes under water to see the air forced from her lungs rising in transparent bubbles to the surface. She fought her way back up, kicking her legs like a comical imitation of a frog.

"Whew!" Sheldon's head broke through the surface, spraying droplets of water in all directions. "Is it cold in here or what?" He blew heavily through his nose. She flashed him a grin.

"You'll get used to it fast."

"Yeah, we will." In a few sure, strong strokes, he reached her, knees bumping into hers as he treaded water.

"Why didn't you take me here before?" she asked, wiping water out of her eyes.

"I hadn't thought of it until we were driving aimlessly around wasting gas. I did a fair amount of exploring these parts a few years ago, just haven't been here in a while. I love it." He glanced around them.

"It is beautiful." The falls weren't so loud in the pool, and they could hear each other distinctly without having to shout. Sheldon floated on his back, drifting around the little pool luxuriously, eyes closed. She played with the idea and then couldn't contain herself any longer. He inhaled lungful of water as she pushed him under, and he frantically came alive from his lethargic spell and thrashed to the surface, sputtering and coughing. She was laughing so hard that her effort to get away as he gave determined chase was weak at best and he returned the favor. He dunked her a second time for good measure as she came up for air.

"Sheldon! Stop, I can't breathe!" she gasped, still laughing. Her hair was plastered to her head, water streaming over her face as she tried to wipe it away and kept slipping back under water. He held her up as she caught her breath, both of them laughing.

They adjusted quickly to the change in temperature; the sun was hot, the day was young, and they had nearly three hours to spend together. Time passed, but they were oblivious to anything but one another and the fun they were having, happy laughter bouncing off the walls of the rocky cliffs to be drowned in the roar of the rushing water.

Richelle clambered out up on the ledge of sun-baked rock and dangled her feet in the cool water. Sheldon wasn't finished swimming and took a few laps around the enclosure. He popped up close to her and swam over, his chin dipping into the water and making a V-shaped trail behind him as the water curled away. He pulled himself up beside her and then scaled the wall deftly, standing at the very edge, measuring the distance between himself and the rippling water. He poised for a heartbeat, arms extended over his dripping head, and then leaped, arching gracefully though the air. He broke the surface, speeding like an arrow just out of sight, his skin pale in the dark water. The dive was executed perfectly, the only evidence of his presence a steady trail of white bubbles and widening ripples lapping against the stone. She saw him bob up at the opposite end of the pond and strike out across it.

With a fluid, easy movement of his muscular arms, he was beside her, the touch of his body cold after the warmth of the sun and the rock. Gooseflesh shot over her skin, and she shed away, rubbing her arms vigorously. He grinned and lay gingerly back on the ledge, the heat burning his bare back momentarily, and he drew a sharp hissing breath at the contact.

"Ouch, that's hotter than I expected!" But it had passed, and he was already accustomed to it. She looked down at him, smiling.

"Yeah, but it feels so good!" She had a shower hair, towel-dried appearance, her hair drying quickly, and her coral tank top clinging to her trim figure. Slender and lovely, his summer queen. "Do we have to leave soon?" she asked quietly, hating to bring up the subject. His hand flopped lazily against his stomach.

"Oh no, we got a while yet." He sat up, leaning back on his elbows, kicking his feet in the water, splashing them both. Playfully, she splashed back, hitting his feet with her own. Grinning, he held on to the rocky shelf and paddled water steadily all over her, soaking her drying clothes.

In the natural course of things, he was pushed in, and he grabbed her ankles and pulled her in after, dunking them both as he held onto her. They chased each other the length and breadth of the pool. She'd wriggle free for an instant; then he'd catch her, tickling her until her laughter rang out. In the climax, she whirled in the water, slamming into him with the full force of her momentum, knocking the wind out of his lungs. Her smooth leg brushed against his, and he paused, watching her strike lithely across the small pond, inviting him to give chase.

In a flash, his mood changed, the levity disappearing as his desires morphed into something more serious. Not hearing him splashing in pursuit, she glanced round and stopped, seeing him remain stationary in the water, sending it in wide ripples around him as he treaded it. He began moving slowly toward her as if she was a skittish colt that would bolt if he was too fast. She hesitated, her eyes wide, then he was beside her. Contact broke the spell and he moved swiftly then, his legs tangling through hers as he pressed her against the stony wall, the solid rock holding them afloat in the water. Her curvy waist seemed to flow with the water into rounded hips, the satiny skin of her thighs warm against his open palms. Ready, willing and yielding lips asked tremulously for a kiss, and she gave in, swept away in the red-hot fire invoked by his insistent mouth. The water closed over their heads, the silence enfolding them, not a sound in the liquid world. Her hair streamed behind her in the gentle current, ethereal, her eyes searching his hungrily, bubbles escaping from parted lips rosy from contact with his. He reached for her, and she came willingly to him, her pliant body seeming to melt into his. His hands on her hips locked them together as he kissed her again.

They lay on the ledge drying in the sunshine, her head on his bare chest, one leg across his. She watched the play in the muscles as he reached an arm over and stroked her back, lingering on the downstroke soothingly. He gave a sudden lurch and then hooked the arm round her waist and gently pulled her up as he propped back against the wall. "I'm sorry. I shouldn't have . .," she murmured, sitting up. His mouth quirked.

"Not your fault, I shouldn't have invited it." He held her gaze, forcing himself to look at her, knowing full well the struggle it had been. "Chelle—stuff like that, we gotta help each other out!" He shrugged. "Things aren't helped by, well, you know, I liked lying here, but . . ." His cheeks flushed red.

"I understand everything you're trying to say." She drew her knees up to her chest, looking at him, a question blossoming in their troubled depths. Her lips parted but not a sound came out.

"What is it?" he asked, anxious lest there be any secrets between them. He wanted to be straightforward with her, and she with him, and the hesitancy between them had to be overcome.

"Well," she bit her lip "what we just did, did that make it more difficult for you?" She looked at the deep green water. Difficult. She was asking if he felt a pull, an urge that was hard to say no to? He knew the full extent of her tentative inquiry. He looked at her, her slim arms drawn tight around her lightly tanned legs, little feet splayed out on the rocky shelf.

"I wouldn't be a guy if I didn't feel the way you make me feel sometimes, Chelle. I . . . I don't know . . . I guess the water made it different. It was, easier, I . . ." Two red faces peered studiously into the dark depths of the pool. "I shouldn't have . . . Oh, darn it all, Chelle! Let's face it. I'm sorry! Sorry for putting you into a vulnerable situation. Sorry for being lax in my defenses, I swear it won't happen again! I shouldn't have touched you like that or even began to lie down, and I shouldn't have invited you to either." His pupils had dilated, and his eyes were midnight, the crush of emotions giving themselves away and leaving a telltale story in his eyes.

"We were wrong," she stated simply and then looked him squarely in the eyes. "Do you not want to . . . kiss . . . anymore?" She ran the tip of her tongue over her lips, still freshly stinging from his. He pushed his hand over the length of his face.

"No. I . . . Chelle, ignoring it, this passion, covering it over, won't make it go away. Yeah, it is passion. It's a strong term, but it's what I feel. But what we've been doing, it isn't helping." He paused, collecting his thoughts. "Kissing you, I mean there's nothing wrong with it, Chelle, but too much of anything can be unhealthy. Do you get what I mean?" She nodded slowly. "I just feel like the more we do it, the less special it will become. It's all a beautiful, wonderful, thrilling thing, but I don't ever want it to become the old familiar same-old, same-old." He shook his head and pulled her face up to look at him with a finger on her chin. "Can you understand that? Am I making an ounce of sense? Tell me if I'm doing the right thing! I feel like I am."

"You're making perfect sense, Shel. You're right." She flipped a pebble into the pool. "Anyways, the less we kiss, the more special it will be when we do." She smiled faintly and was silent for a while. He didn't speak. "Thank you." It was so soft that he wasn't sure if he'd heard right. "Thank you for being a man and saying no when I couldn't. You're like no one I've ever met. I . . . I don't deserve to be your girlfriend." Her eyes filled with tears.

"Oh, don't be silly!" he ejaculated, scooping her up in his arms, rocking her gently. "You're a lovely girl, and it's a *privilege* to even be your friend. I wouldn't trade you in for anyone else in the world. You know that." He held her tight and then pulled back, smiling at her as she sniffed and wiped her eyes. "We'd better go now. I have to get changed for work."

Chapter 21
Brothers in Arms

He saw her look back at him from the doorway. She raised her hand to wave, her mouth curved in a halfhearted smile, and he beeped the horn as he drove past her house.

He hoped his landlady wouldn't see him sneak shirtless into the garage. She was one of those ridiculously silly women who pretended to be scandalized by everything. If she was born in another era, she might have been constantly fainting and inhaling smelling salts, rather like Aunt Pitty in *Gone with the Wind*, but she made due with pop eyes and pursed lips, and noises of obvious disapproval were certainly not exempt. In reality, there were probably a very few things on the face of the corrupted planet earth that would give her a good proper shock.

He bounded up the creaky old stairwell and burst into his apartment, rushing for the chest of drawers. He was cutting it close and didn't have time to waste or spare. He buttoned up the white shirt and fussed with the tie hurriedly. He was in the car within ten minutes and went roaring down the road. It had always been a point with him to be on time as much as was possible, and his job provided no room for exceptions.

He glanced down the neat precise row of baggers, but Josh was nowhere to be seen. He was slightly disappointed. *Oh, well,* he thought, *there will be some other time to ask him*. Things were busier than usual; from the food he was tucking into bags, he concluded that most people were shopping for Sunday afternoon barbecues. The unrelenting onslaught of hamburgers, hot dogs, and all sorts of potato chips made his stomach growl. He was already hungry and there were hours to go. He felt like someone on a forced starvation diet and couldn't help the pious sensation of martyrdom and self-denial as a double-decker chocolate cream cake slid toward him. Was it only his imagination or could he smell it through the plastic cover?

Sheldon didn't get a chance to talk to Josh over the whole beginning of the new week; in fact, the young man was hardly there. Once, in passing, he managed to get his phone number because he told him he wanted to talk to him. The smile he gave him along with the scrap of paper was tired, and he looked exhausted. Sheldon noticed strained lines of tension about his pleasant brown eyes; they were more and more hollow in his sunburned face every time Sheldon saw him.

Sheldon kept an eye out for him, worried. He could sense something was wrong. It had to be Josh's mother; he could just feel it. It had to be what was stressing him, more like consuming him. He was glad when the two of them got paired up together. Josh was looking quite downtrodden and was a mere ghost of his former cheery self as everyone had known him only days ago.

"Anything new?" Sheldon struck up a conversation.

"Nothing much," he didn't feel like talking, and his tongue was heavy in his mouth, like lead.

"You're a poor liar, Josh," Sheldon intoned quietly. "You need help." He met the older boy's eyes. "You need to talk to someone." Josh grunted and cans clattered against each other as he deposited the bag into the waiting cart. His mouth was a hard thin line.

Sheldon was a little uncomfortable and unsure of himself, but he said, "You're not working tonight after this, are you? Want to come up to my place and get supper?" Josh weighed his suggestion carefully and in silence.

"Sure, why not?" He sounded raspy.

"Cool. Don't take off without me," he said lightly, earning a grimace which hardly passed for a smile. He hadn't noticed the dark shadows under the brown eyes. Josh looked worn out and pale under the harsh revealing electric lights, and Sheldon was relieved for both their sakes when the store closed for the night.

Headlights shone in his mirrors as Josh shadowed his tail. Sheldon couldn't help feeling just a little nervous; Josh was clearly not getting enough sleep, and he was driving too close for comfort. He gradually increased pressure on the gas.

"This is totally sweet, nice little place." Josh perked up as he looked around the small suite.

"Yeah, thanks!" Sheldon's key chain jangled as he chucked it through the open door of his bedroom. Arms crossed, he looked at the young man and then set about making supper.

"Looks like it's frozen pizza because I'm not in the most creative mood ever." He ripped open the cardboard box. "So what's up, Josh? You don't look so good."

Josh watched the pizza disappear into the oven. Sheldon fiddled around with knobs and dials, and the appliance gave a click, beginning to come to temperature.

They sat on the couch, the TV droning in the background. Sheldon looked at him expectantly, and Josh stared at his fisted hands.

"Well," he said slowly, "Mama isn't doing well. Things are stressful. Beth doesn't want to work. I can't do it all, you know? I wish she'd just start. She keeps dragging her feet! I . . ." He ran a long brown hand over his face. Sheldon laid a friendly hand on the hunched shoulder.

"Yeah, there aren't really words to make it better. But somehow, it'll all come together." He shrugged. "It always seem to. Things weren't the best for me all that long ago." He told him of his father. "I'll be praying for you, man." Josh raised his head, meeting his eyes.

"Pray?" His mouth quivered into a rueful smile. "To what? Who?" He leaned back, waiting for Sheldon's answer.

226

"The God who hears," he said firmly. "Jesus Christ." A broad grin spread over his weary face, lighting it up suddenly.

"You're a Christian? How awesome is that?" He clapped Sheldon on the back. "I knew there was something different about you, just wasn't entirely sure what."

They grinned at each other and suddenly had a lot of things to talk about. Sheldon was glad he was able to encourage a struggling brother.

"So I had this idea the other day," Sheldon sank his teeth into his pizza "my girlfriend and I were talking, and we'd like to get to know you and your sister, hang out when we get the chance and do stuff together, and we wanted to know your thoughts. I know you're really busy and all," he added hastily. Josh looked thoughtful.

"Yeah, I don't know. I mean, I'd love to, but I don't know about Beth . . . I'll talk to her. She's gotta chip in! She's gotta!" He smacked a fist against his thigh. "I can't support us all, and she gives me flak about not having the kind of life a girl her age should have, but what can I do? I mean, she never made any friends at school. Maybe she and your girlfriend would get along. Sorry for the rant," he said with a grin. Sheldon shrugged, his mouth full. "But anyways, I work every day but Sunday, so maybe we could work something out then."

"Yeah! That's what I was thinking. I thought it would be good for you. I get that—sometimes you need to get away, just go somewhere." Josh nodded, rising to his feet.

"Well, all good things must come to an end. It's been really good spending time with you, Sheldon." There was no mistaking the sincerity of his words.

"You too. Anytime. So lemme know if tomorrow will work for you. Text me," he said casually.

"Gosh, it's Saturday, isn't it!"

"Yup. Do you go to church?"

"Yeah, I found a good one. So, yeah, I could come over tomorrow. I don't know about my sister, but I'll be there. Should I come here?"

"Sure." He and Richelle could deal with a little inconvenience of driving back and forth once in a while. "Come hungry!"

"Will do." Josh grinned. "See ya, man!"

Sunday turned out to be very fun. Richelle liked Josh a lot, and he was able to relax and let himself be caught up in the Callahans' energetic family life.

The younger folks trooped down for ice cream.

"So, guys, what do you think about this?" Sheldon passed Richelle his maraschino cherry and disclosed the plan for the water park. Matt, who was easily excited, grinned like Cheshire cat.

"My treat." Sheldon put in quickly before Josh could look uncomfortable. "Something to beat the heat and celebrate it at the same time, hum?" He bumped his foot into Richelle's under the table and smothered a snicker as ice cream slid down her wrist. He earned a glare. "What do you think, Josh? Next Sunday?" The young man blinked.

"Sure, I guess," he stammered.

"Good! We'll pick you up, or you wanna come to my place?"

"I'll come your way." Sheldon was reminded instantly of himself in months past and became lost in a flash back. That time when he'd had Evan drop him at the head of his street because he was so ashamed of where he lived, he couldn't bear to have him see it. Oh, it seemed like a lifetime had passed since. Things were so much different, so much better. He didn't negotiate with his friend, for he understood him very well. Some people lived two lives, and only let you in on one. That had to be respected. He'd been in Josh's position before and understood that one had to keep one's head up somehow.

"Good-bye, Josh. It was ever so nice meeting you. Tell Beth I can't wait to meet her too! Does she have a phone? We could work something out together. No? Well, I'll just text you and you can pass it on. Have a good week, and I'll be praying for you too!" Richelle lowered her voice so only he could hear her last words and gave him a quick hug.

"Nice to meet you too, Richelle. Matt." He shook her brother's hand. "Thanks for having me. See you at work, Sheldon."

"See you! Drive safe!" A quick wave and the old car was gone.

"He was awfully nice, and I'm glad he came." Richelle took Sheldon's hand. He smiled down at her.

"Me too. Poor guy, I hope his sister gets this job. He needs help. He can't support all of them." Sheldon sank onto the leather couch. "This is the place to be. I'm kinda tired, that ice cream made me feel all droopy." He grabbed a cushion and settled down with a yawn. "I'm taking a nap," he mumbled. Richelle sat down at the opposite end, pulling his feet onto her lap as she did so. She felt content and shut her eyes, happy to be with him, even if he was slipping off into semiconsciousness.

Beth was a timid, quiet little creature, dark like her older brother, only her eyes were a pale blue while his were deep brown. They stood out like moons in her tanned face. Josh had been right in saying she'd be relieved to know someone in the working world of complete strangers. It was something like having his own younger sister, the way she trailed him when her real brother was absent. Although she didn't speak often, she had a shy but friendly smile that said a thousand words. She and Sheldon were frequently teamed up, she being new and inexperienced and in need of instruction. He rather enjoyed showing her the ins and outs of her job.

"So, Beth," he said conversationally one easygoing day, "how do you feel about coming along with Josh and me and hanging out sometime? I've got a girlfriend who really wants to meet you. She says hi, by the way." The girl blushed.

"Really? I would like that." She was so shy!

"Sure, we'd love to have you! It'll be fun." Beth carefully turned back the cuffs on her sleeves.

"I'll think about it, thanks." Sheldon yawned and hung his hands behind his neck.

"There's like nobody here." She made a noise in agreement, resting against the counter.

Some people, you just have to give up on them after a few futile attempts; having a two-sided conversation with them is akin to pulling teeth out of a chicken. Chickens having no teeth, it's more or less impossible, and Sheldon didn't enjoy talking to himself.

Chapter 22

Future Plans

"I don't know, Chelle." They were walking hand in hand down a forest trail. "She's awfully shy! Maybe she will, maybe she won't, at least I tried."

"We'll see. You're right. It's OK. You extended the invitation, and it's up to her now." He tilted his head back and gazed up at the leafy green canopy spread high above them.

"Oh, Sheldon, look!" She pressed his hand eagerly, her attention riveted on a small doe and her twin fawns grazing in an open space, the sunlight filtering through the trees making patterns on their hides. The deer had not yet scented them and were oblivious to their presence. The two of them stood still and observed the graceful fluidity of their movements.

"Too bad I don't have a gun." Sheldon joked in a teasing whisper. She elbowed him in the ribs.

"You're terrible."

"What I meant to say is, boy, do I wish I had a camera!" Richelle wasn't convinced.

"Let's turn back. I don't want to disturb them." With as little noise as possible, they turned and backtracked. "Perhaps you should look into one."

"Look into what?" he asked.

"Why, a camera! Why ever not?" she protested at his objective expression. "You have a deep appreciation for the beauty in nature, Sheldon. Haven't you ever wished you could capture some of it?" He kicked a pebble down the gravely trail.

"Now that you mention it, yes, I have." A thoughtful look crept over his features. "That's an idea, Chelle. It's something I love." She smiled at his quiet enthusiasm.

"I wonder why you never considered photography before." The corners of his mouth twitched.

"I don't know. I never really thought about what I wanted to do futuristically. There was a lot going on, but now, I should be thinking about it. I mean, I don't really want to be working at the same place five years from now."

"Maybe something will come of this. I can see you, tramping through the woods at four in the morning to catch a sunrise." He laughed.

"Am I really as crazy as you make me out to be?"

"I like you crazy," she said coyly and smiled up at him.

"You're a goose," he said matter-of-factly, pulling her affectionately to his side as they walked.

"Hopeless goose."

"Hmm." He squeezed her shoulder, wrapping his arm snugly around her.

That night, just for the sake of knowing, he did a little research on cameras and choked over the prices. If he was going to drop that kind of money, he needed to invest in it. Photography would be serious, not just some hobby born of a passing whim. And he knew scratch about the whole thing. There would be programs to purchase, books to study, techniques to master, classes to attend . . . and the list went on. Sheldon scrolled through pages of recommended photography books, chin lowered on his chest, a scowl of concentration wrinkling his face. He ordered a few from the local library and went to bed with thoughts of signing up at the community college floating through his active mind.

He closed his eyes and began to talk out loud as he asked God for direction. He didn't want to waste time, money, and energy on this if he rashly plunged into it on an impulsive notion.

Sheldon talked to his grandmother about his ideas, asking her to pray for him and needing someone to listen to his ambitious ramblings. He was greatly encouraged by the end of the conversation. She had advised him not to waste too much time, and he dutifully enrolled in a college class. He found himself anticipating it eagerly, even if it was two weeks away.

Hours of research and time spent in devouring books made up Sheldon's schedule. He felt like this was what he was meant to do, and his naturally driven personality honed in on his new interest purposely, everything else put off as second priority. Work was when he reviewed everything he'd learned, turning it over and over in his head, accustoming himself to the language of this new realm. The different techniques light played in capturing images he found fascinating. To his profound embarrassment, his preoccupied demeanor got him taken aside for a hasty admonishing lecture to apply himself.

One night, when he got home, there were several voice messages from Richelle. He knew he'd been scarce and felt a pang of self-reproachful remorse. He acknowledged that he was none too good at multitasking and wasn't proud of it. More relationships than one had suffered that week. Beth and Josh, he knew his conversations with the siblings had been halfhearted at best. He dialed Richelle's number.

"Hello?"

"Hi, Chelle, calling you back."

"Hey, you, how have you been?" The preoccupied tone in her voice disappeared, and he could almost see her push aside whatever it was she had been doing to give him her undivided attention. It didn't help him feel any less guilty.

"Oh, things have been crazy. I'm totally serious about this whole photography thing." Richelle smiled as he dove into an animated detailed narration of everything he'd been doing, from his research to discussing it with his grandmother.

"Wow, you're totally psyched! This is great!"

"I am! Totally excited. I really feel like this is where God wants me to go, even though I know next to nothing about this. But I really can't wait to begin! You wouldn't believe the kind of stuff that's available on the Internet. YouTube, oh, how I love YouTube." She giggled.

"You're so crazy about this. I can't stop smiling."

"Don't ever stop. You're adorable when you smile. I'm missing this!" Sheldon grinned, hearing her stammered objection. "Hey, I'm sorry I've been so preoccupied this week. Hope the water park will make up for it."

"Shel, you don't have to apologize, sweet. This is so important. This could be your career!"

"I know, but you're important too. You're the most special person in the world to me."

"But this is your priority, your future, and I understand. You need to invest in the things that will matter." Sheldon opened his mouth to parry her argument but realized he was in no place to say what was burning on the tip of his tongue; he had no right.

"Whatever, Chelle," he improvised lamely.

But the conversation made him consider once again; he'd told her father that he basically wanted to marry her, but he had no idea when. Richelle complimented his nature and encouraged him in many areas of his life. But what if she felt different and what if her love for him wasn't of the kind to last a lifetime? What of her dad? If he actually out and asked for her hand in marriage, was Evan ready to part with his daughter, to give her over to another man's care? Sheldon's palms were slick with sweat at the very thought. The way he was budgeted, he felt confident he could support her, but did he have it in him to be the kind of husband she deserved? That she needed?

Sheldon slept restlessly that night, even though he had poured out his heart in earnest prayer and supplication for hours. He knew

God was leading him; he knew his life wouldn't be the same for much longer.

Animated chatter rose over the beat of the radio as the navy blue Honda zipped down the highway. Richelle glanced back at the boys in the backseat and shared a smile with her amused boyfriend. Matt was chewing Josh's ear off. Natalie had made it down, and she was chattering away; the nearer they got to their destination, the more excited they both became. They all were anticipating it, but Matt couldn't contain himself. He rambled on and on about the thrill of the water roller coaster. Sheldon grabbed the rearview mirror and glared into it, scowled at him.

"Quit gabbing, Matt! I'm wishing we left you home!" It was no good, everyone knew he was kidding. "You sure he's nearly sixteen?" he asked Richelle. She tapped the side of her head, green eyes twinkling merrily.

Extra clothes were tossed into the trunk, and soon, they'd gained admittance. The water park was enormous, and they consulted a map to determine where to head to first.

"So I guess we'll try to stick together for the most part, unless someone doesn't want to go on a particular ride," Sheldon said. The others nodded in agreement.

Hours later, their clothes damp, they sat outside a restaurant sharing a large sausage pizza. There was a veggie in reserve, its delectable aroma drifting out from its cardboard box.

"Wow, what a day!" Josh took a swig of his root beer, wincing slightly as the fizzy soda burned his tongue and throat. Natalie nodded in agreement with him and suddenly leaned over the table and tipped his can up, laughing as he spilled some down his shirtfront. Josh scrunched his face up and playfully threw his napkin at her.

"Totally a blast!" Matt cried, wiping damp hair off his forehead. Richelle's wet bathing suit stuck to the picnic table's wooden bench, and she peeled her legs off it one at a time, watching Natalie attempt to flirt with the older boy. *She isn't usually like this at all,* Richelle thought and couldn't help smiling at her friend as she looked up and met her eyes.

"I'm so glad we have a water park relatively close to home! I really really enjoyed it today. Thank you, Sheldon," Richelle said, turning her head toward her boyfriend.

"Yeah, thanks!" the other three echoed, each taking another piece of pizza.

"You're welcome, guys." Richelle leaned her leg against his as he shifted uncomfortably. Sheldon didn't really know what to do with himself and fiddled with a piece of cardboard he'd torn from the pizza box. He shot a sheepish smirk at Richelle and snuck a hand under the table to poke her side. Sometimes, he wondered if she knew how awkward he felt when he was put on the spot. He only got a playful jab in the ribs for his troubles.

That was a hundred dollars well spent, he thought as he slid into the car and gripped the steering wheel in one hand. He reached back around his shoulder and pulled the seat belt across himself. The parking lot was packed, row upon row of cars shimmering in the hot sun, heat waves radiating off them. Sheldon maneuvered his way carefully out of the lot, breathing a sigh of relief when they got to the road again.

Richelle's loose hair blew in the breeze as she leaned out the window. She loved the cool air blowing on her skin from the speed of his car. Sheldon shot a tender glance in her direction. He was grateful for the time they had been able to spend alone that day, as well as sitting next to her on several rides. He hadn't realized how much he'd missed her dear sweet company. Reaching out, he clasped her little hand in his and squeezed her fingers. He loved her. She could feel it in his touch, sense it in the way he treated her, and hear it in his voice when he spoke to her. She responded to his touch but did not turn her head to look at him. He understood her reserve; three people sitting in the back seat made them both feel awkward, and he put both hands on the wheel.

Richelle saw from the look in Sheldon's eyes that he wanted her to stay in the car when they dropped her brother and Natalie off at her house. Matt stood uncertainly on the side-walk, regarding her expectantly.

"You coming, Rik?" She shook her head with a smile.

"I'll be home soon."

"OK, bye," Matt snorted and followed Natalie up to the door. His sister and her boyfriend didn't act stupid or anything, but he felt like they were alone a lot and knew it wouldn't matter as much if he wasn't friends with Sheldon. He didn't feel like an awkward third-wheel for the most part, but he couldn't help a tinge of annoyance at their eagerness to get rid of him. He called hello to his parents and ran upstairs to rinse off the chlorine from the water park in the shower. Natalie stood on the doorstep, waving good-bye to her friends. Richelle knew enough about being a girl to know she was hanging around for as long as she could just so she could get one more glimpse of Josh. It was obvious to Richelle, who was her best friend and knew her very well, that Natalie had a crush on him.

Sheldon and Richelle said good-bye to Josh and went up to the apartment. Sheldon could feel her damp one-piece through her thin T-shirt as he pulled her close to him, sitting down on the couch. She leaned into him with her head resting on his chest.

"I had a lot of fun today," she said, twining their fingers together.

"I did too. But I wanted to see you, for a little, just you and me. Talk about whatever, you know. That OK?" Her slightly damp hair smelled good, and he laid his cheek on top of her head.

"I missed you this week." Her thumb gently caressed the skin on his knuckles. "But I'm glad you've figured out what you want to do for a career."

"Yes, it's pretty much settled in my mind. It's going to take a lot of money, all that equipment and the classes. This is serious. If it takes off as a business, I'll be a professional photographer, and there're probably hoops to jump through. I wonder if you have to get certified . . . I'm kind of leery about the money. I mean I've worked a lot this summer and made a few thousand to put into savings. But I don't know if I'll have enough."

"Sweetheart, you're not there yet! You haven't even taken the first class. Take it one step at a time. Don't worry about the money just yet. I take that back. Don't worry at all. God will provide." Their eyes met for a long moment.

"This is why I'm so blessed to know you. You are a treasure, Chelle."

"Do you really think so?" He pressed his lips to her hair.

"I know so."

Richelle and Natalie were able to spend a few days with each other before she had to go home, and Richelle's suspicions were confirmed; Natalie found herself inexplicably attracted to Josh. She was annoyed but strangely grateful when Richelle found ways for them all to get together. Josh liked her as well, she could see, but he was twenty-two to her eighteen, and she knew it was silly, wishful thinking to hope anything could possibly come of it. Anyways, Natalie didn't believe Josh returned her feelings in quite the same way she felt for him. *Which is probably for the best,* she thought with a sigh, stealing glances at him as they sat on the couches in Sheldon's apartment watching a movie after a long day. Josh was talking with Matt and was oblivious to the ardent attention he was receiving through no fault of his own.

Before too long, Natalie found herself at the train station, saying good-byes to the gang all around.

"Bye, Sheldon. Be good to Richelle! I'm not sure I like sharing her, but you're a great guy!" She winked at him and gave him a quick side-hug to show him she was totally kidding. Richelle held her tight and let her go with a smile, whispering something in her ear as she pulled back that made Natalie blush, which was rare with her. Matt shook her hand awkwardly and scuffed his foot on the sunbaked asphalt. Natalie found herself face to face with Josh and for once in her life had nothing to say. Luckily for her, Josh wasn't at all uncomfortable and stepped close to her with his sunny smile, catching her to him in a hug.

"Bye, Natalie, come back soon. Things are a lot of fun with you around." Natalie returned his smile eagerly but found that her reply sounded funny getting past the catch in her throat. She was actually a little grateful for the urgency of pressing time that forced her to go before she lost her cool, and she turned and waved once more as she stepped onto the train that would bring her home.

The little gang of friends stood on the platform and watched the train puff down the tracks, carrying Natalie away from them. Josh glanced at the faces around him.

"Call me crazy, but I'm gonna miss that girl. She's a lot of fun bound to happen. Crazy little kid," he muttered the last words under his breath, casting one more slightly wistful look down the tracks before turning away and calling the rest of them to follow him back to the car.

"I agree with you, Josh. Nat is a blast. I wish she didn't live so far away." Richelle glanced at her brother in surprise. "What?" Matt lifted his palms out of habit. "She is! And it would be awesome if she lived here. Don't deny it, Rik. After all, she is your best friend, besides lover boy." Sheldon scowled, wrinkling up his nose at the younger boy with an expression of disgust that didn't quite hide his affection.

"Lover boy. I mean really, Matt? Gosh, is that just stupid." he snorted. Josh looked at them and shook his head, grinning.

"You guys are all nuts," he laughed as he hopped into Sheldon's car and shut the door.

The classes on photography had only increased Sheldon's interest all the more, and he attended all the classes that the college had to offer. Frequently, he was out of town at some event or lecture.

Richelle was happy for him, even while his absence made her restless and ache inside. She was wrestling with her feelings for him and many fears concerning the unknown future. Sheldon never talked about how he felt about her; she didn't know where their relationship was headed. He loved her, she knew, but sometimes, a new love grew old and you moved on, other things becoming more important. Did he really need her anymore? She pulled her pillow to her chest and shut her eyes, trying to block out the thoughts.

He was a man. His career was picked out; he was used to being a loner. She wasn't necessary, was she? God had absolutely used her in Sheldon's life, and she'd been privileged, but perhaps that was her only purpose. And she couldn't say she was all right with that.

"Do you trust your Lord when He says He has a plan for you?" Her mother had asked when she told her about the turmoil raging inside of her. Richelle's tearful outpouring tugged at her heart. She remembered going through a similar journey, all those years before. And the Lord had been faithful and true in her life; she knew He would be so in her daughter's.

"He has someone for you, sweetie. You don't have to afraid. It may not be Sheldon," she said gently. "You can't hold onto him. You have to hold him with open hands and give him to God. And ask the Lord to guide you where He will. People fail you, honey. God won't." Mrs. Callahan's words sliced into her daughter's heart like a knife and everything in her wanted to reject the advice, but she knew her mother was right. Sheldon was only a man. Perhaps not even *her* man, but regardless, he was a fallible human being just like she was; he wasn't perfect, and even someone who loves you, even your best friend, can hurt you.

"Mom, I'm scared. What if I can't let him go? What if I can't trust God?" Despair colored her words. Mrs. Callahan tipped her head to one side.

"I know you're scared, dear. But listen. Would you want to make a mistake and marry the wrong person because you couldn't entrust your future to God's care?" The question hung heavy in the air.

"No," Richelle whispered.

"Wait. Pray. Don't focus on Sheldon and your feelings for him." She laid her hand on Richelle's. "Focus on Jesus. He won't disappoint you, honey. Not ever." She gathered the distraught girl in her arms and rocked her gently. "It's all going to be fine Richelle. I remember going through the same thing with my first date, and then I met your father, and yes, it hurt to let go of the other boy, but I'm glad I did because I never would've noticed my husband if I was blinded by romantic illusions for someone else. But God had

His hand in my life, even my love life, and He'll guide you through yours. Let Him." She kissed her cheek and looked into Richelle's eyes. "I love you, honey." A tear slid down the flushed cheek, and her voice quavered.

"I love you too, Mom."

"Richelle." Mrs. Callahan turned at the door. "Don't worry."

Funny, Richelle herself had advised Sheldon the very same thing all those months before. Perhaps it was not coincidence, perhaps deep down she knew the answers to her questions already. She did, she knew she did. But would she listen? Would she heed the voice of instruction and wisdom? If worry didn't fix anything, then why was she so tempted to indulge in it? She was so tuckered out, so emotionally drained that she fell asleep on top of her blankets.

Chapter 23

Camera Flashes and Salt Air— Older and Wiser

The pressure of a finger, a bright flash, then move to a different angle to try it all over again. There was a deep sense of fulfillment in making a living from doing something you love. Sheldon was making a profit from his photography. A year had passed since he had first become interested in capturing moments of beauty in creation, and now it was a main source of income. Many happy hours were spent trekking through the evergreen forests of New Hampshire, camera in hand.

The current project was providing photos of native trees for a scientific arboreal textbook. For a young man of twenty, it was like having a star in the hall of fame. At least it was to this boy from the backwoods of upstate New Hampshire; it was the beginning of making a name for himself. Things were going so well with the business that he was renting out a studio. Although he mostly did landscapes and nature shots, he didn't turn down an opportunity to take portraits, and several people in town sported his photos of their children's senior pictures on their mantels, along with family photos. Yes, life was good. Another long winter had come and gone; he still had kept his shoveling clients for the extra cash, only now he'd upgraded a bit and bought himself a snowblower.

One day, at an odd hour between the afternoon and the evening, Sheldon stood outside Evan Callahan's study door. His hand shook slightly as he knocked.

The leather chair was deep and comfortable, but he sat on the edge. Steady gray eyes met his. Sheldon's answers to the man's polite inquiries after his health and work were curt and vague.

"There is clearly something on your mind. Tell me about it." He watched the young man snap to his feet and pace the length of the small room. A moment slipped by and another; then he gripped the edge of the desk, knuckles white as he leaned over it. Evan started at the dark color of Sheldon's eyes as they stared boldly into his own.

"Sir, I've got a steady income, a lot of money in the bank. I know I can provide for a family, easily. I've waited nearly two years, and my feelings have not been altered. I love your daughter, and I want to be her husband. Sir, I've prayed and prayed over this, but there is such a sense of certainty in my heart. I know she's the one for me." He ran his tongue over dry lips. "I understand this is no small thing I'm asking you to do, sir, but will you give me your blessing to ask for her hand in marriage?" Evan ran his hand over his chin, the stubble sounding scratchy.

"So you've finally screwed up the courage to ask, have you now?" Laughter lines crinkled around his eyes as he rounded the desk and put his hand on the tall young man's shoulder. "Sheldon, this is a serious undertaking . . . Marriage is, well, nothing to be taken lightly."

"I know it is not. Richelle is someone whom I have always deeply admired. She's always supported me and encouraged me in my faith and in everything I do. I . . . it's deeper than that. I love her, and I can't go on like this."

"Both my wife and I have prayed about your relationship. Richelle has struggled so long with her feelings for you, with so many questions. We were all fearful that your intentions would alter. Sheldon, my boy, I can only answer you with a hearty 'yes'! Yes, marry Richelle. You can make her happy again. She needs you. You are both intensely attracted to one another and it would be wrong to keep you apart. You have my blessing." Tears shone in the gray eyes as he pulled his future son-in-law into a tight embrace, slapping him on the back. Sheldon couldn't speak, a channel of joy ran through him with such intensity that he wanted to both laugh out loud and cry at the same time.

The Callahans were accustomed to having Sheldon over for dinner on Fridays if his work permitted. He had a few photos to edit, but there was such a flurry of emotional anticipation inside him he simply could not concentrate or stand being cooped up in front of his computer for another moment. For all his striving to act normal, Richelle kept shooting anxious yet curious glances at him. It was a struggle to finish the food on his plate, and he didn't recall eating most of it.

"Is everything all right, Sheldon? How is work?" He couldn't help smiling at her obvious concern when they were alone and pulled her tight into his arms.

"Everything is fine, Chelle. I missed you this week." To his surprise, she gave a hiccupping sob, and he could feel her body tremble against him as she strained him closer. "What is it?" he asked anxiously, quickly cupping her chin in his hands and forcing her to look at him. Her eyes were miserable. "Oh, Chelle, did I do this? I'm sorry!" She stood on her tiptoes and kissed his mouth hungrily. Sheldon did not respond, and she began to cry as he stepped away from her. "Not like this," he whispered. Stunned, Richelle dropped her face into her hands, her shoulders hunched.

"Shel, I can't do this! I can't!" she cried passionately, stamping her foot. Sheldon didn't understand.

"Can't do what?" Her hands twisted over and over, tears streaming unheeded down her face.

"It's been a year, Sheldon." His heart stood still. "Things aren't like they used to be. I think they've changed for you. You won't even . . . even kiss me anymore." She turned away from him, unable to speak for a weighted moment. "I need to move on, Sheldon. Maybe we should have just stayed friends." He couldn't say a word. "I don't want to hurt you, but I can't live like this any longer. And I won't."

"Richelle, please! You're wrong!"

"Wrong? Then why did you turn away? Why didn't you kiss me?" She became louder, and he shot a fearful glance toward the door.

"I wasn't ready . . ." She cut him off, her eyes huge in her white tear-streaked face.

"You weren't ready? Weren't ready?" her voice broke. "I thought you loved me!" She whirled and made as if to run from the room, but Sheldon caught her arm in a desperate grip.

"Chelle, wait! I can't let you go, please. You're doing everything wrong!"

"No, I'm not! I can't take this anymore!" He took both her arms and stared into her face intently, forcing himself to be calm.

"Do one more thing for me. Just one. Then you can say goodbye. You can do whatever you see fit." His breath shuddered in his dry throat as he drew it in. "Tonight, I want you to pray, really pray about our relationship, and tomorrow, I want to take you out. Give me one more chance, Chelle, please!" She didn't speak, but the look in her eyes spoke of wavering determination. He plunged on in desperation. "I know I've screwed it up. I've been so caught up in my work, but you're everything to me, the more I'm away, the brighter you shine. I miss you, I really do, and won't you let me have another try? Just tomorrow, Chelle. Please!" He couldn't breathe. When she slowly nodded, he wanted to kiss her so badly it hurt. "Thank you," he whispered, taking her hand and raising it to his lips. "I'll be here at three-thirty. Good night, Chelle."

"Good night, Sheldon." She closed her eyes as his hand brushed her cheek, his touch caressing, and then watched him walk from the room. The electric thrill when he touched her was still there; it had never left. She wondered if it ever would.

He didn't leave right off as expected. He took Mrs. Callahan aside and told her what had happened.

"Mom, I came so close to losing her, I still am. I've been so stupid and caught up in other things. I have to propose to her tomorrow. I need to. I'm ashamed to say it, but I . . . I had to stop kissing her. I'm drawn to her so strongly, it's just becoming harder." He found it difficult to meet her eyes.

"That's nothing to be ashamed of, Sheldon. It's natural. And you are very wise to draw lines in the physical aspect of your relationship. Take my advice and don't drag out your engagement."

"If she'll have me, that would be suicidal."

"I should start planning a wedding then, shouldn't I?" she laughed.

"I wanted to show you something." He took out his phone and showed her a snap shot. It was the ring he'd bought for Richelle.

"It's lovely, Sheldon. Unusual for sure, but a stunning piece."

"I thought it was perfect, like it was made for her. She is an unusual girl, Mom." He slipped the phone back into his pocket. Mrs. Callahan smiled at him. "I need to get going. Could you pray for me tonight?" he asked hesitantly.

"Of course, I will, honey. Bless you, I pray for you whether you request it or not." Sheldon drew a shaky breath and hugged her.

"Thank you." He pressed a hasty kiss to her cheek and stepped to his car. Mrs. Callahan stood in the driveway for a long time, looking up at the stars and praying. Like Evan, she was confident that God had chosen Sheldon as their daughter's husband. But they weren't married yet!

"Hi." Sheldon opened the passenger door for her. She was wearing his favorite dress, sleeveless, a soft silvery green, its hem not quite reaching her knees. The color brought out the stormy green of her eyes and made her hair stunning. Richelle was quiet, and he was so nervous that his hands stuck to the wheel.

Sheldon had passed a sleepless night planning this crucial date; it had to be perfect. It was a long drive to the ocean, but it was a favorite haunt of theirs, for they both loved the roar of the surf crashing on the sand, and the sting of the salt breeze. The cry of the wheeling gulls, the tall swaying sea grass, and the beautiful sunsets would never grow old.

"How was your day?"

"It went well. How was work?" He ground his teeth.

"I don't want to talk about work, Chelle. This isn't about work. It's about you. You and me, OK?" That made her smile.

"OK." There was a lilt in her voice that was heart-wrenching. He slid his hand down her bare arm and reached for her fingers. Stiffly, she let him hold her hand, her face turned to watch the scenery passing by.

"You're not letting me in, are you?" He tried to pay attention to the driving. She didn't speak. Fear touched his soul with an icy finger. What if she was through? Had he screwed up so terribly that she'd severed all the bonds they had shared? "Chelle? Come on, girl, don't do this!" She shook her head, and he saw she was biting her lip to fight back tears. He squeezed her hand and could breath again as her fingers closed about his tightly.

Not many people were at the beach, and he and Richelle walked over to a sub shop and ordered their regular preferences.

"We'll be back in twenty minutes to pick them up," Sheldon called as they left. "Come on, Chelle." He couldn't wait any longer and, catching her hand, ran with her along the boardwalk down to the sandy beach, finally making her laugh. It was beautiful, and they sat on a huge boulder in a clustered rock formation and gazed out at over the rolling white caps. They sat in silence, listening to the scream of the gulls and the wind, and then Richelle turned and found him searching her face ardently. Hesitantly, he passed his arm around her slender shoulders and leaned his head close, his breath warm on her cool skin.

"I'm sorry, Chelle. Won't you forgive me?" Her resolution crumbled as she felt his soft mouth on her neck.

"Yes." Her voice was barely discernible, and she turned in his arms and wrapped her own around his torso, nestling her head against his chest. Sheldon pulled back and kissed her deeply, his hard lips arousing a fire that was both pleasurable and painful.

He tried kissing her tears away but began to cry himself. The thought of losing her was too much to bear. She lay cradled against him and held his head in caressing hands as her sweet soft lips wandered over his face, lingering on his mouth. He closed his eyes as her gentle fingers rubbed over his cheeks, drying the streaking tears. The skin of her legs was satiny smooth as he hooked his arm beneath her knees and swung her closer to him. He laid his head on hers and gently ran his thumb up and down her lower leg.

"I wish I was better at dividing my time, but I've got such a one-track mind." He caught his breath as she smoothed her hand over his chest.

"Darling, you don't have to keep on apologizing. I love you." She kissed his chin.

"Oh gosh, Chelle! Quick, our subs!" She laughed, springing lightly to her feet.

"One-track mind indeed. Boys, all you think about is food!" He looked at her quickly, but she was laughing up at him, eyes sparkling with a joy that had been absent too long.

The brisk wind made her dress cling to her thighs as they clambered down from the lofty perch and set out across the damp sand close to the lapping waves. Sheldon chased her across the beach, sea spray stinging their legs and then the grainy sand sticking to their skin as they moved further inland.

They returned to the boulder to eat dinner, sitting close together. Richelle rubbed sand off her legs, her dress bunching about her thighs. The honey-tone of her skin shimmered in the dying glow of the sun as Sheldon laid his hand on her knee and kissed her cheek.

"You're beautiful tonight, Chelle." She gave that sweet, shy smile that made him want to kiss her. But he didn't and drizzled dressing on his sub.

"Can I tell you something?" he asked when they'd finished. He had his arm around her, and they were admiring the fiery sunset reflected off the rippling ocean.

"Of course," she replied, leaning her head on his shoulder.

"I love you, Chelle. I can't deny it any longer, nor do I wish to." She was stunned. He'd finally told her that he loved her! "Do you love me?" An unbelieving smile touched her mouth.

"Very much so," she whispered. Sheldon took her hand.

"Richelle, I've known you for nearly two years now, and I've never met a sweeter, more beautiful girl than you, and God knows I never will." He felt his throat tightening, but there was such a light in her eyes that her face was all he could see and he could think about nothing other than her. "I was so used to being alone, so accustomed to it. Then you came into my life, and being a loner wasn't so much fun anymore. Darling, I don't want to be a loner any longer. I can't. I don't want to go through life without anyone by my side. I need someone to share it with. Doing it all on my own is pointless. I need to do it all together with another. God said it wasn't good for man to be alone. Chelle, I want to be your husband. I love you. I can't live without you." He knelt in front of her, holding both her hands, his face level with hers. "You've always been God's way of pouring blessings on my life, from the moment we met, and I don't want that to ever change. Would you make me the happiest man on earth and marry me, darling?" The red sun struck the sparkling diamond he held in his fingertips, making it a tiny flame of a million colors. Richelle's eyes searched his face for a tense moment. A smile sparked somewhere deep in the depths of those beautiful eyes and blossomed all over her face.

"Yes," she said firmly. Sheldon realized he'd been holding his breath when his lungs emptied with a gasp, and he flung his arms around her slender waist, both of them laughing and crying for joy.

"I thought you'd never ask me!" she cried, burying her face in his neck.

"I couldn't until I could provide for you. I love you, baby, oh so much. It hurts I love you so much!" The passion in his kiss echoed the longing in her. His breath was hot and sweet, and his lips were hungry and not to be satisfied.

The engagement ring he'd bought Richelle was, as Mrs. Callahan had observed, unusual. But it was gorgeous, and Sheldon glowed at Richelle's delight as he slipped it on her finger. The diamond was cupped in an intricate twist of worked silver, the Celtic knot as beautiful as the precious stone it held. The ring itself was a narrow band of silver, the design wonderfully proportioned and pleasing to the eye.

"It's beautiful, darling. I don't know what to say!" His lips curved in that dear, crooked grin.

"Then don't speak at all." There couldn't have been a more suitable substitution for speech; their lips and tongues did everything but speak.

Chapter 24
I Do—Epilogue

Everyone else thought the two months until the wedding flew by, everyone other than Richelle and Sheldon. They couldn't wait; September seemed ages away, so far in the distance. This time it was Richelle who was more cautious; Sheldon was over at every opportunity and small window of time he could spare, and she resolved demurely to stay at home with the family more times than not when he tried to take her out. Her parents confirmed her in her decision to protect both herself and her fiancé when saying no became so very difficult. Sheldon put up a calendar in his studio above his desk and methodically crossed out the months until the wedding . . . the weeks . . . then the days . . .

Josh was, of course, Sheldon's best man, and Matt and one of Richelle's cousins from North Carolina made up the remainder of the groomsmen. It was a small wedding party, but the whole church was invited to share in the celebration. Natalie was exuberant and smiled constantly so that she positively glowed. She was the maid of honor, and she and Richelle had had hardly enough time to pick out the dresses. Sheldon felt kind of awkward meeting Richelle's relatives and the other friend that was her bridesmaid (also from North Carolina), especially as one of her cousins was his groomsman, but he didn't have a plan B.

Other than the dresses, he and his fiancée planned most of the wedding, sitting up late at nights poring over bridal magazines and paging through websites for pictures and ideas. For the most part, Sheldon let Richelle decide on what they wanted, but he was adamant concerning one thing: one of the wedding colors must be silvery green. They both thought it would look lovely with a soft shade of rose. Mrs. Callahan proved herself to be a capable organizer, which was fortunate because the star-crossed lovers had a difficult time focusing on anything but one another the closer the wedding date came.

Afterward, people said it was a lovely wedding; the weather was perfect, the sea breeze was gentle even coming off the ocean, and so on, but all Sheldon knew was that the sun was bringing out the auburn lights in his bride's hair, and she was the most beautiful woman he'd ever seen. The white gown she wore for him was gorgeous, the short flowing train sweeping over the sand as she walked toward him with a smile that outshone everyone. She was all he could see. The rhinestones and sequins in her gown were nothing to the light in her beautiful green eyes. He remembered her sweet face looking up at him as she held his hand, repeating the sacred vows after the minister. (Sheldon Eric Trindell, will you take this woman to be your lawfully wedded wife . . . I do . . . for better, for worse . . . for richer or poorer . . . to love and to cherish . . . until death do us part . . . Richelle Alyssa Callahan, will you . . . I do . . . Son, you may now kiss your bride.) He'd carefully raised his wife's veil and leaned in to kiss her. The applause was enough to drown out the sea, and the crowd of smiling faces would've been enough had the sun disappeared behind a cloud, especially his dear grandmother's.

They'd returned to the church building for food and dancing, the day rushing by in a joyous blur. Now here they were, arrived at a resort hotel suite, the steward closing the door behind their piled luggage. The two of them stood there with the most foolish grins on their faces and gazed at the other jubilantly. Somehow, Richelle unpacked while he showered; then they switched.

It was dark, and a moon shone through the open window overlooking the bay when she came out, a light robe covering her silk negligee. She went to him as he stood by the window. The cool early autumn breeze rippled her robe close around her as she slid her hand over his lower back, laying her head on his bare chest as she pressed a kiss to his skin.

"Hi, sweetheart." He looked her over admiringly. "You look absolutely exquisite. Should we leave the window open?"

"Sure, it's lovely out." She gave a sigh and walked over to the king-sized bed. "Today was wonderful, wasn't it? But I'm so tired!" Her robe dropped to the floor, and she lay back on the pillows, tucking her little pink toes beneath the folded back sheets. Sheldon swallowed hard.

"It was! But it's a good kind of tired, baby." He turned from the open window, the full moon casting shadows over his bare chest, and looked back at his wife, watching him from the huge bed. His wife! He wouldn't admit even to himself just how nervous he was. But it was overcome when a shiver of delight rushed through him, and he crossed the thick carpet, stretching his lithe body on top of hers. Richelle squirmed slightly under his weight and then lay perfectly still, love glowing in her entire face as she smiled dotingly up at him.

"My dear Mrs. Trindell," he murmured, raising his body so he could cradle her face in his hands. Her smooth shoulders pressed against the insides of his forearms, and he bent his head and let his lips feel her soft skin. She wrapped her arms around his waist, and he felt her fingertips lightly caressing his lower back.

"I love you, baby."

"I love you too, ever so much. I can't believe this is really happening. I mean we're really married!" Sheldon's voice was low, but if he'd shouted, it wouldn't have carried the effect of the unmistakable sweet desire she heard so clearly. Her hands moved quickly over his broad shoulders, and they clasped each other with ardent urgency, their lips fused together for an eternal moment. They drew apart, and Richelle drew Sheldon's head down on her breast, stroking his fair hair. He twined a strand of his bride's hair around one finger and his eyes flickered up to hers. The pupils had dilated until his eyes were huge and a deep midnight.

"You know what they say of the effects of a full moon." His teeth flashed in that roguish grin that made her heart beat all the faster.

"What do they say?" she murmured, pulling his head down until their foreheads touched. Smiling, he rubbed her nose with his own.

"I'll show you." He kissed her lingeringly, bringing a caressing hand to her cheek.

"Cedee, don't fight over the sand bucket!" Richelle stood in the summer heat balancing a plate full of ham and cheese sandwiches in one hand and a pitcher of lemonade in the other. "Come and get your lunch, you two."

Little four-year-old Mercedes dropped the red bucket and tumbled out of the sandbox, racing over the grass, her short red pigtails flying in the wind. Her two-year-old brother toddled on fat legs, crying "momma" and reaching out plump arms to Richelle.

"Hey, baby, I'll take one of those." Her husband kissed her full on the mouth before she knew he was there and snagged a sandwich as she lovingly returned his affectionate gesture.

"Who's a big boy, Joshy? Come see Daddy!" Sheldon knelt, and the little boy toppled into his strong arms. Richelle smiled down at her family and sat down in the grass to share a moment of peace with them.

Things were busy, but going well. She and Sheldon had been married for nearly six years, their anniversary coming up in a few short months. Sheldon put his free arm around her and kissed her neck the way he knew she loved.

"How you doin', honey? Everybody OK out here?" She nodded, and he put his hand on the slight swell in her belly, laughing as he leaned his head against it as if he were listening for signs of the life within.

"Are you nearly finished with that photo shoot you're editing?" He sat up and ran a brown hand through his sun-bleached blond hair.

"Nearly done. Hey, your mom offered to take the babies for a few hours. Want to skip out tonight for a dinner date? Yeah, I thought you would." He tilted her face up to his with a finger under her chin and nuzzled his nose against her cheek. "I love you, sweetheart."

"I love you too, Sheldon. I always will." He smiled and kissed her.

"Until death do us part." Richelle wrapped her arms around her husband for an instant before Joshy, who was sandwiched between them, pushed his mother away. "Looks like someone wants to keep Daddy to himself!" Sheldon laughed and gave her a hasty peck on the cheek before he turned his attention to his little son.

The walls of the little yellow house saw many years of joy, and a few more faces added to the family. There were hardships; yes, life is not without them, but love overcame obstacles. Richelle and Sheldon were knit together, their marriage firmly grounded in their faith in the Lord, and they both said when they were old and gray, as they sat in the proverbial rocking chairs on their front porch, that they would never have made it through all those years if it hadn't been for the Lord. Sheldon always said and advised his sons that no marriage would last if there were only two people apart of it. "The Lord is the glue that holds you together. If He's not present, then it won't last. Your mother and I know a marriage takes three." He'd say this with a smile and look at his wife with a love that was a testimony in itself.